ADVANCE PRAISE FOR

WHERE I
BELONG

"A thought-provoking book. Filled with courage, Millie will show us the way to a kinder, more compassionate way of being in the world."

—Guadalupe García McCall, Pura Belpré Award-winning
author of *Under the Mesquite*

"In *Where I Belong*, Guatemalan-born Milagros Vargas finds herself in the spotlight of our nation's immigration debate. Her name is Spanish for 'miracle,' an apt description of her character, but the real miracle is this novel, which takes on the racism and classism that plague our society while never forgetting that this is also a place for love. In Milagros Vargas, author Marcia Argueta Mickelson has brilliantly captured a voice for our times."

—Diana López, author of *Lucky Luna*

WHERE I
BELONG

WHERE I
BELONG

WHERE I
BELONG

MARCIA ARGUETA MICKELSON

carolrhoda LAB
MINNEAPOLIS

Carolrhoda Lab®
An imprint of Lerner Publishing Group, Inc.
241 First Avenue North
Minneapolis, MN 55401 USA

For reading levels and more information, look up this title at www.lernerbooks.com.

Cover and interior image: Jenny Dettrick/Getty Images.

Main body text set in Janson Text LT Std.
Typeface provided by Linotype AG.

Library of Congress Cataloging-in-Publication Data

Names: Mickelson, Marcia Argueta, 1973– author.
Title: Where I belong / Marcia Argueta Mickelson.
Description: Minneapolis : Carolrhoda Lab, [2021] | Audience: Ages 13–18. |
    Audience: Grades 10–12. | Summary: "Guatemalan American high school senior
    Millie Vargas struggles to balance her family's needs with her own ambitions,
    especially after her mother's employer, a Senate candidate, uses Millie as a poster
    child for 'deserving' immigrants" —Provided by publisher.
Identifiers: LCCN 2020009207 (print) | LCCN 2020009208 (ebook) |
    ISBN 9781541597976 | ISBN 9781728417363 (ebook)
Subjects: CYAC: Family life—Texas—Fiction. | Immigrants—Fiction. |
    Guatemalan Americans—Fiction. | Dating (Social customs)—Fiction. | Politics,
    Practical—Fiction. | Texas—Fiction.
Classification: LCC PZ7.M581924 Whe 2021 (print) | LCC PZ7.M581924 (ebook)
    | DDC [Fic]—dc23

LC record available at https://lccn.loc.gov/2020009207
LC ebook record available at https://lccn.loc.gov/2020009208

Manufactured in the United States of America
1-47986-48667-4/13/2021

GRACIAS A MI PAPI, JOSE ARGUETA,
POR TRAERNOS A ESTE GRAN PAÍS.

CHAPTER ONE

MAY 2018

Girls who were born in Guatemala can never be president of the United States. This is all I can think about every time I see Mr. Brody in one of his yellow button-downs. He crosses in front of me in the hall and turns into his classroom. As I watch him enter, I catch a glimpse of the huge U.S. map that covers his windows. I guess the oversized map he treasures so much is vastly more important than the sunlight we might receive on that side of the building.

He never actually said the words, but it's the message I came away with. Freshman year, he asked for volunteers to run for president in a model election. I volunteered, only to be told that he wanted to make the elections realistic, with only natural-born citizens. I wanted to point out that it couldn't possibly be realistic because none of us were thirty-five. Of course I didn't say that, because I still wanted an A in the class. I did get the A, but I never quite forgave Mr. Brody.

I shake the bitter thought away as I head outdoors to the bus. It's not that I actually want to be president, but I don't like being told I can't do something just because of where I'm from. I was only a few months old when my parents left Guatemala, but sometimes those few months feel like an anchor weighing down my entire life. Getting my citizenship two years ago, getting my college acceptance letters this spring—none of it erases the fact that I wasn't born here.

Charlie Wheeler comes up right behind me as I step outside and head toward the buses. "Hey, Millie. How's it going?"

"Hey, Charlie." That's all I say. Charlie Wheeler doesn't actually want to know how it's going. He's just one of those people who is surface-level friendly toward everyone. Convenient for the son of an aspiring U.S. senator, I'm sure.

"So I know it's still a few weeks away, but I'm having a pool party the day after graduation," he says. "Just thought I'd let you know in case you'd like to come."

Leave it to Charlie to not see the irony of his invitation. During the summer, I have to stay home to babysit because *my* mother is babysitting *his* sister. My mom has been the Wheelers' housekeeper since Charlie's little sister, Caroline, was born seven years ago. Mami does more than just clean their house and cook their meals—she's practically raised Caroline Wheeler. "I can't, Charlie, but thanks." I turn to face him as I say this, out of politeness, but quickly redirect my gaze toward the buses.

Charlie steps into the bus line with me. "Well, let me know if you change your mind. You'd be welcome to bring Chloe or Jen or whoever, really." He gives me one last hopeful smile before turning toward the path that leads to student parking.

Imagine being rich enough to host an unlimited number of people for a graduation party at your house. And then paying my mom to clean up afterward.

I board the bus and take my usual seat next to my friend Chloe. Our school is right in the middle of Corpus Christi,

Texas—two miles away from both the richest part of town and the poorest part of town. Currently, it's headed to the latter.

Chloe's concentrating on her latest sketch. She carries a small sketch pad everywhere and ninety percent of the pages are filled with drawings of horses. It's her dream to own a horse, probably not something that will happen soon. Her family is only slightly better off than mine.

"Hey," I say, sliding in next to her. "Let me see."

She angles the notebook toward me. "I'm not finished yet . . ." she says tentatively.

"It's great, Chlo. You're amazing. I could never draw anything like that."

"You have to say that because you're my best friend." She pulls the notebook back in front of her and starts shading in the horse's mane.

"I say that because I have eyes and can see how good you are."

She smiles because she knows it's true. "You going to the dance this Saturday?"

"No. My mom has to work late."

"You never get to do anything." Chloe shakes her head.

"I'm used to it, I guess," I say even though I'm not.

"How late does she work? Can you go after she's done?"

"No," I say. "The Wheelers are having a dinner party, so she's going to be there until way after midnight, serving and cleaning up." They've always been big entertainers, especially Dr. Wheeler, Charlie and Caroline's mom. And now that Mr. Wheeler is running for Senate, they spend a lot of time courting big donors.

"Well, I don't think I want to go anyway." Chloe pulls out her phone, checks it, and then shoves it back into the pocket of her jeans. "Maybe Jen and I can come over and help you with the kids. We can watch a movie after they go to bed."

"You don't have to do that. You should go. I bet Ivan will be there."

"Yeah, I know Ivan will be there, but that doesn't mean anything really. He just wants to hang out with his stupid friends."

I know all about his stupid friends, especially Jay Hernandez, who was my boyfriend until ten months ago. "You really should go, though," I say to Chloe. Just because I don't have a life outside of being an unpaid nanny doesn't mean she shouldn't either. For the most part, I try not to throw myself pity parties, but when I do, Mami is usually there to remind me that missing dances were not her teenage worries. She tells me about how she spent her youth avoiding assault and theft every time she rode the autobus. Or she'll bring up her nineteen-year-old uncle, who was dragged out of his bed and arrested for sympathizing with insurrectionists who opposed Guatemala's dictator during its thirty-six-year civil war.

"We're almost done with stupid high school boys anyway," I remind Chloe, since I can tell she's still thinking about Ivan. "I can't wait until we meet some college guys, you know."

"I know, girl. And I can't wait for our road trip. I just put away another fifty bucks that I got for my birthday." Chloe and I are saving for a trip out west this summer. Chloe will visit her older sister in Arizona and then drop me off in California to start my fall semester at Stanford.

So far, I've told my mother nothing about this.

Mami doesn't know that I was offered—and accepted—a full ride to Stanford. She thinks I'm going to the Texas A&M satellite school right here in Corpus Christi, since they've also offered me a full-ride scholarship. And I was tempted to stay here. I really was. But I turned them down, without telling Mami. I'm waiting for the right time to break it to her that I'll be going almost two thousand miles away.

Chloe looks at me as if she can tell what I'm thinking. "Your mom is going to flip when you tell her about California. How's she going to keep your virginity intact from so far away?"

I laugh. "Stop it." Although she's barely more than an in-name-only Catholic, Mami lives by a lot of Catholic values—no stealing, no taking the name of the Lord in vain, no sex before marriage.

"Girl, I'm going to miss you," Chloe adds. "Never mind your mom, what am *I* going to do without you?"

"Oh, I'm going to miss you too. Everyone at Stanford is going to suck compared to you."

The bus pulls up to our stop. As Chloe and I get off, I pull my long hair into a ponytail. All the women in my family have straight black hair that only slightly curls with the Texas humidity.

We walk together until Chloe gets to her house. I have two more blocks on my own. Two blocks of perfectly alone, quietly mine time. It's the only time I get completely to myself—to breathe, to think, without someone wanting something from me or wanting to tell me something. I take in the hot, humid air, pretending, for just two blocks, that it isn't stifling. For those two blocks it's fresh spring air—cool and calming.

And then I get home.

Sele has done the best a thirteen-year-old can do to hold things together for the past half hour, since she and the younger two got home from their schools. It's my siblings' free time to watch TV or play before the homework battle begins with nine-year-old Javi and six-year-old Ceci.

I dump my heavy backpack on the floor by the door, not to be picked up until seven-thirty, which is when I usually start my own homework. For now, it's time to play mami.

"Okay, guys. Let's turn off the TV. Time for homework."

"But this show's almost over!" Javi says, jumping up from the couch.

"Five more minutes, and that's it," I say. After I take a quick trip to the bathroom and the five minutes have expired, I try again.

Javi groans.

"Wait!" pleads Ceci, grabbing the remote from Sele, who's about to turn it off.

Sele rolls her eyes and lets Ceci have the remote. She's been dealing with them since school let out, and she's tired of it. She settles in at the table with her math book.

I focus on prying Javi away from the TV. He hates home-work almost as much as I hate making him do it. "Come on, Javi. Spelling test is tomorrow. It won't take long."

"But Millie. I haven't had much free time."

"More free time than me. I still have to help you and make dinner. Now, let's go!"

Javi stomps his foot and sets off to find his backpack. He's named after our dad, Javier Vargas. Papi worked for an oil refinery out in the Gulf until he died of a heart attack almost three years ago. Now, Mami works a lot more. She used to work part-time at the Wheelers, but after Papi died, they gave her a raise, more hours, and the chance to clean Mr. Wheeler's law office as well. Sele and I have picked up the slack at home. It's just what you do; there's no choice. When a tragedy happens, you pick up the pieces and move on. That's what I learned from Mami, who's cried only once in my eighteen years—the day my papi died.

Ceci comes into the kitchen too now. With Javi resigned to do homework, she has no one on her side, and she surrenders. She starts with her preferred assignment—reading—delaying the math worksheet and spelling words until later, when I'll have to threaten to call Mami if she doesn't do them.

She grabs her Beverly Cleary book from her backpack and a flashlight from the counter and crawls into a cupboard by the stove. That is where she reads, where she has space to herself in this tiny house.

As a first-grader, Ceci is already reading at a fourth-grade reading level. I think back to my first-grade experience. It was nothing like that. I was speaking English, but barely learning to read, sounding things out. I didn't start reading Beverly Cleary until I was in fifth grade, after four years of pull-out sessions with the school reading interventionist, Mrs. Lacey. Mrs. Lacey had a sound board that showed all forty-four sounds that make up the English language. I remember asking her how there could be forty-four sounds when there were only twenty-six letters in the alphabet.

I've come a long way since then. The summer after sophomore year, I spent countless hours going through SAT prep books from the library and taking online practice tests. But I still found time to start teaching Ceci to read. She wasn't even in kindergarten yet, but I didn't want her to suffer through embarrassing reading pullouts once she did start school. And now, we have the result of those efforts sitting in the cupboard diving into a two-hundred-page book.

An hour later, I've successfully plowed through homework with Javi and Ceci, and they've been rewarded with thirty more minutes of TV while I get dinner ready. Mami has called to remind us that she's working late because the Wheelers are at a campaign function. This Senate run is keeping both Mr. Wheeler and Dr. Wheeler busier than ever, which means more responsibilities for Mami, and by default more responsibilities for me.

After dinner, once Javi and Ceci have cleared the table, I remind them to take showers and get ready for school tomorrow.

As I start the dishes, I try to think of a way to tell Mami that I'll be leaving. At first, I didn't tell her about Stanford's offer because I assumed that I couldn't take it, that I couldn't leave her and the kids to manage by themselves. But then the deadline came, and I had to decide, and I found myself accepting. Afterward, the guilt overcame me, and I just could not bring myself to tell her.

Time is running out, though, and I'll have to break the news to her—to everyone—soon.

CHAPTER TWO

This Sunday is dollar day at the Texas State Aquarium. It's the only time we can afford to go. Half the city has come to the same conclusion, I realize as we stand in a slow-moving line two blocks long. We even came early, but not early enough it seems. Slugs move faster than this mass of ice-chest-toting, stroller-pushing parents.

Mami had to work. She's watching Caroline Wheeler while Mr. and Dr. Wheeler are at a political appearance in Austin and Charlie is out of town with some friends. I try not to be mad that she has to spend her whole Sunday carting Caroline around to her art lessons, dance lessons, soccer games, whatever activities that overscheduled child is enduring. I know it's overtime, extra money for us. Sele is going to need braces soon, and I'll be going to college next year.

Chloe drove us here, in exchange for me paying for her ticket and bringing lunch. She's the youngest of three, so she doesn't have younger siblings and enjoys hanging out with us. We're in line behind a young mom who's trying to hold on to her wiggly toddler while the baby in her stroller wrestles in his seat and yelps every time he realizes he's being restrained.

Groups of people walk past our winding line toward the entrance. They're members who have a yearly pass to get in any time they want. They get to use a special entrance. I can tell they're relieved that they don't have to wait like us.

It's worth it, though. It's life changing; it was what changed my life when I was in third grade. Our class came on a field trip, and I was torn between watching the graceful jellyfish with their dancing tentacles and sitting out on the deck by the dolphin exhibit, breathing in the sea air from the bay.

That feeling of belonging comes every time I get near seawater. It's what keeps me going back to the beach every chance I get, what brings me here every year, what compels me to strive for straight As in hopes of getting into a marine biology program.

"Millie!" Javi says. "I'm tired. Can we just go home?"

"No, Javi. We're going inside. We just have to wait."

"But Millie. Look at the line."

"I know," I say, thinking he stood in a line twice as long to meet the Spurs point guard. I'm not about to give up on today's outing. This will be the last time I get to go to Dollar Day—the last time I get to share the aquarium with my siblings—before I leave for Stanford. Though they don't know that yet.

I swing my backpack off my shoulder and pull out a Frisbee. I've come fully prepared. "Here. You can go out in the field and throw this around. Ceci, you want to go with him?"

"Yeah." She grabs it from me and takes off for the large field next to the building.

"Wait, Ceci. She gave it to me!" Javi catches up to her and takes it from her hands. He throws it across the field, and Ceci runs after it yelling out his name.

Chloe laughs. "Nice way to get rid of them," she says.

"It's the only way we're going to survive this wait."

"It's not so bad," Sele says. She pulls out her phone and starts texting. I can always count on her to be the one without complaint. Mami and Papi named me after the Spanish word for "miracles," while they named Sele after the Tejano singer from Corpus, but Sele's the real wonder. Sometimes, Mami calls her "mi cielo," *my heaven*, and I wouldn't disagree. She never argues with the little ones; she never asks for anything.

Still, I hate to think about how she'll have to take care of them all on her own after I leave for college. She's even younger than I was when Papi died. And she's not expecting it; as far as she knows, I'll be living at home and going to TAMU-CC for the next four years. Telling her about Stanford will be almost as hard as breaking the news to Mami.

Another boy has joined Javi and Ceci in the field, and the three of them are running toward the fallen Frisbee. I fear a collision as the three dive for it, but the new boy holds it up victoriously over his head as Javi and Ceci spread apart, ready for the throw.

"You have anything to eat in here?" Chloe asks as she digs through my still-open backpack.

"Yes, but I didn't think you would be the first one asking for it," I say, laughing. I put the backpack on the ground at our feet so she can reach it more easily.

"Girl, I didn't have any breakfast. My mom sleeps in till ten on Sundays, and you made me wake up extra early."

"Phsh. You picked us up at eight-thirty. How is that extra early? Besides, you're perfectly capable of making your own breakfast."

"I'm missing out on my mom's eggs, so don't get on my

bad side," Chloe says as she pulls out a granola bar. "And just so you know, I'm not waking up at five to watch those turtles this summer. You're on your own for that."

"Noted," I say with a snort. Last year, I took Chloe with me to the National Seashore to watch a bunch of baby sea turtles drag themselves the thirty feet from their nests to the ocean. She wasn't impressed.

The young mom in front of me looks at her phone and then at the slow-moving line in front of us, probably questioning her decision to come here. Her toddler is on the ground draining his sippy cup, but the wrestler in his stroller is now grunting loudly. He's either going number two or seriously ticked off. She sighs and bends down to unbuckle his stroller.

"Can I hold him?" I offer.

She looks up at me, wipes a hair off her face, and smiles. "Sure." She picks up the squirmy baby and holds him out to me. I try to remember the last time I held a baby. It was Ceci. I take the baby and try to balance him on my hip. "What's his name?"

"Christopher."

"Hi, Christopher," I say in a cheerful voice I've never heard myself use.

"I didn't expect the wait to be this bad," Christopher's mom says. "I'm not sure we're going to make it."

"It hasn't always been like this, but every year it gets more popular as more people find out about the discount."

"You've done this before?" she asks.

"Every year for the past nine years. It's awesome."

Chloe scoffs. "You're asking a girl who's obsessed with fish, so it's kind of a biased opinion."

"I'm not obsessed with fish, Chloe. You make it sound silly."

"She's *obsessed* with fish," Chloe repeats to Christopher's mom. "And sea turtles. And jellyfish. She'd live with them if she could."

Christopher squirms in my arms and reaches out to grab a fistful of my hair. I gently pry it out of his hand and throw it behind my shoulder. His hand goes to my nose and he starts poking it.

"You sure you're okay with him?" Christopher's mom asks.

"Yes, just fine," I say. I really want Christopher's mom and her little family to make it inside the aquarium. I want this little baby with the worn, hand-me-down tennis shoes and the faded stroller to see the dolphins and jellyfish.

The toddler, Christopher's brother, is now running toward the field where Javi and Ceci are playing. His mom runs after him, which makes him go faster, squealing with laughter. The line moves up a little, and Sele pushes the stroller a few feet. We continue like that for about ten minutes, until Javi and Ceci come running back, sweating and begging for drinks. I give them each a juice box from the backpack, knowing I'll still have enough for lunch.

The moment I knew was coming has now come: Ceci says she needs to go to the bathroom.

"Ceci, you're going to have to wait until we get inside. We're only about ten people away from the entrance."

"Millieee," Ceci says, using the squeal-y tone that usually makes me submit to her pleas, but not today.

Christopher's mom looks at me in sympathy and takes him back. I kneel down to look at Ceci. I know she can hold it; she knows she can hold it. Now, I just have to convince her to do it. "We're almost there," I say.

"You want to play Angry Birds?" Chloe asks her.

"Oooh," Ceci says, grabbing the phone from Chloe's

outstretched hand. The novelty of a smartphone is a welcome distraction to her. She quickly figures out the game with a few pointers from Chloe.

"Thank you," I mouth to Chloe, though I wonder if the aquarium will have any appeal for her now that new technology has found its way into her hands.

"You're welcome," she says. "So, by the way, the dance was totally stupid last night. Be glad you didn't go."

"Why was it stupid?"

"Ivan is such a loser. I see why you dumped his best friend."

Jay had a tendency to forget when we'd made plans. He'd spend ten hours straight surfing at the beach while I sat at home, waiting.

"When I got there, Ivan comes right up to me, starts talking to me. We dance for three songs straight, and then he spends the rest of the night hanging out with his friends."

"That sounds about right," I say.

"I'm just going to forget about him. I know he likes me, but what's the point if he's going to do exactly to me what Jay did to you?"

"Did he even say good night?"

"No. Stupid dork," Chloe says. A second later, her phone announces a text, and she grabs it from Ceci's hands. "Stupid dork just texted me."

"What did he say?" I ask.

"*Where did you go last night? I didn't see you anymore.*" Chloe starts typing. "Right in front of your face," she says even though I know that's not what she's writing.

I look over her shoulder.

Was just hanging with Jen, she's said. *I thought you'd left.*

I was looking for you, his response says.

"Yeah, right!" Chloe keeps texting as we finally reach the front entrance.

At the counter, I hand the attendant a five-dollar bill, a fraction of the usual cost. After the attendant admits us, Javi and Ceci run toward their favorite exhibit, the touch tank.

"I'll go save seats at the dolphins," Chloe says, not taking her eyes off her phone.

Sele follows her. "I'll go with you."

"You guys sure?" I ask. The dolphin show won't start for another forty minutes, but the seating always fills up quickly and if you don't go early, you end up standing.

"Yeah, take the little ones to do their thing. We'll see you soon." Chloe waves me away and walks off with Sele.

Before I can catch Javi and Ceci, their hands are immersed in a touch tank inhabited by hermit crabs, starfish, and an assortment of other small creatures. I won't admit it, but this is one of my favorite parts of the aquarium as well. The area is surrounded by small hands searching for something to touch or pick up. I find a small spot to squeeze through and pick up a hermit crab. It crawls around my hand in short, unsteady steps.

When Javi and Ceci have had their fill, I make them clean their hands with sanitizer before moving on. Next up are the enormous tanks that hold large fish and small sharks, and I slip onto a bench to watch them. I quickly find my favorite small shark. I savor its graceful movements as it glides through the water, unique among hundreds of different kinds of fish and sea animals in this tank. They pass each other undisturbed, in harmony.

Nearby, moving slowly and deliberately through the water, is a man in a wetsuit who's cleaning the tank. It's always fascinating to watch the aquarium staff at work. One day, I will wear a wetsuit like that and I will dive deep into the sea, surrounded by hundreds of species of fish.

Javi taps me on the shoulder. "Let's go, Millie. I want to see the stingrays."

I check my Mickey Mouse watch, a gift from Papi that I always wear even though my phone could tell me the time just as well. We have fifteen minutes until the dolphin show starts. "We'll see them after the dolphins. We just barely have time for the jellyfish before that."

In the jellyfish room, I press my fingertips against the glass and focus in on a tiny one in the center; it dangles in the water, reaching its tentacles out as far as possible. I move on to the next window to stare at the angelic white jellyfish, larger than the first, the umbrella-shaped bell squeezing in and out. Ceci, somewhat afraid of the darkened room, grabs my hand and asks if we can leave. I resist for a minute as I watch a purple-striped jellyfish dancing through the water.

Finally, Javi joins forces with Ceci, and together they manage to pull me away from the jellyfish and out into the bright foyer. We hurry outside and squeeze onto a bench between Sele, immersed in her book, and Chloe, who's sketching. As I sit down next to her, I see that she's drawing the Harbor Bridge on the horizon. It's a familiar scene, but I never get tired of it. I'll miss it next year. I'll miss all of this.

But that's the future. Right now, the small seating area is full, and the announcer begins talking. Right now, as I breathe in the smell of the seawater that surrounds the aquarium and watch the marine animal trainers preparing for the show, there isn't anywhere else in the world I'd rather be.

CHAPTER THREE

W ho takes weekend trips to Cancun? My weekend revolved around babysitting my siblings; the aquarium visit was the most excitement I got. Charlie Wheeler, on the other hand, spent two days ziplining, kayaking, and scuba diving with his friends.

"We zipped down past these trees and then plunged right into the water," Charlie tells our entire row in AP English class. "It was so amazing."

My friend Jen, who sits a couple rows away, turns to look at me and rolls her eyes. I just smile and shrug. With Charlie sitting in front of me, I can't avoid hearing his vacation recap. I have, however, been able to avoid glancing at any of the pictures he's scrolling through on his phone.

"And *this* line was more than a hundred and thirty feet. Can you imagine that plunge?"

Mindy Stincil grabs his wrist to get a better look at the picture on his phone. "Okay. I am definitely going next time."

I look at Ms. Cope, hoping she'll put an end to Charlie's already too-detailed account of his trip, but she's still at the door, summoning in the stragglers.

I double my efforts to review my chapter outline before class starts and it's quiz time.

Nearly every girl in our school who likes boys at all has had the obligatory Charlie Wheeler crush, and each one of those girls has eventually come to the realization that he is completely out of her league. I had my obligatory Charlie Wheeler crush when I was twelve. It was extinguished rather quickly and only occasionally resurfaces when he flashes me that orthodontically perfected smile.

There's only one girl who seems eligible for the Charlie Wheeler seal of approval, and that is Mindy Stincil. She's the smartest *and* prettiest girl in our senior class, in addition to having a family almost as rich as Charlie's. I've often asked God how that could possibly be fair, but I'm still waiting for my answer. Her only flaw seems to be that she's terrible at layups; Chloe and I can't help secretly laughing at her in PE.

Charlie turns around in his seat. "Hey, Millie. How was your weekend?" He combs his sandy brown bangs to the side with his fingers and smiles, pocketing the iPhone.

I keep my eyes on my outline. "Not as good as yours, apparently."

"It *was* pretty cool," he says, missing the passive-aggressiveness in my voice. "We toured two Mayan ruins. Have you been to some of the ruins in Guatemala?"

"No," I say. "The few times I've been back were to visit family. We don't really have time to do, you know, touristy stuff."

"Well, the tour guide in Cancun told us that the ones in Guatemala are awesome too. I'd love to go sometime."

"Knock yourself out," I say, turning the page in my notebook. "Most people I know are trying to leave Guatemala to come here and escape, you know, poverty, gang violence, and political corruption, but I guess when people like you go there on vacation, you don't have to see that type of stuff."

"People like me? What do you mean, like, white?"

I let out a long sigh. He's only half right. "People with money. So, sure, go to Guatemala. Take your tours. Take your pictures. Just don't feel like you have to report to me because I happened to be born there."

"What are you so pissed about?" he asks me.

"I'm pissed," I say, trying to lower my voice, "because it was America's intervention that started our civil war, which is the reason so many of us left. And now Americans who don't even know the history want to vacation there and have a good time? I just don't want to hear about that."

"Okay . . . sorry," he says and turns around just as Ms. Cope starts our lesson.

Some people might think it's strange that I'm in AP English when Spanish is my first language. My first year of school was a nightmare. I didn't understand anything, and I hated it. I was only five years old, but it was in Miss Smart's kindergarten class that I resolved not only to learn to speak English, but to learn it well—to learn it better than the bright blond kids who surrounded me. And with Mrs. Lacey's help, I eventually got there, with a near-perfect score on the reading section of the SAT to prove to colleges that I belong in my advanced classes.

I don't love this class. It's not that I don't like to read. I do. But I don't like to beat a story to death, which is precisely what Ms. Cope does. It takes us weeks to get halfway through a book, choking the life out of what little symbolism remains.

Currently, we're doing that to Corrie ten Boom's *The Hiding Place*. Corrie and Betsie have just been forced into a concentration camp. I would prefer to read quickly through this harrowing and painful part, but Ms. Cope is dragging us through the experience.

"Why do you think the ten Boom sisters risked harm, risked their lives, to help all those people?" Ms. Cope asks as she walks down the aisle between two rows of desks.

A few people raise their hands, but I lean my head down, bury it behind my open book. Ms. Cope waits a moment, wanting us all to have thought about it. I myself cannot answer the question because I honestly don't know how Corrie and Betsie could have been so brave.

Such bravery and selflessness is beyond what my brain can comprehend. Betsie dies at Ravensbrück. She actually dies. I wouldn't have blamed Corrie and Betsie if they'd chosen not to be part of the resistance movement, not to hide Jewish people during the Nazi occupation. I cannot imagine opening up my home, sacrificing my family's safety that way. My instinct is toward self-preservation. Some people might think of that as selfishness, but I don't. I don't believe it's selfish to make sure you and your family are safe. So, no, I cannot answer Ms. Cope's question.

But Charlie Wheeler can, of course. Ms. Cope calls on him.

"It was their desire to help others," he says. "Corrie ten Boom once said something about how a person's life is measured by its donation, not by its duration. What matters in your life is what you do for others."

Ms. Cope smiles. "Yes, Charlie. Yes! It was their belief in helping others. And that stayed with them through hiding people in their home, through the concentration camp, and through everything else that happened."

When she's finished with her excessive praise of Charlie's answer, Ms. Cope asks another question that I don't hear. I'm still thinking about what Charlie said, about how he can so easily say something like that. Donation. Giving to others. It sounds impressive, but it's not practical. At least not for me or hundreds of others at this school. Sure, it's totally doable for Charlie Wheeler, who spent spring break building houses in Costa Rica. Dr. Wheeler works at a clinic in the poorest area of town. Charles Wheeler's law practice represents lots of pro bono cases. And of course, Charlie goes to school with people like me because his parents believe in public education. Philanthropy, generosity—that's easy for the Wheelers. Well, what do you do when you have nothing to give?

CHAPTER FOUR

When I get home from school, I see Javi outside playing football with the boy who lives down the street. Justin. I know Javi idolizes him. I also know Mami's opinion of him. "Ese niño es muy malcriado," "No tiene respeto," "Se porta muy mal." Justin is rude, has no respect, and behaves very badly. She has told Javi, in both English and Spanish, that he is not to play with Justin.

"Javi," I yell out, walking toward him. "Come here!"

Javi catches the perfect spiral from Justin and turns to me. "Millie, go away. Just leave me alone."

"Why is your sister such a downer, man?" Justin asks, catching Javi's return throw. "Tell her she needs to get a boyfriend and get a life."

I take a deep breath, trying to decide which boy I will turn my wrath on first. "Javi, get in the house right now. Justin, why don't you go do your homework? You want to stay in the fifth grade again next year?"

"Screw you, Millie," says the two-time fifth-grader. He grabs his ball and walks into his house.

Javi storms past me. "You ruin everything!"

"You know what Mami will say," I tell Javi, following him home.

"Because of course you're going to tell her," Javi screams over his shoulder. He flings open the front door and runs to his room.

Ceci is combing her Barbie's hair with her eyes fixed on the Disney Channel. "Five minutes and homework, Ceci," I say.

"'Kay," she says without taking her eyes off the TV.

"Sele," I yell out as I dump my backpack by the door.

She comes into the living room from the kitchen. "What?"

"Javi was outside playing with Justin."

"Sorry. He must have snuck out." She walks back into the kitchen and sits down to finish her homework.

I sink into a kitchen chair and sit there trying to guess the contents of the refrigerator, grasping at some idea of what to make for dinner. I eventually pull myself to my feet and start boiling water for spaghetti.

Javi walks in a few minutes later, carrying his backpack to start homework. Normally it takes a half dozen requests and threats from me before he even starts. "I'm sorry, Millie. Please don't tell Mami."

I sigh. "Javi, you can't hang out with Justin anymore. You know how Mami feels about him, and I completely agree with her."

"I won't. I won't. Just don't tell her."

I shake my head, knowing I will probably keep his secret. "Just do your homework."

The three of them finish their homework, and Sele helps me make meat sauce to go with the spaghetti. After dinner, they take turns showering while I start the dishes. The landline phone rings just as I submerge my hands in the soapy, warm water.

I wipe them off on the terrycloth apron Mami made years ago.

"Hello?"

"Millie," Mami says in a rushed voice. "I'm trying to call the Wheelers. I can't reach them. You have to go down to Heritage Park to look for them. Mr. Wheeler is giving a speech down there."

"Why? What's the matter?"

"Caroline hurt her arm. She was doing a cartwheel and fell on it. It might be broken. I'm taking her to the emergency room, but they need to meet me there. They're not answering. I even tried Charlie's phone. I think he's down there too."

"Okay, I'll go. I'll get Chloe to take me."

"Tell Selena to watch the kids, put them to bed."

"I'll tell her. Are you going to be all right?" I ask her.

"Si, si. Fine. Just please hurry."

Five minutes later, I run outside, locking the door behind me, and climb into Chloe's dad's pickup.

"Thanks for coming so fast."

"Sure," she says backing out. "So, you said Heritage Park?"

"Yeah. If you can't find parking, maybe you can just let me out."

As Chloe drives, I fiddle with my phone in my pocket, hoping Mami will call to tell me she's reached Dr. Wheeler and I can go back home. But there is no call, and I picture Mami having to wait in the emergency room with Caroline.

Chloe pulls up behind the small plaza surrounded by old Victorian homes-turned-mini-museums. The parking lot is completely full, so I get out, and she says she'll wait for me in the truck. I take off toward the crowd that is gathered around the hundred-year-old Victorian house in the middle of Heritage Park. I slow down as I reach the back of the crowd.

Mr. Wheeler is at the top of the house's steps. Dr. Wheeler and Charlie are standing next to him as he speaks into a microphone. Charlie's looking debonair in his navy suit and red tie. There are TV cameras and lights glaring at the Wheelers. At least a couple hundred residents of Corpus have gathered to hear him speak on what is quite possibly the most humid night in any of their lifetimes.

I weave through the crowd, working my way toward the front. I try to make eye contact with Charlie, but he doesn't see me. There's a tall man in front of me, with his arm around a woman, and his cowboy boots almost trip me. I walk around them, leaning low so I don't block their view. "Mr. Wheeler," I hear a reporter say, "what would you say to concerned citizens, here in South Texas, and also around the country, who question your opposition to current immigration policy, and your support of amnesty for illegal immigrants?"

Mr. Wheeler nods as if he expected this question. "Let's be clear. Many of the people who are trying to enter this country are fleeing crushing poverty and terrible violence. And they're arriving at the U.S. border without documentation because our current policies make legal immigration an extremely complicated and long process. These people's lives are in danger; their children's lives are in danger. They're coming here because they have no choice. They're simply seeking a safe place where they and their children can work hard, study hard, and contribute to society. I don't think that's too much for them to ask."

I keep pushing through the crowd. I'm at the front now. I don't want to climb the short set of stairs to where the Wheelers are standing, but I can't seem to get their attention. I wave at Charlie, but he doesn't see me. I take tiny steps forward until I reach the banister and place my hand on it, gripping it tightly. I do another small wave, and all three Wheelers look down at me.

Mr. Wheeler stops speaking for just an instant before continuing. Dr. Wheeler joins me at the bottom of the steps.

Perspiration has accumulated under her blond bangs, and she wipes it away with her hand. "Millie, what is it?" she whispers.

"My mom's been trying to call you. Caroline may have broken her arm; they're on their way to the emergency room."

"Oh no." She grabs for both pockets of her ivory-colored jacket, feeling around. "My phone. I left it inside." She turns to look at the house, and Charlie gives her a questioning look.

Dr. Wheeler turns to a woman standing near the bottom of the steps. I recognize her; she's one of the Wheelers' friends. They whisper together for a minute before Dr. Wheeler turns back to me. "Jane is going to give me a ride. Can you tell Charlie where I went and tell him to grab my purse and phone? They're inside."

Before I can answer, Dr. Wheeler and Jane dash around the side of the house toward the parking lot.

". . . hardworking immigrants," Mr. Wheeler is saying, "can achieve great things. For instance, my housekeeper's family—they were undocumented when they first came here, fleeing violence in Guatemala. They applied for asylum and were among the lucky few to receive it. They've spent their lives working hard, hoping to achieve the American dream for their children. And now, eighteen years later, their daughter is a U.S. citizen about to graduate from high school. A straight-A student, and she had her pick of universities."

I'm frozen in place. I feel strangers' eyes on me, scrutinizing me, even though none of them could possibly know that it's me he is talking about. The man with the cowboy boots is watching me, or at least I feel like he is.

Mr. Wheeler continues. "That's why so many undocumented immigrants, so many asylum seekers detained at the border, are risking their lives to get here. They want to work hard and give their children the education, the safety, the futures they deserve, so that they can make their own contributions to our country." I look around, and it feels like everyone is staring at me, but they're watching him.

I can't move. Instinctively, I want to run away from this crowd, from Mr. Wheeler's words, but I can't. "Our country is better with them in it. That's why I oppose current policies at the border, and that's why I'm in favor of a path to citizenship for undocumented young people who attend college or join the military. They're here to work. They're here to serve. And we need to let them do just that."

Tremendous applause follows his last statement. The man in the cowboy boots whistles with both his pinkies in his mouth.

I turn and sprint back toward the street, where Chloe is waiting for me in the truck.

"Millie, hang on," I hear behind me.

I spin around, and Charlie Wheeler catches up to me.

"Are you okay?" he asks me. He tugs at his collar and tie.

"What is wrong with your dad?" I burst out. "How could he do that to me?"

"He didn't mean anything bad by it," says Charlie, plainly confused. "He was praising you."

I turn away from him. "He shouldn't have said something so personal about me."

"But everything he said was positive." Charlie pops up beside me, matching my stride. "And, I mean, nobody knows it was you. He didn't use your name or your mom's."

I shake my head, focusing on the pickup truck ahead of me, its lights illuminating the street. Suddenly the humid air feels even more stifling. I let out a breath I'd been holding since I heard Mr. Wheeler start talking about my family.

"He just told everyone in that crowd something very private about my family. That's nobody's business." I can't stop my voice from rising. It's hard enough to know that people look at me differently because I wasn't born here, but it's even worse for them to know I was technically an undocumented immigrant when I first arrived. Papi applied for asylum right away, which gave us legal status, and we got green cards soon afterward, but people will hear *undocumented* and jump to their own conclusions.

"I'm sorry if it upset you, Millie. My dad loves your family. He was just—"

"Stop it, Charlie!" I look back at the crowd, still cheering at whatever Mr. Wheeler is saying. I don't hear his words anymore; I just drown out his voice.

Taking a deep breath, I suppress the urge to scream at Charlie. "My mother is in the ER right now with your sister and her broken arm."

"Wait. What hap—?"

"And I left my siblings home alone so that I could chase your parents down, and then your father stands in front of hundreds of people, on camera, and talks about my family like he has a right to tell our story."

I turn away from him.

"Oh, and your mother said don't forget her purse and phone. She left them inside." I don't wait for him to answer before I run the rest of the way to Chloe.

I fill Chloe in on what happened as she drives me home.

"Wow," she says, "Mr. Wheeler said all that without getting your family's permission first? What was he thinking?"

"He *wasn't* thinking. It's like he assumed that just because he was saying positive things about us, he had a right to make us a talking point for his campaign."

"What's your mom going to say?"

"Nothing!" I say, throwing my hands in the air. "She never gets mad at them for anything they do."

"I'm sorry," Chloe says. "You going to be okay?"

I shrug and lean my head against the window. I am filled with shame, and I don't even know why. I haven't done anything wrong.

Chloe doesn't say anything the rest of the drive. She probably doesn't know what to say. She was born in Texas. She's always been an American. She doesn't speak Spanish and neither does her mother. Chloe is my friend, and she knows I'm hurting, but she doesn't truly understand why.

I stare out the window at the passing houses. Small, weather-beaten homes lifted up on cinder blocks, no foundations. These are the homes we live in. The Wheelers don't know what it's like. They live in a house that's rooted firmly to the ground, with a cathedral ceiling reaching high into the sky.

≈

I'm lying on the couch when Mami comes in. My physics homework has long been abandoned on the floor.

"Mija, thank you for your help tonight. It turned out that Caroline's arm isn't broken, just sprained. Caroline was really scared, though. She wanted her mother." Mami sits on the couch by my head and runs her fingers through my hair, smoothing it down.

I want to tell her what happened at the park, but the words don't come easily. My lungs are burning as though I'm swallowing mouthfuls of water. Shame is pressing down on me, even though I haven't done anything wrong. And anger, but I'm not sure whom it's directed at. Mr. Wheeler, I think, but not just him.

"Que paso, mija?" she asks.

My tears come quickly, which brings more shame because Mami never cries. Except for three years ago, right after Papi died.

I manage to tell her what happened, how Mr. Wheeler told everyone about our lives.

"Mija, eso no es nada." She says it's nothing, but to me it is everything. Everything about me has been exposed for strangers to hear. "He told the truth about where we come from, why we're here. That's something to be proud of."

How can I be proud of something like that? I know what others think of people like us. Wetbacks. Mojados. Illegal aliens. No matter how complimentary Mr. Wheeler was, those words will still follow me. I shake my head, but don't say anything. She doesn't understand; she can't understand. She made the choice to come here, to bring me here. I had no choice.

"Mija, Mr. Wheeler is trying to help people like us—people who don't have our luck, who don't have their papers."

Why does being helped feel like crap? I want to ask her. "I know that, but why did he have to bring me into it?"

"You said he didn't use our names, though. Nobody will know he was talking about you."

"Plenty of people could figure it out! It's not a secret that you work for him."

"But why is it a problem if people know it's you, mija? Everything he said about you is true."

"I just . . . I just don't want people thinking of me as only an immigrant."

Mami absorbs this in silence for a moment before she says, "Are you ashamed of being an immigrant?"

I don't answer right away; I can't tell her how I'm really feeling, because I don't want her shame for me to match the shame I feel. "No. I'm just very private. That's all."

She runs her hand over my forehead, smoothing down my hair and kissing the top of my head. "I'm sorry, mija. I'll talk to Mr. Wheeler to make sure he doesn't do something like that again."

I nod, thinking that there isn't anything else that can be done about it. Mr. Wheeler's words can't be unsaid. They're still hanging out there in the humid air, making their way around Corpus Christi for everyone I know to hear. "I'd better get ready for bed." I rise up from the couch, wanting to be in my room right away because more tears are very near, and I don't want Mami to see me cry.

Mami gets up and walks across the room with me. "You're such a good daughter, Milagros." She doesn't call me Milagros very often because she knows I don't like my full name. She loves it, though, and I feel very loved when she calls me that. "I'm very proud of you, of everything you do."

The guilt stabs me again. I have to tell her about Stanford. Soon. But I don't have the emotional energy for that conversation tonight.

CHAPTER FIVE

In the morning, I try to find a reason to stay home. I ask Ceci twice if her stomach hurts. Ceci has bouts of constipation sometimes. We give her medicine juice, as she calls it—apple juice mixed with a powdered laxative that makes going to the bathroom easier for her. She says she thinks she's okay, but heads to the bathroom just in case. I silently plead with Ceci's bowels to be stingy today, so that I can stay home with her as I've done in the past when she's been sick.

Javi's on his back looking under the couch for his shoe, and I tell Sele to go help him, but she's in the kitchen making her lunch. The cafeteria is serving fish sticks, and she hates fish sticks, so she's making a sandwich. Javi and Ceci will just have to hold their noses while they eat fish sticks. I don't have time to make lunches today.

Mami leaves at seven-thirty every morning. She takes our neighbor Mrs. Rosario to work before heading to the Wheelers' house. After she leaves, Sele and I walk Ceci and Javi to school and head to our different bus stops. I already know we're going to be pushing it to be on time. I kneel down next to Javi just as I hear the doorbell.

I take a quick look under the couch before getting up. "Go check your room again," I tell Javi.

He growls and storms into his room, one shoe in his hand. "I already looked there!"

When I open the door, Charles and Charlie Wheeler are standing there. I instinctively glance behind me, surveying the mess of backpacks, Barbies, and breakfast dishes on the living room floor.

"Hi," I say, but I don't invite them in. I look over my shoulder and take a step to my left, attempting to block their view of pants-less, headless Malibu Barbie. "My mom just left. She's on her way to your house."

"That's fine, Millie," Mr. Wheeler says. "I came by to talk to you for a minute, if that's okay."

I want to tell him it's not okay, but I don't. We never tell the Wheelers it's not okay.

"I can't find it!" Javi yells from his room. "Millie!"

"I'm sorry," Mr. Wheeler says. "I know this isn't the best time, but I really wanted to apologize about last night. I feel terrible."

"Millie!" Javi yells again.

"Sele, go help Javi," I call into the kitchen.

Mr. Wheeler rushes on. "Charlie told me last night how much I upset you, and I just really wanted to apologize."

I look at Charlie. He smiles awkwardly. It's that smile, that look that says his full attention is on you. He has this way of making you feel like he's actually interested in what you have to say. Which is possibly why so many of us think we might actually have a chance with him, until we realize that's how he interacts with absolutely everyone.

I refocus on his dad. "I just wish you hadn't said all that,"

I say feebly. All my feelings from last night come flooding back. Heat spreads to my face, and I feel my chest thumping. I suppress the angry words, letting them die before they fully form in my head. I want to say them, but I know I can't. The man in front of me pays my mom's salary. Everything that surrounds me comes from him.

"Millie, I'm sorry. If I could take it all back, I would. I wasn't thinking. I think so highly of your mom and this family. You demolish every single stereotype out there. People need to see that, to get a true picture of what immigrants do, what they can accomplish. But I'm sorry I used you for my platform without your permission. It won't happen again, I promise you."

His words, his idealistic intentions don't soothe me. My heart is still thumping. Inside, I am still screaming at him.

"Millie, I can't go!" cries Ceci from the bathroom.

"Ceci, be quiet!" I yell down the hall.

Mr. Wheeler frowns. "I'm sorry, Millie. I don't want to make you late. Just know that I'll do anything to make this better."

What could he possibly do to make things better? "Okay. I . . . appreciate it." I reach for the doorknob.

"There's one more thing," Mr. Wheeler says.

I look behind me to see if the others are ready to go, but they haven't made it to the living room yet. "What is it?"

"One of my campaign staffers called me this morning. There's a blogger turned internet troll from San Antonio named Michael Winter. He started tweeting lies and conspiracy theories about me when I first announced my campaign."

"What about him?" I ask. "Why are you telling me about him?" *At this hour on a school day*, I want to add. I resist the urge to glance at my watch.

"I guess he was there last night," Mr. Wheeler says. "He comes to some of my events, records them, distorts the videos and uploads them to YouTube. I guess he stayed around after my speech last night, and . . . I don't know who he talked to exactly, but there must have been someone there who knows you, knows that I was talking about you. Somehow he got your name, and he uploaded a video . . ."

"What kind of video? What is he saying about me?"

Mr. Wheeler lowers his eyes. "He gives your name, and the video shows some footage of you last night. I don't know how he figured out it was you I was talking about, and it must've just been a coincidence that he managed to get you in some of his footage . . ."

My hand flies up to my face, and I hide my eyes behind my fingers, wishing I could keep them there for the rest of the day.

"My staff are already starting to do damage control, but I wanted to let you know, so that it doesn't hit you by surprise. Millie, I am very sorry. I never intended for this to happen."

I look up at him. I believe that he's sorry, but his apology does nothing to allay my pounding heart or the sinking feeling in my stomach. I want to slam the door in his face and slide down against it on the other side, but I don't. "Well, we have to go."

"Can we give you a ride to school?" Charlie asks.

I shake my head without looking at him. "No, I have to walk Javi and Ceci to school." Actually, there's no time for me to do that now. Sele will have to take them on her own, and I'll need to run to catch my bus.

"We can take them too," Charlie says, gesturing toward the silver Mercedes parked in our driveway.

Mr. Wheeler nods. "Of course."

"No, thank you."

"Okay, well, again, Millie, I'm so sorry," Mr. Wheeler says.

I nod, but don't say anything. If he's waiting for me to tell him it's all okay, he's going to be standing on our front steps for a long time.

I close the door as soon as they turn toward their car.

≈

I'm out of breath by the time I reach my bus stop, and I'm the last to board. Chloe has saved me a seat, and I sink down beside her, trying to catch my breath.

"Are you okay?" she asks.

I shake my head and take a deep breath. "The Wheelers ruined my night and had to ruin my morning too."

I tell her about the Wheelers coming over and about what Mr. Wheeler said.

Chloe's face darkens when I mention the internet troll. "Who is this guy?"

"Some blogger. His name is Michael Winter, I think."

Chloe pulls out her phone and does a search for Michael Winter and Charles Wheeler.

Up pops a long playlist of videos. "One was just uploaded last night," Chloe says. She presses play, and I grab the phone from her.

The guy in the video looks like he's in his early twenties. He's blond and lean and seems to be holding a phone on a selfie stick as he talks. He's on the street right across Heritage Park. "Failed attorney and senator-wannabe Charles Wheeler is here in his hometown of Corpus Christi tonight. I will be filming to make sure we get all of the points from his liberal agenda that he's trying to bring to the good old state of Texas. Those of us who have been in Texas for generations do not want lefty politicians changing our sacred and time-honored beliefs. I am here to bring the truth of his agenda to all Texans."

Next, we see video of Mr. Wheeler onstage. He starts talking about immigration, and Michael Winter turns the camera to himself and shakes his head, slowly and firmly. The frame cuts back to Mr. Wheeler as he talks about his housekeeper, my mom, and Michael Winter scoffs softly in the background.

Next we see Michael Winter standing on the steps where Mr. Wheeler spoke earlier. "So, I've been asking around about this wetback housekeeper and her daughter. I just asked some of the crowd, pretending I was interested in meeting this so-called admirable young woman. A little flattery goes a long way, and people start talking. Well, apparently her name is Milagros Vargas. That's the girl. Her mother, the housekeeper, is Sandra Vargas." The video cuts to a shot of the crowd that shows me talking to Dr. Wheeler. A digitally drawn red circle frames my face.

I look away from the screen, feeling a sharp pain in my stomach.

He continues, "I'm going to do some digging around, try to find out if they're even legal or if we can call ICE on them. I'll be back with more very soon. Thanks for tuning in. This is Michael Winter, truth-teller and justice-seeker."

"Ugh! Gross," says Chloe. "This guy is disgusting."

After the video ends, another one automatically starts. It's Michael Winter again, and I can tell from the date of the post that this is an older video. "In a big step last week, the White House set forth an important immigration policy. Illegal alien children crossing our borders will now be housed separately from their parents, often in different facilities. This step, already in effect, will deter future lawbreakers from illegally entering the United States. If they know they'll be housed away from their children, then maybe they will stop illegally entering this country. Those are their consequences now, and the message is clear to illegals. Stay away."

Chloe turns the screen off. "Pendejos." The one word in Spanish that she knows.

In my head I see a vivid image of myself as a baby, being pulled out of my mom's arms. I know that a lot of the people detained at the border are asylum seekers from Central America, just like we were. The idea that I could have been separated from my parents upon entering the U.S. is cruel, crushing. I think about those kids, scared, not knowing the language, feeling abandoned. How is this an acceptable way to treat people? I feel such a sense of despair, even worse than what I felt moments ago, when I was watching the video specifically about me.

≈

I walk into class with my head down and slink into my chair, hoping for invisibility.

Charlie swivels around to look at me. "I'm really sorry about last night," he says.

"Shut up, Charlie," I mutter.

Had Mami heard me say that, she would've popped me in the mouth. We don't talk to the Wheelers that way. From the look on Charlie's face, he's probably thinking the same thing. Perhaps he's never been talked to that way in his life. For the briefest moment, I'm afraid he'll tell his father and it will get back to Mami, who will be furious and embarrassed. But Charlie Wheeler isn't like that. He may be a spoiled rich kid, but he doesn't think of himself as one. He thinks of himself as a good person. I'm sure that's why he and his dad keep apologizing to me—hoping I'll say that there's no harm done.

But there *is* harm done. That despicable man knows my name now, told all his followers my name, because Mr. Wheeler couldn't resist using me as an example of a model immigrant. What he doesn't get is that for people like Michael Winter, someone like me can never be a model immigrant. Nothing about me—my 4.0 GPA, my full-ride scholarship to Stanford, my U.S. citizenship, the values of integrity and hard work that my parents instilled in me—could ever convince him that I deserve to be in this country, that I'm the equal of white people. The Wheelers are more concerned with being on the right side of this issue, and feeling good about themselves, than they are about me.

CHAPTER SIX

Somehow I make it through the day. When the bus drops me off after school, I don't enjoy my walk home like I usually do. The stifling heat bogs me down, drains me of the last bit of energy I've managed to conserve.

When I get home, I do something I never do. I greet the kids and go straight to the bedroom I share with Sele.

I pull off my school jeans and put on a pair of cutoff jean shorts, cringing at the full-length mirror that hangs from the back of our bedroom door. It has a small crack on the bottom right corner, and every time I look at it I wonder if it's bringing us bad luck. But Sele won't let me throw it out; we both know we can't afford a new one.

I lie on the top bunk watching the ceiling fan rotate as it cools me. Every so often I check the time on my Mickey Mouse watch. Papi gave it to me for my ninth birthday. It's been through various cheap watchbands, but the timepiece is valuable to me because I know how much it meant to *him*.

Papi had a minor Mickey Mouse obsession, starting with a donated shirt he received in Guatemala when he was eight. Charities ship used clothes to Guatemala to give to poverty-stricken families, and he was the recipient of a purple Mickey Mouse T-shirt. Since the clothes came from America, he'd always associated Mickey Mouse with his dreams about life in this country. He brought that small T-shirt with him when we came here. I vaguely remember wearing it a few times before it was passed down to Sele and eventually disintegrated into rags. Upon first arriving in America and settling in Texas, Papi scoured flea markets and thrift stores for Mickey Mouse memorabilia that he used to decorate my room. All through my childhood, he called me Millie Mouse and kept finding Mickey-related gifts for me.

I wonder what he would say to me if he were here now. If anyone could reassure me, make me feel loved and safe after the day I've had, it would be Papi.

I've been lying on my bed for an hour, and I still don't feel like going to the living room to make Javi and Ceci start their homework. I know Sele has probably finished hers and has even done her chores, but at the moment, I don't really care.

I hear a knock at the bedroom door before it opens. It's Sele, and I'm surprised she knocked. After all, this is her room too.

"Are you okay?" she asks, walking over to me.

I sit up and let my legs dangle over the side of the bunk. "Yeah, I'll be fine." I've told her the short version of what Mr. Wheeler said about Mami and me last night. I hope nobody at her school stumbles across that Michael Winter video and shows it to her. It would horrify her.

"I put some chicken in the oven for dinner and we can warm up the rice Mami made."

"Thanks, Sele," I say, jumping down to the floor. "I guess I'd better go make the kids do their homework."

"They finished already. We saw the ice cream truck on the

41

way home, and I told them I'd buy them ice cream if they promised to do their homework right away." She walks over to the bottom bunk to get the fabric squares she's turning into a quilt.

"Wow. Thanks, Sele. I can't believe they're done. And you made dinner. That was really nice."

"It's no big deal," she says as she sits down on her bed to sort through the fabric. "There's a voicemail for you on the landline phone."

"Who's it from?" I ask.

"*Caller Times*," she says without looking up.

I head to the kitchen, where a little green light is blinking on the phone. I press the button to play the voicemail. "Hello, this message is for Milagros Vargas. This is Ellen Ramos from the *Corpus Christi Caller Times*. I would love to talk with you about doing an interview for the newspaper. Please feel free to call me back at . . ." I delete the message. How did this reporter get my home phone number? We hardly ever use it unless there's an emergency or one of our older relatives is calling from Guatemala.

Well, there is no way I'm calling her back. I'm trying to forget my little brush with fame, not amplify it.

I look behind me to see if Sele has followed me into the kitchen, but I'm alone. Javi and Ceci are still in the living room, and the sound of the Disney Channel filters through the house. Just as I'm thinking about getting my backpack to start my homework, the phone rings. The caller ID screen just says UNKNOWN. I stare at it for three rings before I get the nerve to pick it up.

"Hello, could I please speak to Milagros Vargas?" It's a man, and his voice sounds professional.

"Who is this?" I ask.

"My name is Gilbert Workman. I'm from KIIITV. I'm calling to see if we can get a comment about Charles Wheeler's campaign. I realize we'd probably have to get permission from your parents."

"I'm sorry. I can't. I just can't. I can't even believe you're calling me."

"I understand. Perhaps it would be better if I spoke to your parents."

"My mom's at work. I'm sorry, Mr. Workman, but I can't talk to you. How did you even get this number?"

"Well, Milagros, you may be aware that a certain political blogger posted a video that included your name. Your contact information isn't difficult to find."

I feel physically sick. "I don't want to give you any comments. I wish Mr. Wheeler had never mentioned my family and that this guy had never said my name."

"I do understand, Milagros, but I just don't think this is going to die down. I suspect you'll be hearing from several news outlets."

"I don't understand why they would want to talk to me," I say, frustration bleeding into my voice.

"Well, with Charles Wheeler's Senate campaign picking up steam, everything that he says is going to be very closely followed. He pointed to you as a shining example of an immigrant. Immigration policy is going to be a hot-button issue for some time, especially for us here in Texas. The public is going to want to hear from you."

"They're going to have to find someone else, Mr. Workman. I'm sorry."

"I understand, but—"

"Thank you for calling. Goodbye." I disconnect and put

the phone down on the counter, trying to calm myself. The smell of Sele's chicken is wafting toward me, and I start to set the table. That's usually her job, but since she's done mine today, I will do hers.

≈

Calculus homework is killing me today, and I keep double-checking all my answers. I ignore Javi and Ceci bickering in the hallway and try to concentrate on the last problem, until I hear the sound that I most look forward to every day—the sound of Mami opening the front door.

Javi's and Ceci's argument escalates, and I let Mami handle it.

"Mija, let him finish first and then it's your turn," she says to Ceci in Spanish. The two languages are used interchangeably in our home. "Hola, mija," Mami calls out to me.

"Hola, Mami," I say, looking out to the living room.

She picks up Ceci, walks over to the couch, and sets Ceci on her lap. I can't hear what Mami is whispering to her, but Ceci is happy now.

I turn back to my homework, able to focus properly now that I have officially clocked out of my nonpaying job of taking care of my siblings.

Once the kids are in bed, Mami comes into the kitchen and sighs. "Cómo éstas, mija?" she asks me.

"Bien, Mami." I'm not going to say a word about the Michael Winter video or the calls I got.

She walks over to the stove where Sele leaves her a plate every night. Mami warms it up in the microwave and brings it over to the table by me. Silently, she eats while I finish my homework.

When she's done eating, she gets up, washes her dishes, and places them on the drying rack. "Gracias, mija. Estaba delicioso." She walks over to me and kisses the top of my head.

"Sele cooked tonight, Mami."

"You taught her well!" She watches me for several seconds, during which I fake a half-smile.

"Listen, mija. I met a man at the Wheelers' today. His name is Oscar Zambrano. He's a freelance journalist from Austin, and he would like to interview you."

I look up at her in alarm. "Mami, no. What did you tell him?"

She wipes the counter with a sponge and leans back against it. "I told him I would talk to you. He's staying with the Wheelers for a few days. He's interviewing Mr. Wheeler about his campaign."

"What does he want with me?"

"He's heard about you, mija. He writes about immigration issues, especially immigration stories here in Texas."

"Mami, I don't know. I just want this whole thing to die down." I don't want to be an issue. Why can't I just be a teenager whose biggest problem is a giant zit on my forehead?

"But it won't. And he thinks you may have a lot to say that can help people."

I close my calculus book with three problems left. "I have nothing to say."

Mami sighs. "I won't make you, but I really want you to think about it, mija. It might be your chance to do something for others."

Doing something for others. The discussion in Ms. Cope's class comes back to me, but I shake my head. "No, Mami. I don't think so. I'm just not comfortable with it."

That's the wrong thing to say. I know it as soon as the

words are out of my mouth. Mami has spent her whole life doing uncomfortable things because she felt they were necessary and right.

"He's going to be here for another two days." She walks over to her handbag on the kitchen counter. "He wrote a note that he asked me to give you. Read it, think about it, and tell me tomorrow what you want to do."

I take the folded note from her outstretched hand and read it while Mami goes out into the living room.

Millie,

I know we haven't met yet, but I want to tell you a bit about myself. I was born in San Antonio, Texas, as were my father and grandfather. My grandmother and mother insisted I learn to speak Spanish, and so I still do. I don't know what life has been like for you, but I'm interested in learning. I try to constantly learn more about what life is like for those who come here looking for a better life.

I travel around Texas, meeting people and writing about their lives. My greatest interest is immigration, and it has been so since I was twelve years old and my best friend's family was deported to Mexico. I never saw or heard from him again, but I think about him every day as I advocate for the undocumented in this country.

Let me tell you about a group of people I've recently met. Their names are David, Ricardo, and Marco. They've all lived in the US. for more than half their lives. In their late twenties, they're all *college graduates. David wants to teach school. Ricardo wants to go to medical school, and Marco is nearly a CPA. But none of them is doing what they want to do, what they studied to do. All three of them are working on a beef farm here in Texas. They're undocumented, so they can't get jobs in their fields. Instead, they live in fear of being detained and deported.*

That is something I want to change, with the help of legislators in this country. That is why you are needed. You're a success story of an undocumented person who has gotten citizenship and has gone on to make good choices in her life. People need to see that. Please think about meeting with me, just for a short while. Wherever, whenever you want.

Oscar Zambrano

I refold the note, press it closed firmly. I hear Mami straightening up the tiny living room, and I silently chide the kids for leaving a mess for her. She spends all day cleaning the Wheelers' house and the law office and then has to come home to clean up after us?

As I lie in bed that night, thoughts of what to tell Mami roll through my mind. I want to stand firm in my decision not to talk to Mr. Zambrano; I want to willfully go against what I know Mami wants me to do. But that's not me—and she knows it. Doing what Mami wants is my vocation.

In the morning, I sleepily drag myself to the bathroom. Mami is using a small brush to tame her long, graying hair, pulling it into a short bun on the back of her head.

"Okay, Mami. I'll meet with Mr. Zambrano. I don't know if I'm up for doing an interview with him, but I'll meet him and we can talk off the record. Then I'll decide what to do from there."

"Bueno, mija. You want him to come here?"

I look down quickly at the worn rug, the dulling walls. "No, not here."

"At the Wheelers'?"

The last thing I want is to have Charlie Wheeler around or involved in any way. "No."

"Mr. Wheeler said you could use his law office if you like. Maybe tonight, around seven. I can pick you up. We'll have Sele watch the little ones while we're out."

"Okay, that's fine," I say, figuring most people who work at the law office will be gone for the day by then. I don't want to do this, but it'll be even harder if others are around, watching me, listening to me.

"I'll tell them. Okay, mija?" She leans over to kiss my cheek before she goes to say goodbye to the others.

CHAPTER SEVEN

Mami and I leave Sele, Javi, and Ceci in front of a Disney Channel movie before heading out to Mr. Wheeler's law office. Mami doesn't say much to me on the way. I know what she wants me to do—give Mr. Zambrano the interview. She has reasons that are probably very meaningful to her, but she doesn't share them with me. Mami has a way of silently telling us her wishes. She doesn't have to say something aloud for us to know exactly what she expects of us.

The office parking lot is nearly empty. Mr. Wheeler's silver Mercedes is in his marked spot, and Mami pulls our Toyota Tercel right next to it. His office is across from the children's hospital, and the sound of an ambulance fills the air as we walk toward the glass entrance of the dark brown brick building.

Mr. Wheeler opens the door and leads us into the large waiting area. Red fabric-covered chairs are lined up against one wall. A dark-haired Latino man emerges from the conference room in the back. His smile widens as he walks toward us.

"Hi, Mrs. Vargas," he says, shaking Mami's hand. "And you must be Millie. Hi. I'm Oscar Zambrano." He's wearing a black button-down shirt with the sleeves rolled up to his elbows. He reaches out his hand, and I shake it.

"Hi," I say, knowing that the flatness of my voice will sound rude to Mami, but it's the best I can do.

"You can go on into the conference room," Mr. Wheeler says, pointing. There are windows along the entire back wall, with wood blinds pulled all the way up.

"Okay," I say, eying the large windows, feeling like I'll be on display.

"Want me to come with you?" Mami asks.

"No. It's okay."

"Bueno. I'll wait out here with Mr. Wheeler."

Inside the conference room, I sit down across from Mr. Zambrano in a black leather swivel chair. For just a moment, I think about what Javi would do in a chair like this. He'd swing it all the way around and probably roll it across the wood floor.

Mr. Zambrano's black hair is gelled up a little and he's wearing dark-rimmed glasses. I was expecting him to be older, but my guess is that he's not quite thirty. He sits on the edge of his chair and leans in toward the long conference table, which is empty except for a closed laptop. "Thanks, Millie, for coming to meet me. I know the past few days have been a bit stressful for you."

"You could say that." I hope I don't sound belligerent. I adjust my tone as best I can. "I'm still not really sure what you're after, Mr. Zambrano."

"Well, I talk to a lot of people your age. Last month, I went down to Mexico and met several boys who wish they were sitting right here where you are. Luis is sixteen; he left Guatemala and was working his way from southern Mexico to Mexico City. He and some boys he met along the way ride on top of boxcars through the interior of Mexico just to make it to the border. One of the boys, Rafael, fell off a boxcar, and the train rolled over his legs, leaving him unable to walk. They don't really know what happened to him after that. He had to stay behind, and they left to make their way here. I don't know if they've made it. I don't know if they'll ever make it."

I look away from him, down at the table, the space between us, and I stare at the dark wood, but I don't say anything. I don't think I'll ever be able to look at another train car without thinking about this exact moment.

"Last summer, I went down to Potrillo, which is just north of the Rio Grande, to report on a case where people had crowded into a freight truck to cross the border. Twenty-six people died of heat exhaustion and asphyxiation. That's the kind of risk every undocumented person faces in crossing the border. I want to interview you because, frankly, I think your parents are heroes. They endured so much to bring you here, to give you the kind of life that Luis and Rafael and those twenty-six people want or wanted."

His words cut to the very center of me. My eyes sting. "Then why didn't you ask to interview my mom? Why do you want to talk to *me*, specifically?"

"I actually did talk to your mother for a few hours yesterday, and she told me her story. I don't know if you understand, I don't think *I'll* ever understand the extent of her sacrifice for you, for your siblings. The difficulty of getting here, the time they spent living in fear while their asylum case was under review, the very high chance that they would be denied asylum and sent back to Guatemala—the uncertainty they lived with right up until the day they finally received their green cards. They gave you an incredible gift. A gift that people are dying for. And I'm not saying these things to make you feel guilty or make you cry."

His last sentence provokes increased crying, and I wipe my nose with my sleeve. Mr. Zambrano stands up and brings over a box of tissues. I grab one and wipe my nose and eyes simultaneously.

"I cry about this too, because it's a very emotional issue."

I wish he would stop. I wish I could get up and leave because other than making me cry like a baby, I still don't understand why I am here, what he wants from me.

He's quiet for a moment, magnifying the sounds of the sobs that keep escaping me. I look out of the large window separating the conference room from the waiting room. Mami and Mr. Wheeler are sitting in two chairs across from each other. Mr. Wheeler is saying something to Mami, but her eyes are on me. She is watching me, and I feel fresh shame for crying. Whatever hardship she's had, whatever fears Mr. Zambrano has been talking about, she is stronger than tears, and I know she expects that of me too.

She smiles at me, encouraging me. I manage to smile back and turn to Mr. Zambrano.

"Millie, the reason I wanted to meet you, interview you, is because you've taken the opportunity your parents gave you and done so much. Your mother told me you've never brought home a B on a report card. All As. Do you have any idea how proud she is of you?"

"It's what I'm supposed to do."

"That's what I want to show the world, Millie. That there are millions of people coming to this country for the same damn reason the Pilgrims came here—to make a better life for their families. Those are the kinds of stories we need to tell if we're going to combat the fear, misinformation, and down-right racist attitudes about people like you and your family." He pauses. "I feel like I'm talking too much. I'm sorry."

"I understand what you're saying. But, again, why me?"

"Why not you, Millie?"

"Because I'm sure you've met a lot of other people." Anyone, anyone but me, I want to say.

Mr. Zambrano leans back in his chair, placing both arms on the armrests. "Well, there's Gabriel from Brownsville, Texas, who's the quarterback of his football team. He's shattered every football record at his high school. I've seen him play—he could be in the NFL one day. I'd love to do a story on him, but the problem is that he's undocumented; his family is really scared of being deported. Then there's Manuel, who just served a two-year mission for his church in Laredo, but can't get a job here because he has no papers. And Susana, who was going to be the valedictorian for her high school, but had to move because her family heard they were going to get picked up by ICE. So right now she's not even going to school."

I crumple the tissue into a ball, squeezing it in my fist to make it as compact as possible. "And I'm a citizen, so I'm at less risk than they are."

"That's right."

"I understand that. But I'm just not sure. I don't really want people to know everything about me."

"I know, Millie. And I respect that. Really, I do." He leans back in and spreads his hands on the table between us. "But I want to make things better for Gabriel and Manuel and Susana. And the only way to do that is to change public opinion, and especially the opinions of legislators, about undocumented immigrants. I want to show them you, Millie. You are the face of the young immigrants who will make this country even better."

I cross my arms in front of me and stare down at the table. "Mr. Zambrano, I want to help, but . . ."

"What about this: We do the interview right now, and afterward you tell me how you feel. If you want me to go ahead and print it, I will. If you don't feel good about it and you want me to throw it out, I will."

I wipe my nose and look through the window again. Mami, tired after a long day of cleaning the Wheelers' house and this office, taking care of Caroline, making dinner for the Wheelers, is sitting on the red fabric chair waiting for me. Why? Because it's important to her. What I am doing in here, talking to Mr. Zambrano, is important to her.

I nod and whisper, "Okay."

"Okay, well. I'm going to tape our conversation, if that's all right, because I want to make sure I quote you right." He opens the laptop on the conference table and shows me how he'll record me. "So, Millie. Can we start with you just telling me a little bit about yourself?"

"Okay. I'm eighteen years old. I have a younger brother, Javier, and two younger sisters, Selena and Cecilia. I'm a senior in high school."

"Your mother tells me you love the ocean."

I feel myself relax for the first time since I walked into the conference room. "Yeah, I do."

"Tell me about that."

I resist the temptation to look away from him and stare at the conference table. "When I'm in the water, I just feel like I belong. Like I could float over the waves forever. I love the feel of wet sand between my toes, seaweed rubbing against my ankles, the smell of the ocean. I love how you can look out at the ocean and feel like it never ends, like it just goes on forever. And I love that it's full of so many species, all so different, but also all dependent on each other. That's why I want to study marine biology."

"And I know you will. Your mother says that she couldn't ask for a better daughter. That she doesn't know how she would manage without you, without your help."

The tears I had hoped were gone threaten to re-emerge, but I squash them back.

"Why are you such a good daughter?" he asks.

The question catches me off guard, but I know the answer right away. "Because she works so hard, and she does it for us. She never does anything for herself. I can't disappoint her because if I do, then what was all her hard work for?"

"Where do you hope your family will be in ten years?"

"I'll be done with school, maybe have a job here at the university or something. Mami will be retired and I'll help her pay for everything. Selena will be applying for graduate programs, Javi will be in college, and Ceci will be about to graduate high school."

"I believe all of those things will happen." He pauses and meets my eyes. "Thanks, Millie for seeing me. You're what keeps me wanting to do this job. Just like you love learning about the ocean and ocean animals, I love learning about people and their immigration stories."

I'm not sure how I feel about that analogy, but I nod to be polite. I don't say anything because I know what he's about to ask me—if he can write the story. The question has been hanging in the air between us, but I'm still not sure of my answer.

"I'm scheduled to appear on *Sebastian Smith: In Perspective* next week," he says. "I'd love to talk about you and share some of this interview during my segment."

I swallow hard. Sebastian Smith hosts a long-running TV program that airs on channels all over Texas.

I look through the window at Mami again. She's leaning her head back against the wall, her eyes are closed, and her hands are clasped together against her stomach. Mr. Wheeler is on his phone, pacing the floor in front of her.

"And, you'll want to use my name?"

"Yes. Using your name gives validity to my story, gives it more meaning, makes it seem more real. I'd also like to take a few pictures. Get a short video of you talking about the ocean. There's just something that lights up in your eyes when you talk about it."

I drop my gaze to the table. "Okay," I say, hating every suggestion he just made.

From under the table, he pulls out a black camera bag. He takes a few candid shots of me sitting at the conference table. Next, he switches the camera to video.

"Tell me about the first time you knew you belonged near the ocean."

I force my eyes off the wood floor and try to look toward the camera. "I was five, probably, the first time my parents took me to the beach. I just walked straight to the water in my sundress, not stopping even to take off my flip-flops. I just knew, right away, that it's where I wanted to be."

After I respond to a few more prompts from him, he shuts off the camera. "Thanks so much for coming to see me, Millie. Today's interview has been something special, and I can't wait to share it with the world. I'll be on Sebastian Smith's show next Thursday at eight . . ."

He keeps talking, but I have trouble absorbing anything he's saying. This all seems so unreal. We walk out into the lobby, where Mr. Wheeler is still on the phone and Mami is just opening her eyes. She stands up as we approach her.

"Mrs. Vargas, thanks for bringing Millie to see me. She's amazing, just like you said, and pretty soon everyone's going to know it."

Mami smiles more widely than I've ever seen, and for the first time tonight, I am glad I came to talk to Mr. Zambrano. Mami's satisfaction is what will get me through the news story that will depict me as an undocumented immigrant—something I had hoped to keep secret all my life.

CHAPTER EIGHT

Thursday night, we're all gathered in the living room. Mami has left work early to be here with me to watch Mr. Zambrano on Sebastian Smith's show. She's even picked up Chinese takeout, a very rare treat at our house. Sele and I are splitting the sweet and sour chicken while Mami and Ceci are sharing egg rolls and white rice, and Javi refuses to eat anything but a container full of fried rice.

We sit through the host interviewing a doctor about a flu outbreak in North Texas, and several minutes of commercials, before Mr. Zambrano's segment.

Mr. Zambrano is wearing a button-down maroon shirt with a black tie and the same dark-rimmed glasses.

"Oscar Zambrano, it's good to have you back on the program. You've been following the situation at the U.S.-Mexico border very closely. Tell us a little more about that."

"Thanks for having me back, Sebastian. Yes, I'm deeply interested in the struggles of families seeking asylum from life-threatening situations in their home countries. These people are being held for days, weeks, even months, in detention centers with appalling conditions. Children are being separated from their parents. A campaign of psychological warfare is being carried out against people who are, essentially, refugees. All because many Americans have been fed a false narrative about who these people are and why they're trying to cross our borders."

"Give me some examples of that."

"Well, we hear over and over again that all illegal immigrants are criminals—drug dealers, gang members, or simply people with no regard for the law. But more often than not, the people detained at the border are trying to *escape* gangs and drug dealers. And they bring their children in the hope of securing a safer, better life for them. Sebastian, I wish you could be with me as I travel around the country, meeting young folks, young immigrants who were brought here by their parents, as some would say, illegally. They are doing amazing things. We want these bright young people in our country. There is so much they can accomplish, so much they can contribute."

"And there's one in particular you want to tell us about. Is that right?"

"Yes, I want to tell you about Milagros Vargas."

Sele lets out a little squeal, which brings a rare smile to Mami's face. Javi jumps off the couch and punches the air. I feel like punching something too, but all I do is sit there, wrestling with the knots in my stomach as I absorb the fact that people throughout the state are watching this, hearing my name.

"Milagros, or Millie, as she prefers to be called, is an eighteen-year-old immigrant from Guatemala. She has lived in Corpus Christi, Texas, almost her entire life. She's about to graduate from high school and has been given a full-ride scholarship to a prestigious university. She and her parents were undocumented when they arrived here, and they applied for and were granted asylum because her parents were able to prove they had been specific targets of gang violence. It's extremely difficult to meet the government's criteria to receive asylum; her parents had to prove they'd never been involved in any gang activities—even coerced cooperation with gang members, which happens routinely in Central American countries. And they were lucky that they were deemed 'members of a social or political group' who were at risk of persecution. Often, even people who are in grave danger are denied asylum because they don't fit a narrow interpretation of this requirement."

"So you're saying that Millie's family easily could've been denied legal status, simply because immigration law is so restrictive."

"Exactly. Luckily for Millie, her family did receive asylum status, which made them eligible to apply for green cards. She is now a citizen and has a bright future ahead of her. But many young undocumented immigrants are not so lucky, through no fault of their own."

"That's fascinating," Sebastian says. "And tell me why this story is so relevant right now."

"Well, Sebastian, whenever I hear someone say that the people detained at the border deserve to be sent back, deserve to be separated from their children, because they, quote, *broke the law*, unquote—families like Millie's come to mind. Millie is living proof that immigrants are not a threat to our country. They're an asset to it."

"Thanks for joining us, Oscar. We'd love to have you back again with more about this."

"Thanks for having me, Sebastian. Thanks for letting me tell you about Millie. There are many others who I'd like to tell you about, but most of them are still undocumented, and frankly, they're afraid of being found out, of being deported. I'm really thankful to Millie for letting me share her story with you."

Sebastian concludes the segment by showing a clip of my interview. When the show cuts to commercial, I look over at Mami and she dabs at her eyes. She smiles at me and nods, and then she goes into the kitchen. I hear the faucet turn on.

Javi comes over to sit by me. "So, you're famous now, right? Are you going to be rich?"

I laugh. "No, Javi. Of course not. I wouldn't even say that I'm famous." The opposite of famous is actually what I prefer to be. If no one in Corpus Christi watched Sebastian Smith's show tonight, that would be awesome.

"Oh well," Javi says and gets up to change the channel.

"You did great," Sele says. "It's just what everyone needs to hear. I think it could help change a lot of people's minds."

"I'm not sure of that, but I hope so," I say as I get up to go to the bathroom.

"Don't be scared, Mil. Anyone who thinks anything bad about you after they watch this isn't someone worth knowing. All the people who know you and love you always will. This won't change that." Sele should've been born first. She always thinks the right thing, which is the opposite of what I tend to do.

Of course, if Sele had been born first, she would've arrived in this country without documentation too. Maybe if that were the case, she'd feel differently about this.

Just as I enter the bathroom, I get a text from Chloe that just says *hugs* and a heart emoji. I respond with a smiley face. I'm not in the mood for many words, and by the look of her text, she already knows that.

As soon as I send her the text, I get another one—from Charlie Wheeler. I'm not sure how he has my number; I've never given it to him, but I suppose it isn't that difficult to get. After all, he sees my mother every day.

Charlie's text is wordier than Chloe's. *I saw the segment on Sebastian Smith. You were great. I just wanted you to know that.*

It sounds exactly like what Charlie might say to me in person. Perfect words from the seemingly perfect guy. I quickly type the letters *t* and *y*.

I pull my hair up in a bun to wash my face with my five-dollar facial scrub, wishing I felt better about the interview. I still hear Oscar's voice in my head: *There is so much they can accomplish, so much they can contribute.* We have to be the hardest workers, the brightest students, the biggest achievers, if we want to belong here. We can't just be human beings who mean others no harm.

I try not to think about it anymore, to focus on the ordinariness of my evening routine. After I brush my teeth, I sit on the linoleum floor to scrub the remnants of purple nail polish off my toes. Painting my toenails is the one beauty ritual I never forego. Maybe it's because I wear flip-flops almost every day of the year. That might seem excessive to some people, but not to my ex-boyfriend, Jay, who I'm pretty sure owns more than fifteen pairs. It's just one of the things we had in common. Spending hours together at the beach was another. It made us the perfect couple up until it became the reason we broke up.

By the time my polish is dry and I slip into our tiny room, Sele's pulling clothes out of her dresser for tomorrow, and I start to do the same.

"How was school today?" I ask her, wanting to talk about anything other than the interview.

"Okay. We're almost finished with the first half of our quilt." Sele and two of her friends started a quilting club. They meet at lunch in their school's art room to work on it. "Ms. Morales said we could bring squares home to work on and then put them together at school."

"Did you bring it home?" I ask her as I take off my Mickey Mouse watch and lay it carefully on top of the dresser.

She pulls the square out of her backpack and hands it to me. "We don't have much time to finish it before school ends. Ms. Morales wants to hang it up in her room to teach next year's classes about patterns."

"This is really neat." I examine the tiny blue and green triangles. On the back of the square are tiny, flawless stitches. "And you do this all by hand?"

Sele nods as she takes back the unfinished square. She's easily embarrassed by praise, so I don't say anything else. But I keep thinking about that quilt square as I pull off my clothes, toss them into the hamper in our tiny closet, and put on my purple nightshirt—a find from Goodwill, where we shop often. Sele has put so much patience and care and skill into that project. It's at least as much of an achievement as my top grades and career ambitions, though it will never draw the attention of someone like Sebastian Smith.

I climb to the top of our bunk bed and lie on the comforter, feeling the warmth in the air of our tiny room. I have only one chapter of *The Hiding Place* to read for school. I imagine Charlie Wheeler reading this same chapter. The words are exactly the same, yet his analysis and understanding of them will be so different than mine. In Betsie and Corrie, he sees a sense of worth that comes from helping others. I see the pain and sacrifice of their family.

≈

Just before first period, Ms. Cope is standing by her classroom door talking to Mr. Brody. I slip by them, hoping they won't notice me, and it works. Charlie's already in his seat, and I dig through my backpack as I walk past him, looking for nothing in particular, but making sure to look focused.

"Hi, Millie," Charlie says as I drop into the seat behind him.

"Hi," I say, waiting for him to turn around and say more, but he doesn't. He keeps his gaze on his notebook in front of him.

I look around the class to see if anyone is watching me, but everyone is occupied in their own thing and for a minute, I think I'm home free. Until Ms. Cope comes in, slaps her hands together, and walks toward me.

"Millie Vargas, our star. Did anyone see Millie mentioned on *Sebastian Smith: In Perspective* last night?"

A few people murmur in response, but several others seem completely oblivious. Ms. Cope takes a few minutes to summarize the segment for those who weren't aware of it, while I just stare at the back of Charlie Wheeler's head.

"I think you're very brave to do that interview, Millie. It's going to reach a lot of people." Ms. Cope comes over to me, taps my shoulder, and says, "I'm very proud of you."

I force a smile and drop my eyes to the desk. Charlie doesn't turn around to look at me, for which I'm grateful.

Ms. Cope walks to the front of the room. "Well, from one brave heroine to the next. Today, we're going to finish our discussion on Corrie ten Boom."

Being called a heroine is unsettling. I certainly don't think I should be compared to Corrie ten Boom. All I've done is submit to one embarrassing interview.

Mindy Stincil leans over to me, her long blond hair waving in the space between us. "It was a great segment, Millie. My mom and I watched it last night."

I know that the Stincils are good friends with the Wheelers, so this doesn't surprise me. I smile at her briefly before turning my attention to Ms. Cope.

By the end of the class, the pricking feeling of having all eyes on me starts to subside. I gratefully escape to the chaos of the hallway where I hope to quickly become anonymous once more.

Chloe is standing outside my classroom door, popping her gum and wildly scrolling through her phone. "Dammit. Damn. Damn."

"What's up, Chlo?" I say, approaching her.

She grabs my arm and pulls me against the wall next to her. "You know this world is full of pricks, right?"

I look at her phone screen. Instagram always gets her fired up. She essentially has a nonpaying part-time job defending Jennifer Lopez on Instagram.

Four hundred sixty-two comments. It's getting serious. "What are people saying about JLo?"

Chloe shakes her head. "It's you, Mil."

"What?" I grab her wrist and angle the phone toward me so I can see the screen better. It's my Instagram page, which I never check, which I don't even have access to on my prepaid phone.

"Trolls," Chloe says. "They found you yesterday after the interview. They're commenting on all your photos."

"What are they saying?" I ask, snatching the phone from her hand.

"Stupid stuff about immigration, illegals, the usual crap. I'm fighting with like six different jerks right now. Some of them are probably bots. Not even real people."

I scroll through the comments.

Ruining our country.

Taking opportunities from our people.

Illegals are committing crimes.

Just cuz she's pretty doesn't mean she should get to stay.

Go back to where you came from.

Get out of my country.

For each angry and hurtful comment, there's an equally angry response from Chloe. I scroll through her comebacks. "When did this start?" I ask.

"Last night, I think, or like the middle of the night. I just noticed it this morning."

"Chloe. I can't believe this. Why are they doing this?"

"They hate their lousy lives, and they're always looking for people to put down. Obviously they don't have anything better to do with their time."

"When did *you* have time to post all of your comments?"

"Last period. I hung out in the bathroom." She pulls the phone gently out of my hand. "I can keep this up all day." I watch as she types another reply, letting expletives fly.

"I don't want you to have to do this, Chlo."

"It's fine. I already reported these pricks to Instagram. Maybe we should set your account to private?"

I glance over Chloe's shoulder as another cruel comment appears. "I just want to get rid of Instagram completely."

She looks over at me and slides her arm around my shoulder. "I'm sorry, Mil. You don't deserve this." She logs out of Instagram and hands me her phone.

I quickly log in and delete my account. I hand her back the phone and lean against the wall. Chloe puts both arms around me. I close my eyes. The loudness of passing period dissipates as the last tardy students scramble to their classes.

"Mil, don't let it get to you. You are a million times classier, smarter, and less loserish than these trolls."

I open my eyes and try to smile.

"Besides, before we know it, we will be so out of here, on our way out west. We won't be stuck here forever."

≈

The last problem on the calculus test keeps running through my mind as I walk down the hall to my locker. The prospect of a B looms before me and collides with the vivid memory of Mami telling Mr. Zambrano that I have never brought home anything but As on my report card. I focus on that, trying to shut out the Instagram disaster from earlier today, as I open my locker.

A folded sheet of paper that had been hanging from the top vent of my locker falls to my feet.

I pick up the paper and look down both ends of the hallway. I catch Charlie Wheeler's eye as he approaches me. He quickly averts his gaze and looks past me at something at the other end of the hallway. The thought of how I last spoke to him days ago has stayed with me and probably with him too.

I open the folded sheet of paper. In black pen are scrawled the words: *Go back to Mexico.* My first thought is that it's meant for someone else; I've never even been to Mexico. But in a split second, the realization hits me that these ugly words *are* meant for me. I stare at the message in shock.

"Millie." Charlie is beside me, and he puts his hand on my shoulder. "Are you okay?"

I'm still frozen, unable to respond, feeling a sob building

deep in my chest. He takes the paper from my hand, reads it, and crumbles it up.

"God, Millie, I'm so sorry. Whoever wrote this is an idiot." He stuffs the crumbled sheet of paper into his jeans pocket. "Are you okay?"

I choke back my tears. "Yeah, fine," I say.

"Let's take this to Dr. Gomez," he says.

I nod numbly. The principal should know about the note. But I can't move. I look around the halls, wondering who it could have been.

Charlie gently guides me forward with the hand that's still resting on my shoulder, and I silently walk with him to the office. The halls are clearing out now; most students have made it to their classes.

Charlie lets his hand slide off my shoulder as we walk into the main office. The Wheeler charm turns on. "Hi, Ms. Torres," he says to the admin assistant. "Can we see Dr. Gomez? We have an incident to report."

Ms. Torres looks from Charlie to me and back. "He's got someone in there. Should only be a few minutes. Have a seat." She motions to two worn chairs across from her desk.

Charlie smiles and thanks her. We both sit down. I'm sitting outside the principal's office. I've never had to sit outside the principal's office before. Charlie reaches into his jeans pocket and pulls out the crumbled piece of paper. He smooths it down on his pant leg and folds it in half.

"You don't have to stay here," I say.

"If it's okay, I want to wait." He leans over, resting his elbows on his knees. "I want to make sure Dr. Gomez is going to do something about this. I'm going to tell my dad what happened too. In a way . . ." He hesitates. "In a way, this is his fault.

He's the reason you started getting all this attention. My dad has a way of trying to fix things and messing them up more."

I don't argue with Charlie's assessment. If it weren't for Mr. Wheeler, all I would be worrying about right now would be a calculus problem.

Dr. Gomez walks out of his office, followed by a freshman with low-riding pants. Charlie stands up right away, walks over to Dr. Gomez, and hands him the folded piece of paper.

"Dr. Gomez, Millie found this in her locker."

Dr. Gomez looks at the note, folds it back in half, and motions for us to come into his office.

Charlie waits for me to enter and closes the door behind him. I'm still not sure if I like Charlie being here, but a part of me is grateful to not be alone in all this.

Dr. Gomez sits down behind his large wooden desk, layered with binders, loose papers, and Styrofoam coffee cups. "Do either one of you know who wrote this?"

Charlie says, "No," and I shake my head.

"I'm sorry, Millie. It's disheartening that we have students in our school who would feel this way, much less write something like this." He turns to me. "And it was in your locker?"

"Yes, I think someone pushed it in through one of the slats," I say.

"I'm going to personally visit each classroom and have a discussion with the students."

I squirm in my seat. I don't want him telling everyone what the note said. I've already had too much of my personal information made public lately. And the last thing I need is more pitying looks like the one he's giving me. "What are you going to say?"

"I won't mention your name. I'll speak in more general

terms about hateful letters being put in lockers. How it will not be tolerated. I'm going to tell the teachers to keep an eye out during passing periods too. If I find any students being a party to this, it will call for immediate suspension. There will be no warnings."

He seems so sincere. I wish his good intentions could make the drumming of my heart stop, soothe the tears that want to come. But he can't tell me who did this, can't guarantee it won't happen again.

"I'm going to call your mother to let her know what happened." Dr. Gomez reaches for the phone on his desk.

"Could you please ask her to come and get me? I don't want to stay here right now."

Charlie sits up straighter in his seat. "I can take her home. I don't mind."

"Thank you, Charlie," Dr. Gomez says, "but you should go back to class. If Millie goes home, I'll need her mom to sign her out." Mr. Gomez picks up the phone and starts to dial.

Charlie stands up and walks slowly to the door, where he hesitates again. While Dr. Gomez is talking to my mom, I get up and go over to him.

"Thanks for helping out," I say, my eyes on my purple flip-flops next to his black Vans.

"No problem." He pauses, and I drag my eyes off the floor and look somewhere near his direction. "I hope you know I'm your friend. I'm here anytime you need me."

I nod and finally meet his gaze. "Thanks, Charlie."

"Well . . . I guess I'd better get to class."

"Sorry to make you late," I say.

"I'm sure they'll give me a pass," he says, pointing to the reception desk.

I'm sure they will too because he's Charlie Wheeler, and everyone likes Charlie Wheeler.

As Charlie leaves, Dr. Gomez lowers the phone from his ear and tells me, "Your mother says she'll come by and pick you up, but she wants me to ask if you're sure you don't want to stay."

I know Mami wants me to stay, but this time, I can't be as brave as she is, as brave as she expects me to be. This time, I want my mami to pick me up and take me home, so I can feel safe again.

CHAPTER NINE

Mami brings me home and stays with me until it's time for her to go pick up Caroline Wheeler. My siblings are still at school, so I'm home alone, which is a rare occurrence. I try to think about anything besides the note, besides the Instagram comments, but they are all I can think of.

Part of me is grateful for Charlie's presence and his helpful attitude, but most of me is mortified that he witnessed my humiliation. I wonder how I'll face going back to school. Someone in my school wrote that note, and I don't know who it was. The Instagram comments were written by nameless, faceless trolls who might live several states away, but the note was written by someone I might see every day. The thought sends chills up my back, and that feeling only gets worse when the phone rings.

I jump at the sound and consider ignoring it, but it might be Mami, so I pull myself off the couch and go into the kitchen. I don't recognize the number on the caller ID but decide to pick up anyway. "Hello."

"Hi. I'm looking to speak to the parent of Milagros Vargas," says a man's voice.

Uneasiness spreads through my entire body. "This is Milagros Vargas. My mom can't come to the phone. Do you need something?"

The voice sounds soft but professional. "Hi, Milagros. My name is Thomas Dell. I'm a reporter for *Texas Monthly* magazine. I've worked with Oscar Zambrano before. You know Oscar, right?"

"Yes," I say as the fear starts to wash away.

"Well, we're very interested in doing a piece on you and your life here in America. I think Texas readers would be interested in reading your story."

I take the phone with me toward the kitchen table and sink down into one of the chairs. "Thank you, Mr. Dell, but I don't think I'm going to do any more stories. I'd really like all of this to just die down."

"Well, I hope you'll reconsider, Milagros. I'd be happy to come down there, do the interview, do a photo shoot. We can come anytime."

"Sorry, no."

"You know what? I'm going to send you some copies of our back issues. So you can take a look at our magazine and see what you think. I'll include my contact information in case you change your mind. How's that sound?"

"That's okay, but I won't change my mind."

"All right, Milagros. Thank you for your time. I'll send these out today."

I wait for him to ask for my address, but he doesn't. He says goodbye and I do too. I suppose he already has my address. He could get it from wherever he found my phone number. A shiver spreads through my body as I realize that anyone, anywhere could find me.

≈

I wake up covered in sweat and unable to catch my breath.

I was having the dream again. About Papi dying. I've had it more times than I care to count in the past three years.

I hop off my bed and grab my phone to check the time. Two in the morning. At least it's Saturday—well, Sunday, now—so if I can't get back to sleep, I won't have to worry about dragging through school in a few hours.

As I try to shift to a more comfortable position, I hear a lapping sound, like water, just outside the bedroom window. I move toward the window to peer outside. That's when I hear the shrill sound of our smoke alarm blaring from the hallway.

Sele wakes up with a gasp. "What is that?"

I pull the drapes back from our window and see orange flames dancing on our windowsill. I gasp and pull Sele toward the door.

Mami is in the small hallway yelling in Spanish for us to wake up. She spots Sele and me and pushes us down the hall toward the living room. She goes into Javi and Ceci's room and I hear her screaming at them.

I shove my phone toward Sele. "Go outside and call 911. I'll help Mami get the kids out."

Sele stands frozen in place, fear blazing from her eyes.

"Go!" I say, and she turns and bolts out the door.

I run into the bedroom where Mami is picking Ceci up from her bed. Javi is pulling himself upright, but he's completely disoriented. I run over and grab his arm. "Come on, Javi. We have to go!"

He rubs his eyes, but stands up as I pull on his arm. Together, we run into the hallway as Mami follows us with Ceci in her arms.

The living room has started to fill with flames, and we just manage to escape out the front door as the entryway is enveloped.

Sele is on the sidewalk across the street, in front of Mr. Obregon's house, talking unsteadily into my cell phone. Mr. Obregon has come outside and is on his cell phone too. The neighbors to our left, the Lunas, are standing on their front walk. Mr. Luna hurries to the side of his house, grabs a garden hose, turns it on, and starts to spray the flames that have engulfed the entire right side of our house.

Mami grabs my arm and watches as the flames increase in size. I hear sirens in the background, their volume swelling as the fire trucks draw nearer. Javi has pressed his head against my stomach, and Sele—finished with her 911 call—is crying in her hands, unable to even look up. Mami's holding Ceci, whose face is buried in Mami's neck. We all huddle together, unable to say anything.

More neighbors have started to emerge from their homes—in pajamas, bathrobes, tank tops. People begin surrounding us just as the fire trucks pull up. Justin's family is pretty much the only one on the block that hasn't ventured out, and in the back of my mind I feel a twinge of relief that we won't have to deal with that kid's obnoxiousness right now.

Mami stares at our home. Her eyes are focused, unblinking, as if she has to keep on looking to make it real. The firefighters order Mr. Luna and his garden hose away as they begin spraying the flames, which have engulfed even more of the house and are even billowing out of a hole that has suddenly appeared in our roof.

I feel the heat reach across the street, and I move back, pulling Javi with me. Mr. Obregon motions for me to move onto his doorstep, which I do. Mrs. Rosario, who lives next door to Mr. Obregon, comes out in her housedress and puts her arms around Mami, sobbing and praying at the same time.

A police officer who arrived at the same time as the fire truck approaches Mami and Mrs. Rosario. Mrs. Rosario releases Mami but stays beside her as the police officer talks to Mami. I can't hear what they're saying. Mami is still carrying Ceci, who clings to her stuffed bear, Osito. I wonder if that is the only thing that will be left of our home.

About half an hour later, the firefighters are still spraying the house. The paramedics have checked us all out and confirmed that none of us sustained any injuries. Most of our neighbors are out on their lawns, watching, and I feel like we're all cast members in a horribly sad show. I look down at my short cotton pajama shorts and nightshirt. These clothes, along with the cell phone Sele returned, might be all I have left in the world. Every other item I owned is now in flames, destroyed, turning to wet ashes.

Mr. Rosario takes a now-sleeping Ceci from Mami's arms. He and his wife walk over to the three of us, who are sitting on Mr. Obregon's doorstep.

"Come here, Javi," Mrs. Rosario says. "Your mami wants you to come with us, lie down for a while."

Javi keeps still, as if he hasn't heard her. He digs his head deeper into my stomach and squeezes me around the waist.

Sele puts her hands on Javi's shoulders. "Come on, Javi. I'll go with you."

Javi lets Sele pry his arms from around me, and he quickly grabs her, burying his head against her. He won't allow his eyes to stray to the still-burning house.

"I'll stay with Mami," I tell Sele, who nods. Mr. and Mrs.

Rosario take the three of them to the small yellow house next to Mr. Obregon's.

Flames are still flickering from the windows and the rooftop. My eyes move from the water hoses aimed at the house to the police officer who's pointing out something to Mami. He shines his flashlight on the sidewalk just outside our house. I see Mami nodding. I inch closer to them, hoping to hear what he's saying, but the sounds of the hoses, the fire, and the bystanders drown out his voice.

I take a step closer to the street, stretching out my neck to see what he's shining his flashlight on.

Black graffiti burns my eyes. They are familiar words. And I can no longer fold them up to get them out of my mind.

Go back to Mexico.

I can't tear my eyes away. Mami turns around, sees me, and excuses herself from the police officer.

"Mija," she says and comes over to me, envelops me in her strong arms. I remember when I was a little girl and she would hold me by her side or on her knee.

I bury my face in her shoulder and forget every time she has told me not to cry. She rubs my hair and keeps whispering in my ear. "Mija. Mi hija. Esta bien, mi hija."

Nada esta bien, I want to whisper back. Nothing is okay; nothing will ever be okay. I am the cause of this, and it will follow me around for the rest of my life. There is no escaping it now; the proof will be in the heaps of ashes that will appear beside those words by tomorrow.

Mami keeps rubbing my back, my hair, never once telling me to stop crying.

The police officer is only a few feet away, and I can tell he's giving us a minute, but I know he's not finished here. I pull slowly away from Mami and wipe my eyes. "Estoy bien," I tell her. I'm okay. I point to the officer, letting her know it's okay to go back to talking to him.

She eyes me doubtfully for a moment before turning back to him. The firefighters are still at work. The fire has died down a bit; it's not a roaring surge of flames seeping from the roof anymore. In fact, there isn't much of a roof left, and the whole right side has collapsed inward. It doesn't look like anything can be salvaged. Whatever didn't burn is certainly covered with smoke or water.

I pull my phone out of my pajama shorts and text Chloe that I need her.

I sit down on Mr. Obregon's doorstep. He's on his lawn talking to one of the neighbors. Mrs. Rosario comes down the sidewalk toward me, carrying two water bottles. She gives one to my mother and the other one to me. "Vamos, mija," she says to me, signaling toward her house, but I just shake my head.

A few minutes later, Chloe and her dad come racing around the corner. The image of her running in her cutoff sweatpants and tank top immediately provokes fresh tears. Her face is frantic. I get up and run the half block to meet them.

"Millie!" she yells. "I heard the sirens. I didn't know they were for you until you texted me. What happened?" She turns toward my house, and her hand shoots up to cover her mouth.

Chloe's dad is a few feet behind her, and when he reaches us, he pulls me in for a hug. "Oh, Millie. Is your family okay? Did everyone make it out?"

"Yes, everyone's fine. It's just the house," I say.

"How's your mom? Where is she?"

I point over to her. "She's been talking to the police for a while. It doesn't look like it was an accident." Finally verbalizing this reality brings on more tears.

Someone targeted us—targeted me—for the same reason someone put that note in my locker. It could've been anyone who watched Michael Winter's video or Mr. Zambrano's interview with Sebastian Smith. Anyone who hates immigrants and decided to take it out on one immigrant who's been getting attention.

Chloe puts her arms around me; her dad pats my shoulder and walks off to where Mami is standing.

Chloe pulls me in close. "Mil, I'm so sorry. I can't believe this."

I haven't even told her the worst part. I don't have the words, so I grab her arm and walk her down the sidewalk. The darkened street and the lack of blazing flames make it hard to see, but Chloe manages to make out what's written on the sidewalk.

"That's sick." She shakes her head. "Do they know who it was?"

"I don't know. I don't think so."

"Millie!" I look up and see Mrs. Rosario motioning to me from her doorstep. "Come inside, mija. You shouldn't be out here. The smoke is not good for you." She presses a folded white handkerchief to her mouth.

I nod, and Chloe and I follow Mrs. Rosario inside her house. The lights are dimmed in the living room. Ceci is asleep on the loveseat with an orange crocheted blanket covering her, Osito secured under her arm. Sele is on the couch, shaking with silent sobs, and Javi is lying with his head on her lap. I can't tell if he's asleep. I walk over to Sele and sink onto the floor next to her, resting my head against her legs. Chloe sits down beside me.

A few minutes later, Mami walks in with Chloe's dad and

Mr. Rosario. Sele, Javi, and I jump up and run to Mami, who takes us all in her arms. She holds us tightly for what seems like a long time, and none of us moves away.

"You stay here tonight, Sandra," Mrs. Rosario says.

"Or you can stay with us," Chloe's dad offers.

"Gracias. Ceci is asleep already, so I think we can just stay here."

Chloe grabs my hand. "You can come with us if you want, Mil."

I consider this and almost say yes. "Thanks, but I think we'd better all stay together. There's not much left of the night anyway."

Chloe gives me a big hug, and she and her father leave. Mrs. Rosario tells Sele and me to share the spare bedroom. Mami says she'll stay in the living room with Javi and Ceci. Ceci hasn't woken at all, and Javi snuggles onto Mami's lap on the couch.

Sele and I crawl into the queen-size bed in the Rosarios' tiny guest room. Neither of us can stop crying. Sele grabs my hand and squeezes as we lie under the white crochet blanket.

I don't remember dozing off, but when I wake up, sunlight is streaming through the white lace curtains. Sele is asleep, so I quietly reach for my phone on the floor to check the time. It's seven. I tiptoe out of the room and find Mami sitting at the kitchen table. Mrs. Rosario is at the stove, and something is sizzling in a pan.

"Mami. You okay?" I ask.

"Si, mija. I'm just waiting for the insurance company to call me back." She forces a smile, but all I can see is the worry that frames her eyes.

Mrs. Rosario comes over with a pot of coffee and refills

80

Mami's cup. "Do you want some coffee, Millie?"

"Oh, no gracias, Mrs. Rosario."

Mrs. Rosario pours herself a cup and sits down next to Mami. "Well, I hope you kids are hungry. I made bacon, pancakes, frijoles, chorizo con huevos, and tortillas." This doesn't surprise me, considering the six pounds of pan de polvo cookies she gives us each Christmas.

I smile at Mrs. Rosario despite the overwhelming sorrow in my heart. "Gracias. It sounds good."

As the morning progresses, Mami spends a lot of time on the phone with the insurance company and the police department. Javi, Ceci, and Sele eat most of what Mrs. Rosario cooked, which makes her extremely happy. I eat a piece of bacon and some frijoles. I hear Mami on the phone with Dr. Wheeler, explaining what happened and then thanking her several times—even more than usual.

Soon neighbors start dropping by to check on us. Chloe brings over two spare outfits, one for me and one for Sele, which don't fit either of us very well but are an improvement over our sooty, sweat-soaked pajamas. Meanwhile, Mami meets with the insurance adjuster and the fire marshal. She tells me that they have no leads yet on who set the fire, but it's pretty clear that it was arson. The message on the sidewalk makes it a good candidate for an official hate crime, too. The police have opened an investigation, but I wonder if there is any way they will figure out who did this to us.

In the afternoon Mami gathers us all in the Rosarios' living room. "We're going to need somewhere to stay until I can find us a new place to live," she says in a quiet, wavery voice that worries me.

"Can't we stay here with the Rosarios?" asks Sele.

"They've offered, but there isn't much room, and someone else has offered too."

"Who?" I ask. I know Chloe's family has an extra bedroom, the one her older sisters used to share, but that also probably won't be enough space for all of us.

"The Wheelers," Mami says. "They have lots of room, and it'll be convenient for me—no more commute. I've told them we'll come by tonight, right after dinnertime."

I'm not surprised that the Wheelers have offered to let us stay with them. It's just the type of thing that do-gooders like the Wheelers often do. But I am surprised that Mami agreed. How can she be their guest and their employee at the same time? That will be incredibly awkward and strange for all of us.

"Mami, are you sure?" I ask.

"It's just for a little while, until we find someplace to rent."

I've never seen Mami like this. She can't fix her eyes on anything, on anyone. She's worked her whole life to provide for us, so that she would never be at the mercy of anyone, never have to receive a handout from anyone. She doesn't even take free samples at the grocery store. Nothing for free; never. It's not worth anything if you haven't paid for it, she's told me before. But now Mami has no choice but to accept help from the Wheelers.

Everything she's spent her life working for lies in ashes.

I think about objecting, telling her that I want to stay with Chloe, but this isn't the time. She's already had too much happen in the last twenty-four hours. She needs my support right now, even if that means I have to temporarily move into Charlie Wheeler's house.

CHAPTER TEN

After entering the code to get us through the security gate, Mami parks her car in the circled driveway of the Wheelers' million-dollar Ocean Drive home. We all pile out, and she leads the way up the tree-lined walk to the front door. I follow, carrying Ceci. Her arms are clasped around my neck, and her stuffed bear, Osito, is tucked between us. Sele and Javi are right behind me.

The front door is already open, and the somber faces of Charles, Belinda, and Charlie Wheeler meet us. I'm a little surprised that Mr. Wheeler has made time to be here. According to Mami, he's been on the campaign trail constantly for months, making appearances all over the state, and even when he's home he's busy doing interviews or meeting with his campaign staff or hosting donors. And Dr. Wheeler has to participate in a lot of that stuff too, playing the devoted wife even while she keeps doing her own job.

Dr. Wheeler has been crying; her eyes and nose are red. She and Mr. Wheeler move to the side and let us come in. I step onto the marble floors of the entryway and set Ceci down.

"Sandra, I'm so sorry this has happened," says Dr. Wheeler.

"I don't even know what to say. We want to do whatever we can to help. You and the kids can stay here as long as you need. This is your home now, for as long as you want."

Mami nods and looks down at the floor. My siblings are gazing around the room, taking in everything. The chandelier that hangs over the entryway, the grand piano to the left, the marble floor that leads into the living room, and the spectacular view of the bay in front of us keep them mesmerized, maybe even making them forget for a minute what has happened to *our* house.

"Belinda's friends have jumped right in to help," Mr. Wheeler says, pointing to almost a dozen large shopping bags from Dillard's clustered at the foot of the spiraling staircase. "They weren't sure of the sizes, but hopefully most everything fits. If not, we can return it. I think there are some gift cards in there too."

Sele's eyes dart to the bags, and I know she can't wait to tear into them, but she stays frozen beside me. She won't dare move until Mami tells her to.

"I have a maid service coming in for the next few days," Dr. Wheeler says, "so, Sandra, you take a few paid days off to get everything straightened out with the insurance company. And don't worry about meals at all. I'll have some takeout brought in for all of us. I want you to just concentrate on your family and your life."

"And we want you to stay here as long as you need to," Mr. Wheeler chimes in. "I feel like this might be my fault in some way. We'll do anything to make it right."

Mami nods again and clears her throat. "Thank you both."

Caroline Wheeler bounds down the stairs in red polka-dot pajamas. "Look, Mama. It's my best friend!" She runs over to Ceci and pulls her into a tight hug.

Suddenly remembering why we're all here, she becomes more subdued and steps back from Ceci. "I'm so sorry about your house, Cecilia."

Ceci doesn't say anything. She hangs her head low and swallows hard.

"You can sleep in my bed, Cecilia. I have a princess bed."

Mami is about to say something, but Dr. Wheeler interjects. "Caroline's been insisting that she wants Cecilia to sleep in her bed. And Caroline can sleep in the trundle bed beneath her. There's no use trying to talk her out of it, Sandra."

Mami nods, and Caroline takes this as permission to proceed. "Come on, Cecilia." She grabs Ceci's hand and pulls her toward the stairs.

Ceci turns around and looks at me. "Millie." She holds out her hand for me, and I take it. I force a smile at the others still standing in the foyer and follow the two girls upstairs.

I don't remember the last time I was here. It must have been at least five years ago, and I don't even know where Caroline's room is. How strange that Mami must be so familiar with every corner of this house, yet it's so foreign to me.

Caroline marches into her room and points out her bed to Ceci. It's a tall canopy bed with an ivory eyelet bedcover. The carpets are creamy beige and flawlessly clean. I wonder how Mami keeps them so clean. In the corner of the room is a white wooden dollhouse with tiny furniture that looks nicer and probably more expensive than any real furniture we've ever had.

"Come on, try it out," Caroline says and pulls Ceci toward the bed.

"I can't sleep in your bed," Ceci says.

"Yes, you can! I'll sleep down here." Caroline pulls the trundle out from under her bed. "I always sleep here for sleepovers. You get the bed." Caroline sits down on the trundle and crosses her legs.

Ceci looks at me, a question in her eyes.

"It's okay, Ceci," I say.

I hear a soft knock on the open door and turn around. It's Charlie Wheeler, holding two Dillard's bags.

"Hey, Millie. I just wanted to bring these by. Some clothes for Cecilia." He walks into Caroline's room and sets them down between us.

"Cool!" Caroline calls out. "Cecilia, let's see what they bought you. You need pajamas."

Ceci follows Caroline over to the bags, and Caroline begins pulling out clothes, letting them fall to the floor as she searches.

"Caroline, don't throw them on the floor," Charlie says, kneeling down next to her. He picks up a few shirts and folds them on his knee. "Those are Cecilia's clothes. Let her look through them."

Caroline leaves the clothes and sits on the floor next to Charlie. I bend down to help Ceci search through the bags. Together, we find a pair of pink pajamas. They're made of soft, silky material and have little white hearts all over them. The buttons on the top are heart-shaped, and there's white lace along the hem of the pants.

I check the size and figure they'll fit fine. "Here, Ceci. You can wear these."

Ceci takes the pajamas from me and runs her hand over the soft material, smiling for maybe the first time since the fire.

"I'll show you where to change," Caroline says, bolting off the floor and grabbing Ceci's hand. The two scamper out of the room.

Charlie and I are still sitting on the floor of the now-silent room, and suddenly everything I've been feeling since last night is more pronounced. My sadness, my anger, and my tattered pride are all competing for precedence inside of me. And then there is the feeling that I once had a crush on the boy sitting beside me. I'm so glad that was long ago.

"I'm very sorry about this," Charlie says.

I shrug and finally look up at him. "It's not your fault. You didn't burn our house down."

"I know, but in a way it is our fault."

I want to get up and go somewhere, but I don't know where I'm supposed to go, don't know exactly where I will be sleeping or what I'm supposed to do now.

Caroline and Ceci come back in and crawl into their beds. I stand up and walk over to Ceci. "Good night, Ceci. I'll tell Mami to come kiss you good night."

"Okay, Millie." She leans in closer. "What if this house burns down too?" she asks.

I whisper in her ear, "It won't. I promise."

She nods at me, but tears start to gather in the corner of her eyes.

"You want me to lie down with you for a while?"

She looks down at Caroline and shakes her head, trying to be brave.

"Okay, I'll go get Mami." I turn around and see that Charlie has stepped out into the hallway. Mr. Wheeler has joined him.

"Is Cecilia going to be okay?" Mr. Wheeler asks me.

"I think so. But she'll probably end up finding her way to my mom sometime tonight."

Mr. Wheeler nods. "That's fine, Millie. Whatever she needs."

"Thank you," I say.

"Your mom's going to be taking your brother and sisters

to school and picking them up in the afternoon for the time being," Mr. Wheeler explains. "I know you're used to taking them, but it's too far to walk from here. And Charlie can give *you* a ride to school."

Of course, tomorrow's Monday. All the logistics of everything—I hadn't thought about it before. Apparently, the Wheelers have. Mr. Wheeler is good at strategizing, trying to find solutions to every problem he sees, optimizing results and all that. I guess that's what makes him a politician.

I look over at Charlie, who smiles. I suppose I should be thankful I have a ride to and from school, but it's so terribly hard for me to be grateful to these people. The lingering thought won't leave me—our house would still exist, were it not for Mr. Wheeler's big mouth.

But I don't say what I think. I very rarely do.

Mr. Wheeler nods and taps Charlie and me on our shoulders simultaneously. "Well, you and Selena will be sharing a guest room. Charlie, can you show Millie where it is?"

"Sure, Dad."

Mr. Wheeler goes off down the hall, and I follow Charlie in the other direction.

"It's here," Charlie says, stopping in front of a room with an open door. "And the bathroom's through there." He points inside the bedroom, to a door on the opposite side of the entrance. "That bathroom's connected to another small guest room where your mom will be."

"What about Javi?" I ask.

"I think my mom said he's going to be downstairs in the den. There's a pullout couch down there."

"Okay," I say, wondering if Javi will be okay all by himself downstairs.

"The den is right next to the master bedroom," Charlie says, answering my unasked question. He flips on the light and steps aside, so I can enter the room. The queen bed has plush emerald pillows and a matching bedcover. The dark wood headboard matches a dresser and small armoire. Against one wall there's a flat-screen TV and a tall mirror that stands on wooden feet. I think about our cracked mirror back home, the one I always felt would bring us bad luck. Suddenly I remember the mirror doesn't exist anymore.

"Thanks," I say as I walk farther into the room. I look at the bed but I decide against sitting down. I don't want Charlie to think that I'm eager to be staying here.

"I'm really sorry about this, Millie," Charlie says.

I just shrug. I really don't know how to respond at this point. He probably didn't even expect a response, probably only said it because what else is he supposed to say?

He looks at me intently. "You're safe here, you know. My dad's arranging with the Corpus police department to have someone watching the house for a few days. And he said he may even hire a security guard. He doesn't want anything else to happen to you or your family."

I wonder if Mr. Wheeler's intent is to protect my family— or to safeguard his expensive home and the luxuries contained within it. I don't ask the question, though; I keep it inside like I do all my negative thoughts about the Wheelers.

"Thanks," is all I say, just as Dr. Wheeler comes in with Mami and Sele.

"Oh good, you found your room," Dr. Wheeler says to me. She puts her arm around my shoulder. "Charlie, can you please go get the rest of the bags?"

"Right." Charlie gives me a quick look before he leaves.

"I hope you two will be comfortable sharing the bed," Dr. Wheeler says.

Sele nods and I say, "It's great."

"Well, anything you need, just let us know and we'll take care of it," she says. She claps her hands together. "Anyway, the bathroom is through there. Charlie is bringing up the bags, and Sandra, your room is next door. You can go through the bathroom or just down the hall." Dr. Wheeler points to the hall, and then shakes her head with a smile. "Sorry, Sandra. Of course you know," she says, suddenly remembering that Mami knows every inch of this house, has cleaned every inch of this house.

"Yes, I know. Thank you. Everything is just fine."

"Well, I'll let you get settled. I'm sure you're all exhausted."

"I'll go check on Ceci," Mami says.

"I'll go with you to tuck Caroline in," Dr. Wheeler says before she and Mami disappear down the hall together.

Sele and I sit on the bed. I put my arm around Sele and pull her toward me. She puts her head on my shoulder, and we sit there for a few minutes saying nothing. We both know what the other is feeling. Scared, heartbroken, and unsure of what tomorrow will bring. Everything around us reminds us of what we don't have.

Charlie comes to the doorway and knocks on the open door. Sele hops off the bed.

"Sorry, I just wanted to bring these in." Charlie comes over to the bed and sets four more Dillard's bags on the floor by our feet. He hands me another smaller bag. "And this is shampoos and stuff."

I take the bag and set it on the bed next to me. "Thanks, Charlie."

He shoves his hands into his back pockets. "Need anything else?"

Without looking at the bag to actually see if we're missing any necessities, I shake my head. "No. I think we're good."

"Okay, well. I hope you two sleep well. Just let any of us know if you need anything." He looks from Sele to me. "Millie, I usually leave for school around eight-thirty if that's okay."

"Yeah, that's good." I almost say "thank you" again, but I've already said it so many times, and I suspect I will be saying it a lot more. I don't want the words to lose their meaning.

I study the plush white carpet instead of looking at him. I don't want to be here in Charlie Wheeler's house, subject to his generosity. I want to be in my own home, away from his charitable eyes.

"Okay, good night." Charlie takes a step backward before finally turning around and leaving.

I get up and close the door. Sele sits back down on the bed. "I can't believe Mami is making us go to school tomorrow."

I can believe it. Life has to go on, and she won't give us even a day to dwell on our trauma, to feel sorry for ourselves. We are expected to pick ourselves up and move on just as she will do.

"Will you talk to her, Millie? See if she'll let us stay home."

"Stay home? We have no home." I soften the words as much as I can. "And I think I'd rather be at school than stay here all day, just thinking about the fire."

"But everyone will know. Everyone's probably heard. They'll all be talking about us."

I know that's true. Corpus is not a huge city. Word spreads fast. And not everyone in our school wishes us well, as I discovered recently. Some of our classmates might actually gloat over what's happened to us, thinking we somehow deserve it. "I know, Sele, but our friends will be there for us. It'll be good to go to school, be distracted."

Sele nods and rests her head in my lap. She starts quietly sobbing. I want to cry too, but I remind myself that Mami hasn't cried once. And if there's anyone who should cry about all of this, it's Mami. She's the one responsible for four children and the one who has to figure out how to find us a home again. She's the one with the heavy weight on her shoulders, with no husband to share it with her. She's the one who has to swallow her pride by turning to her employers and staying in the house that she cleans.

I run my fingers through Sele's long, straight hair. "It's okay, Sele. We're all okay. That's the most important thing."

Her quiet sobs continue.

"We made it through Papi's death. We'll make it through this."

CHAPTER ELEVEN

The next morning, I lie in bed for far longer than is usual for me. Mami assured me last night that she would get the kids ready and take them to school. She has the day off, which must seem weird for her because this is where she works. A maid service will be coming in today to do her job, because I suppose Dr. Wheeler can't go a single day without her chandelier getting dusted.

It's seven-thirty, and I know Mami has left with the kids by now. Her incessant punctuality persists despite everything.

I get up and make the bed—a habit ingrained in me since childhood. Mami taught us to make the bed as soon as we get up, even before we go to the bathroom. I know I don't do as good as Mami, and she'll probably straighten everything when she gets back to the Wheelers', but I leave it.

The attached bathroom probably only gets used when guests are here, which I imagine is not very often. The Wheelers are so busy; I don't know where they would find time for houseguests. But if I know Mami, this bathroom gets cleaned at least every other day. She does not let dust accumulate on anything.

The white tile is cold against my feet. I open the white lacy shower curtain and wonder if it's even supposed to get wet. But I can tell that Mami showered already; she's opened the fancy bar of soap. My shower is warm, feels good. Maybe it's something about the expensive chrome showerhead that makes it the best shower I think I've ever had. I hurry through it, though, because Charlie Wheeler is my ride today—my ride for the foreseeable future, I suppose.

I wrap a thick white towel around me and walk back into the guest bedroom. I am naked in Charlie Wheeler's house, and it feels so strange. The Dillard's bags are all lined up near the door. Selena has thoroughly examined hers. She's refolded all the clothes she wants to keep and has put them neatly on the nearby dresser. I look through the remaining bags. There are at least five pairs of jeans, several shirts, and pajamas that I didn't wear last night. I just wore the clothes I was already wearing, the outfit that Chloe dropped off for me to borrow.

Another bag has a pair of Nike shoes I will never wear, packages of socks and underwear, and three bras. The bras are too big, but they'll do. I guess Belinda Wheeler's friends have thought of everything. Benevolence is their occupation, and they will surely feel good about themselves for a long time after this.

The jeans still have price tags on them. A hundred and fifty dollars. I've never worn anything that cost this much, but this is what the Wheelers' friends' daughters wear, what they think everyone wears. The pants are a size too small, but I squeeze into them.

I suppose that's why they'd left the price tags on—so the clothes can be easily returned if they don't fit. That's a kinder

and more logical interpretation than my initial presumption—
that they wanted us to know how much we were indebted to
them. I try to squash that thought, chiding myself for being
unappreciative of what everyone is doing for us.

I look through the shirts and put aside three in varying
shades of pink. I don't wear pink. Purple is my color, and in my
mind they are not the least bit related. That leaves me with four
other donated shirts. Besides the Nikes, there's a pair of black
slip-ons, but I only wear open-toed shoes unless it's below forty
degrees. I shove my feet into the flip-flops Chloe brought me
yesterday and am about to go downstairs when a smaller bag
catches my eye. Inside is an assortment of makeup—the expensive kind, not the cheap drugstore stuff I buy. I take the bag
into the bathroom and spend a few minutes applying mascara,
foundation, and blush, thinking about the thoughtfulness of
Dr. Wheeler's friends.

I wish I could simply be grateful, or even just relieved.
Instead I'm more uncomfortable than ever. We never asked
for charity. And if Mr. Wheeler hadn't planted the seed that
had led that arsonist straight to our home, we wouldn't have to
accept it.

I know the Wheelers feel guilty. I know they want to *make
it right*, as Mr. Wheeler said. But part of me suspects that
what these people really want, more than anything else, is to
feel like the good guys in this situation. They want to give us
these gifts, soothe their consciences, and then forget this ever
happened.

I glance at my watch and think of Papi. This Mickey Mouse
watch might be the only tangible memory I have left of him.
All of the photographs of him, the gifts, the mementos, his
long-sleeved blue work shirts that Mami still kept starched and

95

hanging in her closet, are all gone now. I'm grateful I have the watch, but I wish that everyone else in my family had something from Papi that survived the fire.

I hurry to the kitchen. School starts at nine, and Charlie said last night that he leaves at eight-thirty. Charlie is seated at the kitchen table, and he smiles when I walk in.

"Morning," I say.

He stands up. "Good morning. Did you sleep okay?"

I nod and shove my hands into the tiny pockets of my too-small jeans.

"Want something to eat?" he asks. "I picked up some breakfast tacos. There's bacon and egg, and potato and egg."

There are two white paper bags on the table. Charlie has three tacos in front of him, and it looks like he's just started eating.

"Okay," I say and sit down across from him.

"Everyone else has already eaten," he says. "So have as many as you want."

I nod. "You picked these up?" I ask him.

"Yeah, this morning before everyone left." He walks over to a cupboard and pulls out a glass. "Want some juice or milk?"

"Water is good. Thanks," I say.

He walks to the refrigerator and fills the glass with ice and water from the door dispenser. "Here you go," he says, putting down the glass in front of me and sitting back down.

"Thank you." I reach into the bag and pull out a taco. I don't really care what kind.

I take a bite. Bacon and egg, it turns out. I would have preferred potato and egg, now that I think about it. I'm not really hungry anyway, and I don't feel like eating, but it seems that it's what I'm supposed to do right now. And at the moment, I'm just trying to do what's expected of me because I haven't figured anything else out.

I barely finish my taco in the time that Charlie scarfs down his three. I put away my half-eaten food and clean up the spot at the table where I was sitting. Charlie tucks the bags of the remaining tacos in the fridge and grabs his backpack off the floor. I look around, out of habit, for my backpack, until I remember it's gone, left in the house. I have nothing to carry to school with me, not even a single pencil.

The stark reality of the moment hits me so hard that I want to cry, but I don't. I cannot cry in front of Charlie Wheeler. I cannot give him one more reason to pity me.

≈

Charlie's car is a Volvo sedan, one his mother stopped using last year. He probably could have asked for a brand-new car; the fact that he's driving what's technically a hand-me-down gives me a sliver of respect for him.

He opens the door for me—one more reason to thank Charlie Wheeler, to feel indebted to him. He smiles as he closes the door and walks around to the other side. Once he's started the car, he reaches behind my seat to grab something. I lean over toward the door to give him room.

"Here," he says, handing me a bright red backpack. "My friend Mindy dropped this by for you this morning. It's her backpack from last year. She put some notebooks and supplies in there. She said sorry it's not new, but she hopes it's okay for now."

Slowly, I reach out to take the backpack. It isn't heavy, doesn't have textbooks inside. I set it on my lap and leave it there without opening it. "That was really nice of her."

"She texted me last night when she heard, wanted to know what she could do. I thought you could use a backpack for school."

I nod and turn to look straight ahead. Charlie puts the car in drive. Like the clothes from Dr. Wheeler's friends, the backpack in my lap evokes an emotion I can't describe. It's something more complicated than gratitude.

As we cruise through the security gate and leave the Wheeler house behind, I slide open the zipper of the red backpack's main compartment. There's a small binder full of blank loose-leaf paper, three spiral notebooks, a small pencil bag full of pencils and pens, and a calculator. Mindy is in my calculus class and has anticipated everything I might need. There's also a small pink envelope with my name on it.

I hesitate to open it in front of Charlie, but he's distracted by the road or at least pretending to be. And I want to know what Mindy's note says before I get to school; it's not something I want to read in class.

I slide my finger under the seal and pull out the small pink note card.

Dear Millie,

I am so sorry about what happened to your family. Here are a few things that might help. I know it's not a lot and doesn't begin to replace what you've lost, but I wanted you to know I'm thinking of you and hoping it will get better.

Mindy Stincil

I glance over at Charlie to see if he's watching me, and he is, but only for an instant before he turns his eyes back to the road.

"You have a very nice friend," I say, wondering if she's more than just a friend. But that is not my business and feels kind of trivial to be thinking about right now. So I just resume my silence for the rest of the drive.

When Charlie pulls into a spot in the school parking lot, he asks, "Want to just meet here after school?"

Part of me wants to take the bus home as usual, but the Wheelers' house isn't on my usual route. "Yeah, that's fine. Thank you for the ride."

"Sure." We walk together toward the school's main entrance. I see people looking my way. I wonder if they know about the fire or if they're just wondering why I'm with Charlie.

The red backpack on my shoulder seems foreign, and I want to throw it in the street and run as fast as I can to somewhere, anywhere but here. I don't, of course, because I feel my mother urging me on. There is no time to feel sorry for myself, no place for self-doubt. Even after my dad's death, she pulled herself up and continued on every day. That's what she expects of me, but I am unsure if I can do what she's done. I'm not the Milagros she expected. I am just Millie, and I don't think I can do this.

Just outside the main entrance, I stop mid-step, and Charlie stops just in front of me.

"Are you okay?" he asks.

I look back toward his car, wishing it could take me away, take me back, but I'm not sure where.

That's when I see the curls of Chloe's long hair bouncing in the air as she runs toward me across the parking lot. My ex-boyfriend, Jay, and his best friend, Ivan, are right behind her, walking briskly.

"Millie!" she cries out.

In another instant, Chloe is flinging her arms around my neck. "You okay?" she asks.

I nod, my head resting on her shoulder.

"Hi, Charlie," Chloe says, turning to him.

"Hi, Chloe."

"Is she okay?" Chloe demands.

"I think so."

Chloe looks back down at me, and I nod again. "I'm fine. It's good to see you."

Jay and Ivan catch up to us. "Mil, how are you holding up?" Jay asks, pulling me into a hug. I haven't had one of Jay's hugs since I broke up with him last summer, but his arms around me feel good, safe, and I don't want him to let go. He pulls away slowly. "I'm so sorry about your house."

Ivan's frowning and rubbing his hands together in an absentmindedly anxious way. "Same, Millie. Can I do something for you?"

"I'll be okay," I say, even though I don't know for certain that I will be. I turn to Charlie. He looks like he doesn't know if he should stay with us or keep walking to class. "The Wheelers are helping us out," I say.

He takes this as a cue to nod a greeting to Jay and Ivan.

They nod back at him, and I don't miss the way Jay eyes him up and down before turning back to me.

The first bell rings, and we all go inside. The boys head off to their lockers. Chloe keeps her arm around me, and I feel strengthened by it.

"Did you sleep okay at Casa Wheeler?" she asks.

"It was fine," I say. "They've been really nice."

"I can't believe your mom made you come to school today. She should've just let you stay home, take some time."

"Do you know my mother?" I ask her, starting to relax for the first time this morning. Being around Chloe is soothing, like an old quilt wrapped around your shoulders. The world can go on now; I have Chloe.

"I know your mother, and I love your mother, but you should be home right now with family, healing."

"Ha. When Sele broke her arm, she was in school the next day. Healing happens as you're working, that's what Mami says."

"What can I do, really?"

"Just look for me in the mornings, walk with me. I don't want to be by myself right now."

She nods. "I'll walk you to your locker and then to first period."

On the way, several students I only vaguely know from my classes stop to talk to me. "Millie, you're here!" "Millie, are you okay?" I know I should be grateful that people care, but it's embarrassing to have the entire school know that we're homeless now, dependent on the charity the Wheelers have offered us.

When we reach my locker, I pause for a second, remembering when I found that note. That seemed like the beginning of all of this.

I grab my English binder and hang Mindy's backpack on the hook inside.

"Where'd you get the backpack?" Chloe asks.

"Mindy Stincil," I say, looking around to see if she or any of her friends are within earshot. "She dropped it off at the Wheelers' this morning."

"Lazy Layup? That was nice of her."

"Don't call her that, Chloe. I feel bad now."

"That's just your Catholic guilt, Millie. It's not like we're actually mean to her."

"I know, but I don't think I can make fun of her anymore."

"All right, girl. Whatever you want. Let's get you to English." English won't be so bad. Jen will be there. And after that—well, I'll deal with it as I go along.

By the end of the day half the student body, and every teacher I know, has inquired about my family and my house. Even Mr. Brody stops me in the hall to ask me how I'm doing.

"I saw the segment on the local news," he says, which makes my stomach flip. I hadn't realized the fire got news coverage. "My heart just breaks for your family. Folks like you don't deserve this."

I stop myself from snapping back, *What kind of folks do deserve this? Immigrants who aren't citizens? Immigrants who can't find work? Immigrants who don't get straight As?*

People like Charles Wheeler and Oscar Zambrano keep using me as a case study of an inspiring, admirable immigrant. But what if I were just an average student? What if I'd gotten a speeding ticket once? Every time someone says, *look at her, look at all she's achieved*, they're implying that if I achieved less, I would be unworthy of basic human respect. If my family weren't such a shining example of Good Immigrants, people like Mr. Brody probably wouldn't feel nearly as heartbroken to see us suffering.

I bite my tongue. There's some consolation in knowing that by tomorrow, most people will have already forgotten the fire. They won't think to keep checking in on me, and I'll be able to pretend things are somewhat back to normal.

After school I automatically walk toward the bus line, but as I catch Chloe waving goodbye to me, I remember that I won't be riding the bus home with her today. Today, I am going to wait for Charlie Wheeler by his car. People walk past me, streaming out the doors that lead to the bus lines. I'm thankful that they're in too much of a hurry to notice me.

I head to the parking lot. Charlie's already there, leaning against his car talking to one of his friends, a guy named Dawson. They're laughing, and I immediately wish for something to laugh at, something that will make me forget why I have to get a ride from Charlie Wheeler.

Dawson says one last thing to Charlie before walking away. Charlie sees me and waves.

"Hi," he says as I reach his car. "Ready?"

"Yeah, thanks again for the ride. I almost forgot and was heading out to the bus."

We get in and he starts the car. "Oh, no worries. And if you ever need to stay after school or to get here early, just let me know."

"Okay, thanks." I strap my seat belt on and balance Mindy Stincil's backpack on my lap.

"How was school today?" he asks as he pulls out of the parking lot. "Was it too weird?"

Who is he to ask? I think, but of course, I don't say that.

"I don't know," I say, shrugging. "People I never talk to stared at me and asked me if I was okay. I guess that's the standard protocol for when someone's house burns down."

"They're just concerned. They care about you."

I make a noncommittal humming noise.

"I care too, Millie. I know this is hard, but I just want to be your friend."

I can't let go of the blame I've assigned to the Wheelers. They're the cause of everything bad that has happened to us in the last few weeks. I don't want Charlie's friendship. I don't want anything from him, but I can't tell him that.

"I know. It's just a really hard time for me."

"Well, I'm here if you want to talk."

I bite my lip. He would not want to hear what I have to say right now. "Okay."

Charlie maneuvers through after-school traffic and makes it out to Ocean Drive. I look out the window, partly because I really love the scenery—the palm trees lining the drive, the bay stretching out along one side—but partly because I don't feel like talking to Charlie. It's not because it's Charlie; I just don't want to talk.

A woman runs by in tiny running shorts, her blond ponytail swaying with each step. Just behind her is another woman pushing a baby stroller. People going about their everyday lives, their routines undisrupted by fear.

There's one immense and beautiful home right after the other, with backyards overlooking the bay. We pass several blocks of these expensive houses until we reach the Wheelers' home behind its ten-foot fence.

Charlie keys in the gate code, pulls into the driveway, and parks behind Mami's Toyota Tercel.

"Thanks again for the ride," I say.

"Sure. Same time tomorrow, I guess." Charlie smiles, pulling his backpack over one shoulder as we walk up the stone path to the front door. The lock is another keypad, and I make a mental note to get this house's various security codes from Mami.

Inside, Mami has Caroline, Sele, Ceci, and Javi at the

kitchen table doing homework. It's so quiet that I can hear pencil lead on paper as Javi writes his spelling words.

"Hola, mija. Hola, Charlie," she says to us as we walk in. She leans in to give us each a hug and a kiss on the cheek.

"Hola, Señora Vargas," Charlie says. He puts his backpack down on the table and ruffles Caroline's hair.

"Stop it," she says, swatting his hand away.

Mami asks Charlie how his school day was. "Que tal la escuela, Charlie?"

"Muy bien. Cien en mi examen de Español." *Wow*, I think as he slides down into a chair next to Caroline. I wonder if this is a typical afternoon around here: Charlie telling Mami he got a hundred percent on his Spanish test.

I only see Charlie at school, and sometimes it's hard to remember that he has a life here at home . . . with Mami. They see each other and talk every day, say things to each other that I know nothing about.

Mami walks over to me where I'm still standing in the entryway. "Y tú, mija? Cómo estás?"

I look over at everyone seated at the table, busy doing their homework, and meet Charlie's eyes. He quickly grabs an apple from a fruit bowl in the center of the table and says something to Caroline.

"Bien, Mami," I say even though I don't think I'm okay, but how can I complain about my day at school when I know she's been dealing with the aftermath of our tragedy?

Dr. Wheeler comes in, dressed in scrubs, followed by an African-American woman in a police uniform. "Sandra, this is Detective Blake. She's been assigned to the case."

Mami wipes her hands on a dishcloth and walks over to the two women. "Hello, Detective Blake. Thank you for coming."

"You're welcome to talk in the living room," Dr. Wheeler says, pointing.

I follow Mami and Detective Blake into the living room, where they both sit down on the couch. I linger near the doorway, wanting to hear the conversation. Mami doesn't object, so I take a few steps closer.

"Mrs. Vargas, we are looking into all possibilities. We've had a team out all day looking for evidence, interviewing neighbors. We want to find who did this." Detective Blake pulls out a small notepad.

"Did they find anything?" Mami asks.

I quietly take a seat next to Mami.

"Nothing yet," Detective Blake says. "We're still looking, but I wanted to ask you if you could think of anyone who has made threats to you or your family."

Mami looks at me and nods, but doesn't say anything.

"There was a note in my locker at school," I say, looking at Detective Blake. "It said the same thing that was written on the sidewalk."

Detective Blake turns a few pages. "*Go back to Mexico*?"

I don't want to repeat the words. So I just nod.

"So, when did you find this note?"

"Last week. I gave it to the principal. He might still have it."

She makes a note. "Where do you go to school?"

I tell her.

"Okay, I'll talk to your principal. Was there anything else?" She looks from me to Mami.

I look at Mami again. "On Instagram. There were trolls—a lot of them, saying racist things."

"Okay," says Detective Blake. "We have a team of cyber experts that can take a look at these comments, try to unmask them. I'll need your usernames for all your social media accounts."

I give her that information. She leaves soon afterward, promising to call with any information that turns up.

Mami closes the door behind her and pulls me into a hug. "They'll find something, mija."

"I hope so," I say, holding Mami tightly.

"Mr. Zambrano called today," she says as we step apart. "To offer his sympathy."

I wonder if he's offered sympathy because his story has stoked the hate that's being directed at us. But I don't say this.

"He wants to talk to you," Mami says.

"About what?"

"He wants to do a follow-up interview about what's happened since you first talked to him."

"No, Mami. I can't do that. I'm sorry." I think about elaborating, telling her that I'm afraid more notoriety will lead to more danger for my family, but I don't have the energy to plunge into a long discussion. "Lo siento." I offer the apology before turning around and heading upstairs. She has to understand I've done everything she's wanted me to up to this point. I can't do any more.

CHAPTER TWELVE

Dinnertime at the Wheelers' is going to be another big production. Dr. Wheeler has picked up Chinese food so Mami doesn't have to cook. I overheard Mami tell her that our family can just eat in the kitchen, but Dr. Wheeler insisted that we join them in the dining room. I really hope we won't have to do this every night.

I walk in to find Charlie and Dr. Wheeler setting the long oak table. Charlie looks up at me as he's folding a napkin to place beside a plate.

"Millie! Come in and pick a seat for dinner," Dr. Wheeler says to me. Her hair is in a loose bun, and she has changed into yoga pants and a white tee. "We got you sweet and sour chicken. Your mom said that's your favorite. We have plenty. Please eat as much as you'd like."

I look at the white serving bowls brimming with steaming food, and I think back to the last time I had sweet and sour chicken. It was the night we watched Mr. Zambrano on TV. Which led to the note in my locker and was followed by the burning of my house.

"Thank you, Dr. Wheeler," I force myself to say. I grab the

chair in front of me and lean into it. I'm grateful for everything the Wheelers are doing, but I just don't want to be here.

She reaches out and touches my arm. "You know you're welcome to anything in the house, right? Anything you need. It's your home now. Feel free to go anywhere, do anything."

I'm so relieved that Javi comes bounding in before I have to say *thank you* yet again. Caroline and Ceci are right behind him.

"Come sit by me, Cecilia," Caroline says.

Mr. Wheeler comes in too; his tie is gone and the top button on his white dress shirt is undone. "This smells delicious, Belinda," he says, as if she's cooked it, as if she had any part in it other than making a phone call.

Mami and Sele walk in last and sit down on either side of me. I'm still standing, holding onto the chair. Finally, I pull the chair out and sink into it. Charlie is sitting right across from me, looking at me again. He's probably wondering if I'm going to stop acting weird.

"Sandra," Mr. Wheeler says as he starts passing dishes around clockwise, "have you heard back from the investigators? Do they know anything yet?"

Mami shakes her head. "No, they're going to call me again tomorrow."

Dr. Wheeler reaches over and puts a hand on Mami's arm. "Well, you just focus on that for right now. I don't want you to worry about a single thing around the house. And just let me know if there's anything else that you need."

Mami forces a small smile. "We're fine. Thank you." Javi scoops out a huge spoonful of fried rice, and Mami gives him a look. I only scoop out a little when the bowl of fried rice comes to me.

Caroline leans forward in her chair. "Mama, I want Cecilia

to live here. Can they all just live here?"

Dr. Wheeler smiles at Caroline. "Oh, baby. We love having everyone here, and they're welcome to stay as long as they like, but I think Cecilia will want her own room again."

"But she said she's never had her own room," Caroline says.

Dr. Wheeler's smile shrinks a little. "You know what I mean, baby. Her family wants their own home."

Caroline seems unsatisfied, but she lets the topic go and dives into her fried rice.

"Did the clothes fit all right?" Dr. Wheeler asks, putting her fork down next to her plate.

"Yes, thank you," Mami says with that same small, strained smile. "I'm going to have the kids write thank-you notes to your friends."

"Oh, that's so nice," Dr. Wheeler says, picking her fork up again. "Millie, is it working out okay for Charlie to take you to school?"

"Yes, thanks."

"Well, you just let him know if you ever have to stay after for any extracurricular activities, okay?"

I try to return Dr. Wheeler's smile, but I'm not sure I succeed. My main extracurricular activity throughout high school has been babysitting my brother and sisters. I was on the swim team briefly, but I had to quit after Papi died and Mami started working full time. I would've thought Dr. Wheeler would know that, but such a reality doesn't seem to belong in her world.

≈

After school the next day, Mami needs to call Detective Blake and the insurance company, so she asks me to watch the kids.

"I want you to see my playhouse, Cecilia," Caroline says. "It has a little kitchen in it, and we can pretend to make cookies."

Ceci looks at me, and I smile at her as I kneel down to tie her new shoes. They're pink, sparkly tennis shoes that light up when she walks. Dr. Wheeler's friends guessed right on that one, and I suspect Ceci will never want to wear any other shoes. Caroline puts on her almost identical pair of shoes and hurries us along.

"I keep telling Mama I want to sleep out there one night, but she says no. Maybe if we sleep there together, she'll let us." Caroline pushes the sliding door open, and Ceci and I follow her outside to the tile patio. The girls bound down the patio steps, past the lawn chairs with overstuffed cushions and the large table made of wrought iron and glass. The lawn slopes toward the water's edge, which is only a fence away. Caroline's pink-and-white wooden playhouse is in the far corner of the yard, right next to the pool. I marvel that the little kitchen in Caroline's playhouse has such an amazing view of the bay.

I sit on the cool grass and watch as the two girls disappear into the house. My gaze is automatically drawn to the vast expanse of water before me.

This is the same view I've seen from just down the street at Cole Park, but it never ceases to astound me. This is the Wheelers' backyard; this is what they get to look at every day and into the night. That amazes me. Tonight I'm going to look at it from my bedroom window—watch the moon's light dancing on the ever-moving water. It wasn't something I allowed myself to indulge in last night, and even now I feel slightly guilty about looking forward to it.

Still, my eyes stay on the water. I can see and hear the waves crashing against the rocky shore just below the fence.

I never tire of it. I occasionally glance at the playhouse, but the girls haven't emerged from it. I kick off my flip-flops and rub my feet into the grass, letting the cool blades in between my toes. I wrap my arms around my legs and throw my head back a little, letting the ever-present ocean breeze hit my face.

Javi comes outside, dribbling a basketball. I turn around to look at him. "Charlie said I can use his basketball," he says. He picks up the ball and walks to a concrete half-court on the far end of the yard. I watch as he misses his first few shots. Instinctively I wonder if he's finished his homework, but I don't ask. Mami is here; I don't have to play mami today. Besides, it really is only the second day after the fire. I can't expect everything to be back to normal already.

I hear the sliding door behind me again, but I don't turn around, thinking it's Sele wanting to explore the backyard too. But it's Charlie Wheeler, and he sits down on the lawn right next to me. There are at least ten dozen other places he could sit.

"Mind if I sit here?" he asks me, as if I spoke my thought aloud.

"Of course not," I lie. "It's your house."

"I know, but if you just want to be alone, I don't want to bother you."

I shrug and look back toward the playhouse. "I'm just watching Caroline and Cecilia."

"It's great to see Caroline using her playhouse," he says. "I built her that house."

"Wait, for real? From like a kit?"

"From scratch. I like to build stuff."

I pull myself forward to get a better look at the house, to see it from a different perspective, now that I know Charlie built it. "What kind of other stuff do you build?"

"Well, I was a master Lego builder when I was a kid. You should've seen some of the stuff I made. Bridges were my specialty. I built one that was like four feet long, and I used to drive my Matchbox cars across it."

"Nice."

"Then there was the toothpick one. The Popsicle stick one. That was a suspension bridge, even more difficult."

"So building bridges is your thing then?"

"Yeah. That's what I want to do with my life. So, your thing is like swimming? The ocean, right?"

"Basically," I say. He must remember that I was on the swim team freshman year. Or he's thinking of the interview clip that Mr. Zambrano played on Sebastian Smith's program.

"What do you love about the ocean?"

I'm not sure how I feel about Charlie quizzing me this way. Part of me wishes he'd just leave me alone. Part of me loves having an excuse to talk about this. To talk about anything normal. "Just how vast it is, how varied. There are probably over a million species in the ocean, and so many of them haven't even been classified yet. I just love the idea of being a part of that— learning about different species, you know?"

"That sounds pretty cool. I'm sure you'll be great at that."

"I hope so." I fiddle with my watchband, not sure what else to say.

"Well, I guess I'd better go do my homework . . ." He shifts position on the grass. "Oh, by the way, some of my friends are coming over to watch a movie on Friday, if you want to join us. You could bring a friend too—Chloe or Jen or someone."

"Thanks . . . but I don't really think so." Being around Charlie's rich friends is the last thing I want right now.

"Well, no pressure, but if you change your mind you're

welcome to come. It's just going to be a small group. Maybe four or five people."

"Thanks, but no," I say, hoping this will be the last time we will discuss it.

"Okay," he says, pulling himself up to his feet. "See you at dinner."

"Okay," I say, not looking up as he walks away from me. Another meal with the Wheelers to endure. At least Mr. Wheeler won't be here tonight—he'll be out of town for campaign appearances for the next several days.

Ten minutes later Mami calls out for the girls to come in for dinner. They run, barefooted, toward the sliding glass door, but I send them back to get their shoes from the playhouse. They come back quickly with a shoe in each hand, and Mami sends them to wash up.

"What did the detective say?" I ask Mami as I lean against the counter beside her at the sink.

She places a large, stainless steel pot in the sink and turns the faucet on. "There isn't much evidence," she says.

"They have to know *something*."

Her eyes are focused out the small window above the sink. "They found traces of chemicals."

"What chemicals?"

The water is quickly approaching the top of the pot. "I don't remember the names, but now they know it was done on purpose."

I reach over to turn off the water, and she lifts the pot out of the sink and places it on the counter. "How can they find out who did it, though?" I ask.

"Mija, we may never find out." She turns away from the stove to face me. "Detective Blake said she's going to have her team do some more computer analysis on the people commenting online, try to find out their identities to see if any of them are local. That could lead to something."

The idea that someone who brought so much destruction to my family may get away with it is considerably more than I can process at the moment. I shove the thought aside momentarily. "What about the insurance people?" I ask.

"They're sending people out to investigate and assess the damages. Then they'll let us know how much they can pay."

"Will it be enough to get a new place?"

She leans away from the counter and pats my cheek. She used to do this all the time when I was little and would come to her with a worry. All of a sudden, I feel five again. "Don't worry, mija. We'll have our own home again soon. We just need to be patient right now."

"I'm trying, Mami. It's just so hard to live here."

"I know. It's hard for all of us, but hard things make us stronger." She pulls away from me and walks over to the stove. "Want to help me with the beans for tomorrow?"

I nod behind her and resign myself to cleaning beans, knowing that the brief moment she allowed me to feel sorry for myself is over now.

CHAPTER THIRTEEN

Wednesday morning, while I shower, I think about Stanford. About how far away it is. I think of Sele having to manage the kids without me every day, I think of Mami trying to deal with another emergency on her own.

Maybe I shouldn't go after all. I could take a gap year, stay home and then reapply to TAMU-CC for next year. Lots of people take a year off. And TAMU-CC is a good school. Most of my friends will be going there. I could explore the deep seas of the bay, the Gulf of Mexico, even though it's my dream to explore the Pacific Ocean.

I'm still pondering this as I get dressed. Maybe Mami will take us to exchange some of the clothes today. I would like to get some jeans that fit.

Mami has just left to drop the younger kids off at school when I walk into the kitchen. There's a container of steaming oatmeal and a tray of fresh fruit on the table. I wonder where the Wheelers picked this up from. Or maybe they had it delivered. It looks packaged, like something from one of those "pretend you know how to cook" kits that so many well-off people subscribe to.

I pick up a bowl from a stack on the table and ladle out some oatmeal. It's still hot, so I stir it with a heavy silver spoon and blow on it a bit before tasting it.

I hear someone plodding down the hall and assume it's Charlie. When I turn, though, I see it's Dawson from school.

"Hi, Millie," he says, like we're old friends. "What's for breakfast?"

"Hi," I say, probably looking as off-balance as I feel.

"I crash breakfast over here sometimes. Don't mind me." He has blond hair that goes to his ears, and it always looks like he purposefully messed it up before leaving his house. He sits next to me and picks up a piece of watermelon with his fingers. He puts it in his mouth and then grabs another one.

"I'm sorry to hear about your house. That sucks."

"Thanks," I say, nodding. It really does suck. Though I'm not sure Dawson, whose family owns more than one home, can really comprehend the extent of what we've lost.

I hear footsteps approaching the kitchen again, and this time it is Charlie. "You're here already?" he asks the breakfast crasher.

"I wanted to grab something to eat before we left for school," Dawson says.

"Morning, Millie." Charlie directs his attention to me. "You know Dawson?"

I nod. "Yeah."

"I have a guest, Dawson," Charlie says. "I hope you're using good manners."

Dawson grabs a napkin and wipes watermelon juice from his chin. "Of course," he says and winks at me.

Charlie sits down across from us and scoops some oatmeal into a dish. "Dawson's bumming a ride this morning," he says to me. "Something's wrong with his car. What's wrong with your car today?"

"Battery's dead. Want to take me to get a fresh one after school?"

"Sure," Charlie says around a mouthful of oatmeal.

While I chew my oatmeal, I take out my phone and text Chloe to make sure she's meeting me outside the school. I really need her right now. Usually, I am not a clingy friend, but school feels overwhelming to me; my anxiety kicks in just thinking about it—about everyone watching me, talking about me, talking *to* me. I don't think I could do school right now without Chloe.

"I wish my dad would just buy me a *new* car already," Dawson says to Charlie as he continues to polish off the fruit.

"Ah, Daws. How many new cars have you had since you got your driver's license?"

"Three. So what?"

"So, you wrecked them all. I think I can see why your dad bought you an older car."

"Yeah, but it keeps breaking down on me."

I get up to wash my bowl and spoon. While I'm at the sink, Charlie says, "So, Millie. After school, I'll bring you home, and then I guess I'll have to take Dawson to buy a new battery."

"I can get a ride from someone else. Don't worry about it," I say, not wanting him to go out of his way for me. I already feel so indebted to his family.

"No, it's no big deal. Dawson doesn't mind."

"Yeah, Millie. It's cool."

A few minutes later the three of us walk out the front door toward Charlie's car. Dawson grabs for the handle of the front passenger side.

"Hold up, dude," Charlie says to Dawson. "Let Millie sit in the front."

"It's okay, Charlie. I don't care," I say, grabbing the back door handle. In fact, I am more than okay with sitting in the back, unheard, unseen.

"No, really, Millie. My mom would kill me." At this point, I would be fine with chivalry being dead, but I let go of the back door handle. I mean, the guy is giving me a ride to and from school every day. The least I can do is spare his life.

≈

As we head up to the school's main entrance, I see Chloe walking toward us with Ivan and Jay again. All this week, they've come to find me in the mornings. It feels good to have friends to focus on, so I'm not self-consciously looking around to see who may be staring at me, talking about me. Dawson fist-bumps Ivan and Jay on his way past. He might hang out primarily with rich white guys like Charlie, but he seems to be on friendly terms with almost everyone in school. Charlie's like that too, but right now he seems more hesitant than usual. He just nods at Jay and Ivan, gives me an awkward half-wave goodbye, and keeps walking.

"Hey, Mil," Jay says. "How's everybody doing?"

"We're all okay. Thanks, Jay."

Chloe puts her arm around me, and I feel peace for the first time this morning. "Mil, I miss you on the bus. It sucks now."

"Yeah, a lot of things suck now," I say.

"At least you have the baby turtles to look forward to in a couple of weeks, right?"

I'd almost forgotten about the turtle release at the National Seashore. "Yeah . . . I don't know. I might not be able to get out there this year. Mami might need me to stick around and help with the kids."

"It's at like, the literal crack of dawn," Chloe says. "The kids won't be awake. And you are in serious need of some self-care, girl. Speaking of which . . ." She pulls a small bottle of purple nail polish out of her pocket. "When's the last time you did your toes?" She gestures pointedly down at my flip-flops.

"Thanks, Chlo." I take the bottle and read the color at the bottom. *Grape Expectations.* "It's perfect. My toes look horrible."

≈

After school, Charlie drops me off at the Wheelers' before taking Dawson to get a new car battery. Once again, Mami has the kids at the kitchen table doing their homework. It's so nice having her around more, one tiny benefit of having our house burn down, if you can look at it that way. Technically, she is still at work. She's babysitting Caroline as usual, and she's making dinner at the same time, even though the Wheelers told her she didn't have to. I smell her black bean soup simmering on the stove the minute I walk in.

"Hi, Mami." I walk over and kiss her cheek. "Mind if I do my homework outside?"

"Está bien, mija." She hands me an apple and a cheese stick, somehow knowing that I'm hungry—and knowing that I wouldn't feel comfortable just grabbing something for myself in the Wheelers' house.

Suddenly a cupboard door flies open at my feet.

"Hi, Millie," Caroline says, popping her head out.

"Caroline, you scared me," I say. "What are you doing down there?"

"Cecilia and I are reading," Caroline says, opening the door further to reveal Ceci with her book and flashlight.

I laugh. "Well, good for you."

Ceci waves at me, and I wave back before heading outside. I swing the door open, and the wind greets me. It's not a gentle breeze; it blows my hair across my face. It's the wind I've grown up with. It keeps me company as I sit down at the glass patio table. I welcome the soothing sounds of the waves lapping below as I pull out my calculus homework.

Within minutes, though, the door opens behind me, and I hear Charlie's voice. "Millie, someone's here to see you."

I turn around to see Jay following Charlie out onto the patio.

"Hey, Mil," Jay says. He's wearing long shorts and flip-flops, like always.

"Hi, Jay," I say, getting up to walk over to him. I'm surprised to see him here, and from the look on Charlie's face, he is too.

Charlie lingers off to the side as Jay pulls me in for a tight hug. He smells of sea salt and sunblock, the scents I'll always associate with him. I know he's been surfing today, but that's every day for him. "Thanks, man," he says to Charlie. Charlie nods at him and goes back inside.

"What are you doing here?" I ask Jay as we sit down on two cushioned patio chairs. I notice he's holding a small brown paper bag.

"Just wanted to see how you were doing. You know, I've been worried about you."

I nod. We are still friends; I guess friends worry about each other. But it still feels strange to have him here, visiting me at the Wheelers' house.

"Well, I brought you something," he says, handing me the small paper bag.

I reach into the bag and take out a small heart-shaped jewelry box covered in tiny seashells.

"To replace the one you lost in the fire," he says. He reaches over to run his finger across the smooth shells. His finger almost touches mine, but he pulls his hand away. He bought me a similar jewelry box for Valentine's Day last year. He picked it up at one of the little souvenir shops on the island. I was surprised by the gift at the time; I'd been starting to rethink our relationship, but this unexpectedly thoughtful gesture had convinced me not to give up yet.

"Thanks," I say, opening the box to reveal a soft red velvet lining.

"Sorry, I didn't get you any jewelry to put inside it."

"No, of course not. I wouldn't expect that. I didn't expect *this*." I close the box and clasp it with both hands. "It's so nice of you, Jay."

"I'm just really sorry about the fire, Mil. You're the last person that should happen to." He looks out at a pair of seagulls chasing each other over the shore. "You're the best kind of person there is. Nobody should ever do anything bad to you. It makes me mad that someone out there wants to hurt you."

I know he means it in the kindest way possible, but I find myself feeling impatient with this flawed logic. "Bad things happen to people all the time."

"Yeah, but it makes me mad for what I did to you too." He tears his eyes from the pair of gulls, who've taken off over the water in search of something. "I should've treated you better."

"Jay, I think we just make better friends than anything else. The relationship stuff—that wasn't for us."

"I just want you to know that I'm here for you, Mil. Just let me know whatever you need."

"Thanks, Jay."

"I'd better go," he says, standing up.

"Okay, thanks for coming by. See you at school tomorrow."

After Jay leaves, I open the jewelry box again. I try to remember what I kept inside the other one. There was the tiny gold ring Papi gave me for my first Communion and the gold cross necklace Mami gave me. There was also a broken charm bracelet my tia from Houston bought for me. I don't usually wear jewelry, but those few pieces were special.

"Hey." Charlie comes over to sit by me. "Is this your home-work station?"

"Yeah, it's so nice out here."

"I don't think this yard has ever been used so much, honestly."

"Oh, I'd be out here every day if I lived here."

"You do live here," he says. He looks at me for a second before turning his gaze to the playhouse. "Even Caroline hardly ever plays outside. She's been out here a lot lately, though. She really likes Cecilia."

"Yeah, they get along pretty well," I say, following his gaze. We both keep looking at the house like something might happen, but the girls have yet to emerge since ambling into it almost an hour ago.

"So, uh," he says, "you and Jay still together? I thought you two broke up."

His question surprises me for two reasons—first, that he's aware of my relationship status and second, that for some reason he seems to care. It amazes me that he's paid enough attention to my social life to know that Jay and I were even going out.

I peel my eyes off the playhouse and look at him, but his gaze stays on the pink-shingled roof. "Oh, we're just friends now."

He turns to look at me now. "Oh. That's good—you're still friends. No nasty breakup?"

"No. Very amicable. He's just better friend material than boyfriend material."

"Oh," he says, but I don't know if he understands.

"He just came by to see how I was, you know, as a friend."

"And he brought you something," he says, eyeing the small jewelry box I'm still clutching.

"Yeah, it's a jewelry box." I stuff it back into the paper bag and fold the top down.

"It's pretty," he says, not willing to let this conversation die. Can't he mind his own business, just this once?

"Yeah, it's just to replace one he gave me when we were going out. Lost it in the fire, you know."

"Right." He nods. "Sorry."

I shrug. I don't say it's okay, because I'm not even sure why he's sorry. Sorry he wouldn't let the topic dissipate into the sea-smelling air? Or sorry that his father's overeager mouth is ultimately the cause of my loss? Either way, I don't want to get into it any further with him. He's my mother's employer's son. Yes, I am staying in his house, and yes, I am in his backyard, but that doesn't mean that he has a claim on my personal life.

CHAPTER FOURTEEN

On Friday morning, when we've been at the Wheelers' almost a week, I find a new shopping bag sitting on the floor outside the guest room. My name is written on it with a black marker. Inside are three brand-new shirts. I look down the hall, but no one is there, so I go back inside the room and take the shirts out, laying them on the bed. The first one is a dark purple tee with thin black lines. The second is a two-toned purple shirt with three-quarter sleeves. The last one is a thin white blouse with tiny purple polka dots. I check for a note, but there's nothing.

I pick up the Dillard's bag to study the handwriting on the side. It's familiar; I've seen it on school papers.

My suspicion is confirmed when I walk into the kitchen and Charlie smiles at me.

"Good morning," he says between bites of cereal.

"Did you give me these shirts?" I ask.

His smile widens. "I hope you like them."

Something about the way he says it makes this feel less like his mom's friends' charity and more like . . . well, like Jay giving me the jewelry box. "I love them. Thank you."

He shrugs. "I noticed that my mom's friends didn't get you any purple shirts. They probably didn't realize that purple's your favorite color." He turns back to his cereal.

"How did *you* know that?"

"I think you told me once," he says.

That seems unlikely to me, but I'm not sure I want to dispute it. The alternative explanation is that Charlie Wheeler has been paying enough attention to me to notice what color I wear most often.

"That one looks nice on you," he says.

I feel my neck flush with embarrassment. Charlie Wheeler is noticing how I look? Or maybe he's just being instinctively pleasant, like he is with everyone. "Thanks." I finally sit down, reach for the cereal and pour myself a bowl.

He mixes around the cereal in his bowl. "If you're not busy tonight, you're still welcome to hang out. We're just getting pizza and watching a movie. No alcohol, in case you're worried about that."

I stiffen a little with surprise.

He gives a sheepish smile. "I know your mom is really strict about that stuff. And my dad is too—especially now. With him running for Senate, people are watching him all the time."

"I would hate that. Being watched all the time, I mean."

"Yeah, sometimes it's hard, you know, because it puts our whole family in the spotlight. I feel like I have to be on guard all the time, like I can't mess up."

"I think I know how you feel," I say. I can't mess up since Mami counts on me so much. It surprises me that Charlie and I have this in common because I always thought that he had it made. That he could do anything, free from the pressures of the family responsibilities that I have. "This whole Senate race must be pretty weird for you in general."

"Yeah, it is. But my dad sat down and talked to us all about it before he decided to run. He wanted to know how we felt about it. At the time, I didn't hesitate. I told him he should do it. He has great ideas—ideas that I'd like to see him put into practice."

"And you still feel that way?"

Charlie shrugs. "Yeah, for the most part. I believe in what he's doing. He's going to make a good senator. I don't always agree with everything he says or does, but I agree with what he stands for, and I really want him to win. I know he can make a difference. I'm just sorry he had to drag your family into it."

"Yeah," I sigh. "You and me both."

We eat in silence for a minute, until Charlie says, "He hasn't made any public statements about the fire or anything, you know. Or about your family staying with us. He doesn't want to bring up your family unless he has permission from you and your mom."

"Well, good." I'm not quite done eating, but I stand up and bring my bowl to the sink anyway.

"Although . . ." Charlie twists in his seat to look at me. I turn my back to him so that I'm facing the sink and shove a last heaping spoonful of cereal into my mouth. I have a feeling I'm not going to like where this conversation is heading. "Personally I think it'd be really helpful if he spoke out about what happened to your family—if he could publicly say how wrong it is, how things have to change."

My hands shake slightly as I set the bowl in the sink and turn on the tap. Over my shoulder, I say, "Helpful to whom, Charlie? To my family? To immigrants in general? Or to your dad?"

"I—what do you mean?" He sounds completely taken aback.

I scrub hard at the bowl, fighting to keep my voice steady.

"I don't see how putting my family back in the spotlight would do us any good. But it might boost your dad's reputation as a champion of immigrants. It might get him more news coverage, because the media loves a personal story from a political candidate. It might score some points for him, with the people who agree with him already. And it will do absolutely nothing to change the minds of the people who hate us."

I finish washing my dishes and go to grab my backpack off the floor.

"I don't think that's fair," says Charlie, sounding more hurt than defensive. "My dad isn't just posturing. His beliefs don't make him very popular, but he's standing by them, and I admire that."

"I admire your father for standing by what he believes too, but he chose to do it. I didn't. And my family didn't. We're not interested in being a political talking point."

Charlie holds up his hands in a gesture of surrender. "You're right. I shouldn't have brought it up."

"We agree on that, at least," I say as I turn to walk outside to the car.

≈

I don't know how many more days we'll be here, but I am ready to be out—to be in our own place with only my family. I've wanted to ask Mami how much longer, but I'm certain she doesn't know yet. She still has to meet with the insurance people again to find out how much money we'll receive. And then she'll have to find us a new place, which is not an easy task.

So I don't ask her. I keep the probing questions to myself; she'll update me when she's ready.

At least dinner has gotten more relaxed. Mr. Wheeler's out of town campaigning, and Charlie's home late because of tennis practice, so it's just Dr. Wheeler and Caroline sitting with us in the big dining room. To my relief, Dr. Wheeler has stopped quizzing each of us about our classes and our summer plans; now she just listens patiently while Ceci recaps the plot of the book she's reading or Javi describes skateboarding tricks he's seen people do at Cole Park.

After dinner, when Sele takes Javi and Ceci upstairs to shower and watch TV, I help Mami clean up the kitchen. Mami is officially back to work, resuming her usual housekeeping routine. The Wheelers told her it wasn't necessary, but Mami's still collecting a paycheck from them, and she's determined to earn it.

I'm wiping off the kitchen table with a yellow sponge when Dr. Wheeler comes in.

"Thanks so much for dinner, Sandra. That was delicious." She's carrying three cardboard pizza boxes, which she sets down on the counter Mami has just cleaned. "Charlie's having some friends over. I bought paper plates, so I told them no dishes, no mess."

"That's okay, Belinda. It's no problem."

"No, you go on upstairs. Charlie can take care of his own mess. I'm going upstairs too—just going to leave them to it. Once I've checked them for contraband, of course," she adds with a little laugh. She starts pulling out paper plates, napkins, and cups from a cupboard above the sink. "Millie, you're coming, right? Charlie said he was going to invite you."

"Oh, yes he did, Dr. Wheeler, thanks. But, I'm a bit tired, so I'm just going to head upstairs too." I look over at Mami to see if she approves of my decision, but she's drying off a large pot, not looking my way at all. I surmise she doesn't care either way what I decide.

"Well, if you change your mind, come on down," Dr. Wheeler says. "I know they'd love to have you."

I'm not so convinced. I imagine they would tolerate it, would probably try to be nice, but they wouldn't love it. "Thank you," I say.

I hear the doorbell and imagine my rich classmates coming in, taking off their shoes, and making themselves comfortable on the Wheelers' leather couches. Probably Dawson, Mindy, other people who've tried to show me kindness over the past several days. Other people who can't possibly understand what it's like to live my life.

"I'm going upstairs," I tell Mami, putting the sponge back on the counter and quickly leaving before Charlie or any of his friends come in to get pizza.

I hear laughter rolling down the hallway from the entryway and take the steps two at a time to get upstairs. Javi and Ceci are sprawled out on the bed watching the Disney Channel while Sele is folding clothes on the floor by the bed.

"Did you guys have baths?" I ask, easing down to the floor by Sele.

"Yes, they both did," Sele says after I get no answer from the two little ones, who are mesmerized by the screen. "What's going on downstairs?"

"Charlie's having some friends over, I guess. He invited me, but I didn't want to go."

"Why?" she asks me.

I shrug, trying to figure that out myself. "I don't know. It's not like he's my friend, you know. He was just asking me to be nice. His friends aren't my friends."

Sele folds a pair of her jeans in half. "Charlie's okay, Millie. He's . . . trying."

"I know," I say throwing off my flip-flops and reaching for my new nail polish. "I just don't think that means I owe him anything."

"Do you ever think, without the Wheelers where would we be right now?" my sister asks me. "We wouldn't have anywhere to go." She picks up another pair of her pants.

"Without the Wheelers, our house would never have burned down. They're the cause of everything." I shake the nail polish bottle and open it slowly.

"What Mr. Wheeler did wasn't so bad," Sele says. "He was trying to say that we're good people, that our parents were good people when they came here without documents. How many white people do you know who think that, who would be willing to announce that to the world?"

"Sele, it's not as simple as that."

"Yes, it is. Mr. Wheeler is fighting for people like us. He's making it a focus in his campaign. He's not doing it for himself; he's doing it for people like us."

Maybe so. That doesn't mean I have to bend over backwards to make the Wheelers feel appreciated, to sacrifice my peace of mind for theirs, to make sure they feel comfortable at my own expense. "I really don't want to talk about this, Sele. I'm so tired of talking about this."

I thrust the nailbrush back into the bottle and take it into the bathroom.

"But Millie . . ."

I close the bathroom door before she can finish. I have more than enough to deal with right now. I don't have to listen to my little sister lecture me.

CHAPTER FIFTEEN

The next week, after dinner, I walk into the Wheelers' kitchen, thinking about the looming deadline to register for specific classes at Stanford and the upcoming sea turtle release at the National Seashore and whether Javi is borrowing Charlie's Xbox too often and a hundred other things. Mami is hunched over their granite countertop, wiping crumbs.

"Mami, Ceci's ready for you to tuck her in."

"Okay, mija." Mami rinses the sponge out in the stainless steel sink and places it on the counter. The sink is still full of dishes and pots Mami used to make the Wheelers' dinner.

"I can finish those dishes," I offer. "You should just relax."

"No. I'll be back in a minute to finish them."

"Mami, come on. Just let me do them. It's no big deal. I'd be doing them at home anyway."

Mami smiles at me and pats my cheek. "Okay, mija. Gracias."

All of the pots are stainless steel, and I think back to our pots—old, scratched. But those pots are gone now. Everything is gone now.

The other day, Mami went with the insurance people to

see if anything could be salvaged. She didn't want any of us to come, to see everything, but she told us that whatever wasn't charred or in ashes had been ruined by the heavy water from the fire truck hoses.

I pick up the sponge Mami left on the counter and dig into the large pot where she cooked mashed potatoes. I run the faucet as I scrub the sides, letting the crusted remnants of potatoes slide into the sink and down the drain.

I hear footsteps behind me and figure Mami has come back to instruct me on the particular way Belinda Wheeler likes the pots washed.

"I'm already doing it wrong?" I ask without turning around.

"Looks like you're doing just fine." It's Charlie Wheeler's voice, and he's smiling when I turn around.

"Oh, sorry. I thought you were my mom."

"No worries." He's wearing plaid lounge pants and a white T-shirt. His feet are bare, and I wonder how he can handle walking on such cold, hard tile. "Dinner was really good. Did you help your mom?"

"No. I'm just on dish duty."

"She's a great cook," he says. "You've got a great mom."

Thoughts pop into my mind and break like bubbles, before they can float out of my mouth and do any damage. *My mom is always busy cooking for your family, which is why I make thrown-together dinners for my family.*

"Yeah. Agreed." I submerge the pot in the warm water and scrub it with my soapy hands.

He walks over to the fridge and starts taking things out and stacking them on the counter. Suddenly I feel like an intruder on his privacy, his time to do what he wants in his own house. I begin to hurry, wanting to get the dishes done quickly so I can leave him alone, be out of his way. He's probably been wishing me away since we all moved in here.

"Want a sandwich?" he asks, carrying his stack of items over to the counter near the sink.

"A sandwich? Didn't you just eat?"

"That was like two hours ago. I always need a little snack around nine."

"A sandwich is a little snack?" I rinse out the large pot and put it on the drying rack.

"Yeah. Half sandwich—it's just right."

I pick up the next pan and begin scrubbing it.

"You like tomatoes?" he asks me. He pulls out a cutting board and a knife.

"Ah, sure . . ."

He cuts up a tomato, letting the thin slices fan out across the cutting board. "Is turkey okay?"

"I'm fine. Really. You don't have to make me a sandwich."

"Turkey it is then. Provolone or Swiss?"

I laugh and shake my head. "It doesn't matter."

He turns on a panini press and sprays it. As it's heating up, he slices up some sourdough bread. "The secret ingredient," he says, lifting up a small glass jar that says *basil pesto*.

"You just showed it to me. It's not so secret."

"I know, but I wanted to make sure you weren't allergic or anything."

"I don't think I've ever had basil pesto. So, you never know. I could be allergic."

He takes out a knife and spreads the basil pesto on two of the sourdough slices. "Good thing my mom's a pediatrician then. Any allergic reaction and I'll go get her."

He puts one fully assembled sandwich in the panini press

and closes it. I've finished the dishes in the sink, so I reach for the knife and cutting board he's been using.

"No," he says, putting his hand over mine. "That's my mess. I always clean up after my nine o'clock sandwich."

"Okay," I say, pulling my hand away. I look around the kitchen, but everything else is in order. I was thinking it was time to leave, but I guess I'm stuck waiting for the panini to be ready. I think I'm supposed to eat half of it.

"Done," he says a minute later. He lifts the lid of the panini press, slides the sandwich onto a plate, and cuts it with the same knife he used for the tomatoes. "We can let it cool off for a minute." He pulls himself up to sit on the counter. "So, I guess our sisters have become best friends."

I laugh. "Yeah. Two peas in a pod."

"And what is with the reading in the cabinet?"

"Cecilia's been doing that for about a year now. She just likes having a quiet place to read. She doesn't have her own room—so she can go in there. No one bothers her."

"Those two scared the crap out of me the other day. I didn't know they were in there and all of a sudden they burst out laughing."

"I hope your mom is okay with it."

"Are you kidding? Anything to get Caroline to read. She'd rather be drawing. Mom has to hold her markers hostage to get her to do anything else." Charlie picks up half of the sandwich and hands the plate over to me.

"Thanks," I say and take a small bite. It's delicious. Rich people have some weird taste, but wow it's good. "Yum. The secret ingredient has won me over."

"Not breaking out in hives or anything, are you?"

"I think I'm in the clear." I take another bite and notice that he's already practically finished with his. I bet he usually eats the whole thing. "It's really good. Thank you."

"Anytime." He jumps down off the counter and starts putting the ingredients back in the fridge. While I'm savoring my sandwich, he washes the few dishes he used, cleans the counter, and uses the bright yellow sponge to wipe down the panini press.

"Well, I think I'm going to bed," I say as he takes my empty plate from me. "Good night."

"Good night, Millie. And just so you know," he says when I'm already at the door, "I usually sneak in here every night for a sandwich."

Technically that could be a warning, like *Please stay out of the kitchen when I come in to make my sandwich*, or an invitation, as in *Feel free to come by every night for a half sandwich*.

I'm pretty sure I know the answer.

Maybe it's possible to be friends with Charlie Wheeler after all.

≈

Dr. Wheeler has offered to let me use her laptop to write an English paper. Her office is on the first floor, just off the kitchen behind a set of narrow French doors. First thing after school, I sit down at her wide desk, which is bare except for the sleek white laptop.

I sign in with the password she gave me and start working. Ms. Cope wants us to expound on the themes of *The Hiding Place* and how it resonates with us personally. The rough draft is due tomorrow, and I haven't written a single word.

My thoughts go back to the day in class when Charlie

brought up Corrie ten Boom's quote about how life is not measured by duration, but by donation. I think about Papi's life, how its duration was short, but his legacy of love will endure well past my lifetime. Papi loved his family more than anything, and he thought of us before anything else.

Papi's job at the oil field was dangerous and stressful. He did the work because the pay was good enough for Mami to stay home with us when we were little. She started working part-time when Javi was old enough to go to pre-K, but if Papi could see how hard Mami worked these days, it would break him. He always wanted to provide for his family, to make enough money for us to be happy.

When I was twelve, his arm was severely burned, which required trips to Houston for medical care. He came back from the last trip with two American Girl dolls for Sele and me. Mami was angry that he spent so much money on the expensive dolls, but it wasn't the cost that mattered to me. Instead of focusing on his treatment, his thoughts were on us, on what he could do to bring smiles to our faces.

That was Papi. He was always thinking about others. I don't see that impulse in myself; I see it in Sele. When Mami told me about Oscar Zambrano and how he wanted to talk to me, she said it was my chance to do something for others—and now I wonder if I've done anything at all since meeting him. I did the interview, but has that really helped anyone? I really don't think so.

Once I've wrapped up the rough draft of my paper, I click on the already open web browser so I can log in to my email. Up pops an article about the separation policy at the border. Dr. Wheeler must've been reading this article earlier. There's been a lot of backlash against this policy, and the article has pictures of protesters at the Texas border with Mexico, holding signs with messages about keeping families together. I zoom in on some of the pictures to get a good look at who these protesters are. A priest and several nuns. People of different skin colors, young and old, all photographed outside of a detention center in Potrillo, Texas.

I open a fresh tab, log in to my email, and send my draft to Mrs. Cope.

But after I log back out of my email, I find myself typing my name into the search bar.

My eyes are drawn to the videos in the results. Somehow I knew there'd be another Michael Winter video—a new one, posted just yesterday. I shouldn't click on it. I shouldn't waste my time, my energy . . .

I click.

"So, this little illegal girl in South Texas recently got her family's house burned down. How? She was dumb enough to go on a low-rating news channel and spout off about how illegals deserve a chance. How we should feel sorry for them," he says, pretending to cry and wipe his tears.

I should close the tab. I should walk away from the computer. But I can't move.

"So, her family is crying now that someone burned their house down. All of a sudden, they care about laws being broken. They didn't care about broken laws when they were sneaking into this country. So, it's okay for them to break the law by stealing their way into our country, but now someone breaks the law in a way that inconveniences *them*, and it's not fair."

A picture of me pops up in the corner of the screen as Michael Winter keeps speaking. It's from my Instagram account. Someone must have grabbed it before I deleted my account. "Millie Vargas is her name, high school senior, sup-posedly a straight-A student, but you know they dumb down those bilingual classes. Mother is a single mom of four kids. *Four kids.* The more kids, the more money they can scam out of our government. And you know they're all single moms. The dads are in gangs or prison, or dealing drugs. And now the whole family is shacking up with the mom's boss, bone-head wannabe-senator Charles Wheeler, in Corpus Christi, Texas. So, fellow Texans, we need you to be on top of this one. Make sure to vote against Wheeler come election time. And let's spread the word on social media about Mil-lie Vargas. We're using these hashtags: #moochingmillie and #sendherhome . . ."

My whole body is shaking. I think about all of the people who could've seen this video. I think of Chloe, at home, com-batting the Twitter troll army that's been unleashed by Michael Winter.

The next thing I know, I'm running up to my room. I tell Sele that I'm not feeling well and ask her to let Mami know that I'm not coming down for dinner.

I lie in bed with the covers pulled over my head, trying to clear my mind. About half an hour later, the door opens slowly, and I peek out from under the covers to see Mami walk in.

"Mr. Wheeler just told me about that awful video, mija," she says, sitting on the bed. "His campaign staff let him know about it. And Dr. Wheeler said you left a tab open on her com-puter earlier . . . I'm sorry you had to see that."

"Mami, it was so awful," I say, wanting to also bury my face in Mami's lap, to let go of the tears I'm holding back.

"Eso no importa," Mami says.

"It does matter, Mami! He told people where we're living!

People know where the Wheelers' house is. What if someone targets us again, tries to . . ." I can't even finish the sentence.

"No one will get past the Wheelers' front gate," Mami assures me. "And if someone did, there's the security system inside. We're as safe as we can be right now, mija."

I'm not sure I believe that. Horrible images flash through my mind—somebody waiting outside the gate, ramming Mami's car as it leaves or approaches . . . I try to push those imagined disasters away. "But he still humiliated our entire family, and he's going to keep doing it."

"Humiliated? You have done nothing wrong. We have done nothing wrong." I sit up, and she puts her arm around me. "We have nothing to be ashamed of. This man should be ashamed of himself for speaking so badly about others."

"But he won't be! People like that don't feel shame. And they don't ever change their minds. I'm just tired of all this," I say, throwing my arms up into the air.

Mami looks at me steadily. "You keep your head up, Millie. You be proud of who you are. Mr. Wheeler said there will be plenty of people speaking out for you, for us, even if you don't want him to make any official statements."

"I don't," I say. "I don't want him to draw any more attention to that horrible man." *Or draw any more attention to us,* I add silently.

"Okay, mija. It will all be okay."

I still want to dive under the comforter and hide. I promise myself that I won't check Twitter and that I'll try to forget what Michael Winter said about me.

I expect Mami to tell me to come down to dinner, but to my surprise, she lets me stay in my room. After she leaves, I try to think only of turtle hatchlings and their tiny, slow bodies plodding through the cool sand. I remind myself that in just two more days, I can escape to the beach, where boundaries are not visible, where the ocean in front of me seems endless, where sea turtles are freed to find their way to a new home.

As much as I try to focus on that, the words from the video won't leave my mind.

I shut my eyes and try to pull out my most recent happy memory. Charlie's panini pops up. I focus on the image of Charlie slicing tomatoes and cutting the sandwich in two before handing me a half.

CHAPTER SIXTEEN

I spend most of the next day trying to focus on the chores Mami wants me to do. While she takes care of the Wheelers' housecleaning as usual, we kids are in charge of keeping our own spaces clean, doing our laundry, and making meals with the food that Mami keeps in designated parts of the Wheelers' fridge and pantry. We might be living here, but Mami will never allow us to "take advantage," as she calls it.

I'm glad to keep busy, but Michael Winter's rant against me keeps replaying itself in my head when I let my guard down. Snippets of his words filter in whenever I'm not actively concentrating on pairing socks or vacuuming the guest bedroom. I hate myself for letting his words affect me.

In the evening, I insist on finishing up the dishes so she can get the others ready for bed. I tell myself I really just want to help her out, give her a break—but deep down, I want to be in the kitchen when Charlie comes in.

The sink is full of the dishes Mami used to make lasagna. Once the dishwater is going, I begin scrubbing a pot.

"How does ham sound tonight?" Charlie asks as he comes into the kitchen.

I turn around and smile. "I'm fine, really."

"Okay. So you liked the turkey so much, you don't want the ham." He walks over to the fridge and begins pulling things out.

I laugh. "You really do this *every* night?"

"Most nights, especially during tennis season."

I scrub the sides of the heavy pot, kind of wishing I were upstairs in the guest bedroom. I'm not even sure why I stayed down here. I should have just let Mami do the dishes. I don't need to be here talking to Charlie Wheeler about his tennis team and basil pesto paninis. I've got too much else to think about—helping my mom, registering for college, and above all, the insanity that is following me around.

As I hurry through the rest of the dishes, I tell myself that I won't be back tomorrow at nine. I'll stay in my room. I don't want Charlie to think that I'm coming into the kitchen to see him every night.

He closes the panini press and leans back against the counter next to me. "I'm really sorry about all this," he says, probably for the hundredth time since our house burned down. "I heard about that new video. I didn't watch it, because I didn't want to give that creep more views. But I feel terrible about it. We all do."

I shrug, because what am I supposed to say? *It's okay. We'll be all right. It's not your fault.* All of those sentiments are untrue. It's not okay. I'm not sure we'll be all right, and it is their fault. But I don't say anything. I just keep washing the dishes, watching the water flow down to the dirty pots, washing away the tomato sauce, the bits of meat.

"I think I understand now why you didn't want my dad to mention you on the campaign trail," Charlie says. "It seems like people like that Winter guy will use any excuse to go after someone, and they don't care if they're spreading lies or even putting people in actual danger. They just want a target."

I sigh. "Yep." I hope he doesn't expect me to be impressed that he finally figured this out. I'm finished with the dishes now, so I say, "Well, I'm going to bed. Good night."

"Night, Millie. Sure you don't want a sandwich?"

"No thanks." I turn to walk toward the door.

"I hope you're not turning in early on my account. It's only nine on a Friday night. We could watch a movie or something if you feel like staying up."

I stop at the doorway and turn around. Watch a movie or something. Those are words I would have longed to hear a few years ago, but I'm not sure how I feel about them tonight. "No, thanks. I have to get up early tomorrow."

"Early on a Saturday?"

"Yeah." I'm not sure why I want to tell him, but I do. "I'm going to the National Seashore. They're releasing the sea turtles tomorrow."

"The sea turtles?"

"Yeah. The Kemp's ridley sea turtles. They're releasing some hatchlings into the Gulf of Mexico. Really early, like six-thirty."

"Wow. I've never heard about that. You've been before?"

"I try to go once a year. I just love to watch the little guys work their way down to the water, disappear into the surf."

"That sounds really cool," he says.

He sounds so genuinely interested that I find myself blurting out, "Um, you can come if you'd like."

He looks pleasantly surprised. "Are you sure? Or are you just being nice?"

I flash him a sarcastic smile. "Does that sound like me?"

"So . . . you do want me to come?"

"Yeah, I do. I'm going to try to leave at five-thirty. I want to make sure I don't miss it. They might release them as early as six-fifteen."

"Five-thirty, then. I can drive, if you want."

I want to protest, but when I think about the gas I can save Mami, I agree to let him drive.

CHAPTER SEVENTEEN

I pad softly down the stairs to find Charlie sitting on the living room couch, tying his shoes. He smiles at me. "Hey. Morning."

"Good morning," I say, wondering if anyone else is up. I told Mami when I went to bed that Charlie would be going with me to the seashore. She just said okay and didn't comment further.

"Do you want something to eat before we go?" he asks.

"Nah, I'm not hungry. It's too early to eat."

He gets up from the couch and walks toward the door. "Maybe we can grab something after?"

I shrug and say, "Maybe."

He disarms the security alarm, and we go outside. The morning is cool, but the air is still laced with humidity. I pull my hair up with a hair tie, anticipating the moisture that inevitably accumulates at the base of my neck. Charlie opens the car door for me, the small act sparking a million questions about what this outing means.

It's not a date; he just wants to see the turtles. Charlie Wheeler cannot be interested in me. He sees me merely as a cause that his father is interested in, a cause he cares about. I'm nothing more to him than that.

"So, what makes you want to see the sea turtles so much you'll get up at five-thirty on a Saturday morning?" Charlie asks as we drive.

"You sound like Chloe."

"Oh, yeah?"

"Yeah. She came with me last year. She said it's too unspectacular to justify dragging her out of bed so early on a weekend. So she didn't want to come again this year."

"But *you* think they're pretty spectacular?"

"Yeah," I say, smiling. "There's nothing like it. Tiny bodies moving slowly toward the water, finding their way. It's pretty awesome."

"Well, I can't wait then."

"Don't you ever wonder how amazing it is down in the ocean?" I blurt out. "Way down there where we can't even see anymore?"

"I guess I never thought about it. Do you think about it a lot?"

I look out the window at Ocean Drive. It's nearly empty in the predawn darkness, and I can see the moonlight reflecting off the bay. "It's *all* I think about sometimes," I say, not taking my eyes off the water that seems to go on forever.

Charlie turns to get on South Padre Island Drive, which will take us to the National Seashore. "Have you been scuba diving or snorkeling?" he asks.

"Nope," I say, taking my eyes off the bay just as it's about to go out of view. I suppose that's the kind of question one rich person asks of another.

It's a twenty-five-minute drive, over the causeway and

through North Padre Island. Have we already hit a wall in our conversation?

"Maybe we could go sometime this summer," he says, "before we head off to college."

I decide to ignore this hypothetical invitation and just say, "Mami says you're headed to College Station, going to Texas A&M?"

He sighs. "I was going to. And that's what my dad wanted me to do, but I'm going to Stanford instead."

"Stanford?" I ask, sitting up straight.

"Yeah, Dad hasn't really wanted me to be too vocal about it. He's still pissed because A&M is where he always wanted me to go. He went there, my grandpa went there, his father before him. Our name is a big deal in College Station. Dad wanted me to continue the tradition, especially with the campaign going on. He said it would mean a lot for a Senate candidate to have his son attend school right here in Texas, instead of running off to California. Like his image is more important than what's actually best for me. He also wishes I would be around to help campaign for him, said I should at least wait and transfer next year."

"That sounds rough," I say. "Is he okay about it now?"

He shrugs. "I guess. He's still mad, but not like cut-me-out-of-the-family kind of mad. Just low-key passive-aggressive mad, so back to normal, really. He never misses an opportunity to point out what a good engineering program A&M has."

"Well, doesn't Stanford have like one of the best engineering programs in the country?" I ask.

Charlie laughs. "Yeah, they do. I remind my dad of that almost daily. It's just this power struggle with my dad and me, you know. I've lived so much of my life the way he wanted me to. 'Charlie, you need to try out for the tennis team.' I just wanted to skate. He would take away my skateboard though, and I could get twenty minutes of it for every two hours of tennis I practiced."

"Sheesh."

"Yeah. And he wanted me to play the piano, so I took piano lessons for ten years. I wanted to take guitar lessons, but he only let me do that for about a year."

On one level, it's hard to feel much sympathy for someone whose family can so easily afford sports equipment and musical instruments and endless lessons. But on another, I can see how the weight of his dad's expectations must be unpleasant.

"So Texas A&M was the last straw?" I ask.

"Well, it's funny. I think if he didn't want me to go there so badly, I'd probably want to go there. When I toured the campus and met some of the professors, I was really impressed with their program."

"So, why not just go there then?"

Charlie shrugs. "Because then he would win again. I've been doing what he wants me to do all my life. For once, I just wanted to make my own choice, you know."

I nod even though I don't know. For me, it was different. I had to quit the swim team after Papi died. Mami had to work more hours, and I had to help watch the kids. I didn't quit because Mami wanted me to, but because it's what our family needed.

Charlie parks the car; the lot is already filling up. As I step outside, the briny smell of the sea envelops me. Seagulls, looking for breakfast, tiptoe along the ground and then abruptly dash for the sky. In the distance, I can hear the lapping of the ocean waves. Charlie stretches his arms in the air and yawns as he comes around to my side, and we walk up the wooden steps to the small buildings that surround the wooden patio.

"There are a lot of people up for this," Charlie says, sounding impressed.

"It's a pretty big deal, Charlie. You'll see." I hope he won't be disappointed—that unlike Chloe before him, he won't think he's wasted his time.

We reach the top of the steps. To the left is a small gift shop and some picnic tables, to the right are the bathroom and showers, and straight ahead, there it lies. Beautiful blue ocean that goes on forever. So much prettier than West Beach where we usually go. West Beach is just bay water and it's dark, stony.

We head down the wooden walkway to a large roped-off area of sand. Two park rangers hold a large net in the air to keep away hungry birds that spy the turtle hatchlings from high in the air. The net sways with the strong wind that carries the smell of salt and sea.

The wind pulls strings of hair from my hair tie and whips them across my face. Charlie and I walk halfway down to the shore and stand behind the roped barrier. One park ranger is speaking to the crowd, telling us about the Kemp's ridley sea turtles, explaining the process of releasing them into the sea. About a hundred people have gathered, waiting for the first glimpse of the tiny creatures who have yet to make their appearance.

Next to us is a man holding a sleeping baby in a carrier strapped to his chest. He cradles the baby's head and bounces up and down to soothe her. Beside the man is a woman holding the hand of a little girl who looks younger than Ceci.

"You ever bring your brother or sisters?" Charlie asks beside me.

"I brought them once, but they weren't too impressed, didn't feel like getting up early today. That's okay. I didn't push it. I don't mind coming by myself." I turn up to look at Charlie. "But I'm glad you came today."

"Me too," he says.

A few more park rangers kneel in the sand, holding the hatchlings with rubber-gloved hands. They set the tiny turtles on the ground and urge them forward with gentle fingers and whispered encouragement. I bend down for a closer look, just as Charlie pulls out his phone and starts taking a video.

The turtles begin their slow toddle toward the ocean. Tiny legs carry them inch by inch as they progress toward their new home. I can't take my eyes off them as they move, bumping and crawling over each other toward the beckoning waves in front of them. A gloved woman picks up a turtle and moves it over, off a slower turtle that is in no rush to reach the crashing waves.

I hear Charlie say "Wow," but I don't turn to look at him. I ease my way down along the edge of the roped-off area, following a small crowd of turtles. Collectively, the crowd moves closer to the waterfront, along with the baby turtles. The first few turtles reach the water's edge and the crowd cheers. The rolling waves toss one turtle back, but after taking a moment to adjust itself, the turtle trudges forth, regains its momentum. I keep my eyes on that turtle as it inches into the surf, with no doubt of its purpose, determined to continue despite the strong waves lapping against it. I lose sight of it as the wave rolls over it. Its shell emerges for an instant and is quickly lost again, swallowed up, accepted by its new home.

I turn back to look at the rest of the baby turtles, who will not stop until they're completely submerged by the massive ocean. They vanish into darkened waters, not to return to the sandy shores until some of them—the mothers—come back to lay their eggs in the very place where they themselves have hatched.

"This is pretty amazing," Charlie murmurs. "Thanks for letting me come."

Minutes later, most of the turtles have been pulled into the deep, and only a few especially slow-moving ones remain. Some of the crowd has dispersed, but many of us have squeezed together to watch these unhurried creatures.

Charlie stays by my side as I edge my way to the water, following the last of them. "Come on, buddy," he urges the small one he's filming with his phone camera.

When the last turtle finally disappears, there's a moment of complete silence. Our eyes all face the water's edge, straining for a last glimpse, but they're gone, carried away in the vast ocean, headed to diverse places, unknown to us, unknown even to them.

The watchers behind me begin moving away from the shore. The little girl yawns and turns away from the water, following her mother's gentle pull. She turns back once more and waves her hand at the ocean.

Charlie drops down to the sand and watches some of the footage he's taken. "Want to sit for a minute?" he asks.

I sit next to him, leaning back on my hands behind me.

"It all happened so fast," I say. "I wish it would last longer."

"I know. Me too."

The sun is just starting to rise, and I can feel its warmth on my back. "I just want to stay here all day and never leave."

"Well, I'm in no hurry." He leans back and lies on the ground, his arms crossed behind his head.

I want to lie down next to him, but even more, I want to just stare out into the ocean. I want to imagine what's in there—the sea life that I've learned about from books and documentaries. An infinite number of species lives in there, simultaneously among each other, around each other. And they all belong in there; all of them.

I look back at Charlie, and his eyes are closed. I wonder if he's fallen asleep, but after a moment he smiles. "I can tell you're watching me," he says.

"Don't flatter yourself. I was just trying to figure out if you were asleep."

"No. Just thinking."

"What are you thinking about?"

"That I'm starving. Want to go get some breakfast?"

I laugh. "And here I was assuming you were having deep existential thoughts."

"Hey, don't blame a guy for being hungry." He sits up and scoots closer to me, his knees bent and his arms encircling them. "So, I know a great little Mexican place that serves the best breakfast. It's on the Southside. Do you like Mexican food?"

"Yeah, it's good."

"Is Mexican food similar to Guatemalan food?" he asks. I'm pleasantly surprised that he remembers where my family is from. Most people in South Texas just assume that I'm Mexican, which doesn't really bother me, I guess. Or didn't, before the note in my locker and arsonist's message on our sidewalk.

"Some things are similar, but some are different," I tell him. "Our enchiladas and tamales are different. We eat more black beans than pinto beans, more corn tortillas. But basics are still rice and beans."

"Well then, how about breakfast?" he asks, dusting sand off his pants.

"You don't have to take me to breakfast," I say.

"Come on. You just let me tag along with you so I could see this incredible thing. At least let me buy you a little breakfast. One taco?" he says the word *taco* with his best Spanish pronunciation.

I laugh even though I know he wasn't saying it that way to be funny. He just wanted to say it the right way.

"That's all?" I say, standing up. I dust off my legs and bottom, trying to get all the sand off. "I show you the amazing Kemp's ridley turtle hatchlings being released into the ocean, and that's all the compensation I get?"

"All right, how about . . . three tacos plus rice and beans, and chips and salsa, and a freshly squeezed orange juice? Okay, two freshly squeezed orange juices. Those are tiny glasses." He holds out his thumb and forefinger to show me just how small.

I smile at him as we amble back up the wooden walkway.

≈

The line of cars waiting for the restaurant's drive-thru stretches all the way down the block, holding up traffic. Charlie goes around that lane and turns into the parking lot.

"Seems like a popular place," I say.

"Yeah. Especially on Saturday mornings. So this should take care of any doubts you had about my taste in restaurants."

Inside, a server shows us to a table and asks us in Spanish what we'd like to drink.

Out of habit, and because I believe it's respectful to answer in Spanish if someone addresses me in Spanish, I say, "Jugo de naranja, por favor."

Charlie asks for orange juice too, in his nearly perfect accent.

The woman gives us menus and tells us in Spanish that the drinks will be right out.

"Where'd you learn Spanish?" I ask Charlie, smoothing the paper napkin onto my lap.

"You're laughing at me," he says looking down at his menu.

"No, I'm not. It's good. I was just wondering where you've learned it."

"I've taken Spanish since seventh grade, and I speak to your mom in Spanish. She's helped me with my homework before. I ask her how to say stuff."

"Oh yeah—I noticed that." Until we moved into the Wheeler house, I never thought about what his interactions with my mother might be. I guess I just imagined that she would do her work in relative silence around the family while they went about their lives. But that's not how the Wheelers operate. The Wheelers take interest in those around them. Whenever I've seen Mr. or Dr. Wheeler they've asked me multiple questions about how I'm doing and what's going on in my life. I guess Charlie is like that too.

"So, does my mom ever talk about me?" I ask him.

He looks up from the menu, a smile playing on his lips. "All the time. If you only knew the stuff she tells me." The smile reaches his eyes, and he winks.

"Come on. Really."

He shrugs. "She just, I don't know, tells us when one of you does well at something. Like when Selena won the spelling bee or Cecilia became the top reader in her class or Javi went on that city council field trip. And when you . . ." He looks up from his menu again, his eyes right on mine. "When you went to get naturalized, got your citizenship."

That was sophomore year. I took the day off school, Mami took the day off work, and she drove me down to the courthouse. It was such a day of pride for her; I don't know why I didn't feel that same pride. It was something I wanted—my American citizenship—but I just resented the long and complicated process it required. I wanted it to be mine already, like it was Ceci's, Javi's, and Sele's. They'd all been born in the United States. It was something that was theirs automatically. Some would call me ungrateful, but I just call myself human.

"She talked about that for weeks before and after," Charlie goes on. If he notices the change in my demeanor, the sudden onset of my discomfort, he doesn't let on. "She was so happy that the two of you were finally going to be citizens. She told me about how it took years, most of your life, in fact, to finally get there. I think it's her greatest source of pride—that you're all citizens now."

He says the last word more quietly, almost like he regrets it. And I know why. It's been three years since my father died. He lived his life impeccably, wouldn't go a mile over the speed limit, and couldn't wait for the day when he could call himself an American citizen. He didn't live long enough to see that day. We're not all citizens now. Not him.

"So, what's good here?" I ask quickly.

"I like the huevos rancheros, but all the breakfast tacos are good. Their potatoes are great."

After the server takes our orders, Charlie says, "Your mom was also really excited when you got the full-ride scholarship to the Island University." That's what we locals call TAMU-CC. "She said it was like all her prayers were answered."

I look down at my hands. "I actually got a full ride to Stanford."

"Really? To Stanford? That's amazing. Your mom didn't tell me."

I glance at his smiling face. "That's because I haven't told her yet. She still thinks I'm staying here."

"When are you going to tell her?" he asks.

I sigh, trying to find a way to explain. "Well, after everything that's happened lately, I'm not sure I can go after all. Mami needs me here to help her with the kids, especially now. The Island University is doable if I reapply next year. I could go to school there and still be around for Mami when she needs me."

Charlie absorbs this for a moment before responding. "Millie, I'm sure your mom will be thrilled for you once you tell her about Stanford. She wouldn't want you to give up your dream. Of course your family needs you, but they'll manage."

I shrug. "I don't know. I have to see what happens this summer—if and when we find a place. I have to see how Selena feels about me leaving, if she can handle it all. She'll be starting high school. That's a big thing; I don't want to put too much pressure on her."

"Selena is pretty amazing," Charlie says. "If anyone can take over for you, she can."

I smile at Charlie's kind words. "Please, don't say anything to my mom. I'm just not ready to talk about it with her."

"Of course, Millie. Don't worry about it."

"Great. New topic?"

"Sure. Um, can I ask you something?"

"Yeah," I say, noticing that he's rolling a paper napkin between his fingers. "What is it?"

"So, I know you said you and Jay are done, but he still comes to find you every morning at school. Does he want to get back with you or something?" His expression is neutral enough, but his fidgeting continues.

I decide I don't mind his nosiness at this particular moment. "Jay is still my friend. I don't think he wants to get back together. And if he did, I don't."

A smile sneaks across his face. "Can I say *good*?"

I shrug the tiniest bit. "Sure, you can say that."

"Can I say *why*?"

"Why I don't want to be with him?"

He nods.

"He's a good friend. He's just a lousy boyfriend. He loves surfing more than he could ever love a girl, or at least love me."

"Well, sounds like he's kind of an idiot."

I laugh and reach for a chip, quickly dipping it in salsa so I can pretend that the heat rising to my face is due to the spiciness. "Yeah, pretty much," I say, bits of chip still in my mouth. I swallow and take a long drink of water. "We would have plans, you know, like an actual date planned with a set movie time, and he'd go surfing for just a couple hours, he would say. And then, it's five minutes before the movie starts, and he still hasn't picked me up. And then the movie time comes and goes, and nothing. He's still surfing."

"No way. He did that to you?"

"Many times. More times than I should have let him." I dust some crumbs off the table and continue. "*I'm sorry*, he would say. *The waves were so good; I lost track of time.* So I kept forgiving him. It wasn't like he was cheating on me. The other girl was the ocean. And in a way I can understand. I'd go with him sometimes, hang out at the beach while he was surfing. But I couldn't go with him *all* the time. I love the ocean too, but I don't let it affect how I treat other people, people I care about."

"I'm sorry. You deserve better than that."

I nod. "Yeah, I know. It just took me a while to figure that out. And it's not like I'm a clingy girlfriend. Go out, be with your friends, go surfing, just don't make plans with me if you're not going to keep them. If he were to tell me, *I can't see you this weekend; I'm going to be surfing,* I'd say: fine, no problem, and make plans with my friends. But if he says, *I'll pick you up Friday night,* then he should pick me up Friday night. So I finally broke up with him."

"But you're still friends?"

"Yeah, he feels bad about the way he treated me; he knows he was wrong. And so we're still friends. I just know not to expect much from him. We hang out if we have the chance, but I never make plans with him anymore. He's a good guy, you know. Means well. It's just that surfing comes first with him."

The server brings over our steaming, overflowing plates, and we dig in. "Well, hope I wasn't prying too much," Charlie says before he takes his first bite.

I shake my head and swallow a bite of beans. "That's okay. So what are your plans for the rest of the weekend?"

"My dad wants me to go to San Antonio with him later today. He's supposed to go to some dinner up there."

"That sounds like fun."

He shrugs. "I guess. Sometimes I don't really want to go to those things, but it's hard to say no to my dad."

I know how hard it is to say no to his dad. Mami never says no to him. I wonder if *anyone* ever says no to Charles Wheeler.

≈

Inside the Wheeler house, all is quiet. It's still early, and I figure everyone but Mami is still sleeping. Mami never sleeps in. I remember her saying last night that she wanted to take the kids to the park for a little while today, get them out of the house. She also wanted to take them to the thrift store to get some shorts for summer. I wonder if she's still planning on doing that. I would love to have some time to myself.

Charlie and I stop at the bottom of the stairs.

"Thanks again, Millie," he says. "It was fun. I guess I won't see you until tomorrow. I think we'll be getting back late."

"Okay. Thanks for coming—and thanks even more for liking it. I had a lot of fun with you." I can feel myself blushing, but I try to keep my tone casual. "And you were right about that breakfast place." I head up the stairs, but at the landing, I pause to look down. Charlie is still at the bottom, and he smiles up at me. I flash him a grin before rushing down the hall.

CHAPTER EIGHTEEN

O n Sunday, Charlie and his dad come back from San Antonio, bringing Oscar Zambrano with them. Mami makes a big meal of pot roast and red potatoes, and we all sit around the table to eat while Oscar tells us about what he's been doing the past few weeks.

"I've been to Tornillo, to El Paso. Each time, I take a local member of Congress with me. We've been attending rallies to protest the separation of families at the border. The representative tries to gain entrance to the detention center to get a glimpse of the conditions, but the authorities won't let them in. I've heard that conditions are deplorable, with no access to showers and with very little food. There have been reports of the children being abused or neglected. Young children are being put in charge of infants and toddlers. The whole thing is horrible, just horrible." I notice that Oscar hasn't even touched his food. It just sits there on his plate, getting cold.

Dr. Wheeler puts her fork down. "What is being done? Is there a group that can bring a lawsuit?"

Oscar nods. "A few immigrant-rights groups are working together on a lawsuit, but so much time has passed already . . .

and the worst part is that the government isn't keeping track of where these children are. Some of the kids are being shipped out of state, and parents don't know where to reach them."

"Oscar and I are meeting up with Congresswoman Martinez in Potrillo tomorrow," adds Mr. Wheeler. "Congresswoman Martinez is going to demand to go inside, to get a look at conditions. All the local news outlets will be covering the visit, which will also draw some coverage for the protests in Potrillo. We have to continue to keep this in the public eye, to get more people speaking out, shaming this administration until they reverse this policy."

Mr. Wheeler already sounds like he's making a campaign speech. I imagine his supporters will love seeing him publicly taking a stand on this issue again. I bet even Sele would love it. Maybe I would too, if he were just a random candidate for public office and not someone so closely linked to my family.

"Is there anything we can do to help?" Mami asks, startling me out of my thoughts.

"Yes, actually," Oscar says, setting down his fork. "I wanted to ask if Millie would come with us. She has face and name recognition, and just having her present would add humanity to the event."

The red potatoes feel like rocks in my stomach. I look at Mami, hoping she'll tell him that I can't go. She looks at me silently, with a question in her eyes.

I look back at Oscar, reaching for an answer. "I—I have school tomorrow."

"Millie, there are only three days left in the school year. They're not doing anything," Mami says.

This seems incredibly out of character for her. She's never let us skip school unless we were too sick to move.

I look around the table; every single eye is on me. That is a total of eighteen eyes. I wish Oscar had waited to ask me privately, not here at the Wheelers' kitchen table. "I don't think I can go. I don't see how I could help. I can't do anything there to change the situation."

"Well," says Oscar, "a lot of my fellow journalists and members of the media have asked me about you, about how you're handling everything, how you've been since the fire. There's still general interest about you. I'm hoping that your presence will generate more media attention and more coverage. The more coverage we can get, the better."

My stomach tightens as I feel the pressure he's laying on me. "I wouldn't have to speak or anything, right? I would just go and . . . be there. No interview? No nothing?"

"No interviews. No speaking. Just your presence for a show of solidarity."

I glance back at Mami to gauge her reaction.

"Sandra, if you want to go with her, I can get Jane to pick up the kids from school," Dr. Wheeler offers.

"I can pick them up," Charlie says. "Seniors have a field day tomorrow. It's basically a half day. I'll pick them up and stay here with them until you get off work, Mom."

"Oh, Charlie, that would be wonderful. What do you think, Sandra? You want to go with Millie?"

Mami nods. "Yes, I think I should go with her."

Mami coming with me makes it less scary. I want her with me, by my side, the whole time.

The rocks in my stomach remain rocks, though, and I block out the rest of the dinner conversation while I think about the daunting task of traveling to the border tomorrow.

≈

After dinner, Charlie finds me in the kitchen. "I think it's great that you're going out there, Millie."

"I wouldn't use the word *great*," I say.

"Well, I'm sure it's going to be tough, but that's why it's all the more important to draw attention to it, right? I know you didn't choose the fight, but the fight chose you, and it needs you. I think it would be really powerful for you to speak out."

I shake my head. "I don't know if I can do it, Charlie. Not if it puts my family in danger."

"You just don't see how amazing you are, Millie. You're Rosa Parks."

"I'm not Rosa Parks," I snap. "For one thing, she was already an activist when she got famous. She didn't get caught by surprise the day she refused to give up her seat on the bus, you know. She planned it. I didn't plan any of this."

"Okay, so, maybe not Rosa Parks," he says. "But you're Milagros Vargas. And the world needs to know Milagros Vargas. It needs to see that undocumented immigrants aren't drug runners and criminals, aren't here for handouts and entitlements. Your family is like millions of others, here to work hard and make a difference. I see that, my dad sees that, and this country needs to see that, and you're the person to show them that."

"I'm not," I say, despising his words, his campaign sound bite. "I'm just me. It's not my job to convince people that immigrants are humans. Don't put that responsibility on me."

He looks surprised, even bewildered. "I'm sorry, Millie. I didn't mean it like that. I'm just trying to say that it's a fight worth fighting despite the costs."

164

I almost let it go, let him say what he wants; it is after all, his house. But his last three words hit me, and I am not going to swallow my anger this time.

"The costs? By costs, do you mean watching my house burn to the ground? I get that it was a small, rundown house, nothing compared to this place," I say, gesturing around me. "But it was *our* house. Everything we had was in that house. So, I'm sorry, but this fight is not worth the cost to me!"

"I'm sorry," he says again. "I shouldn't have said that. I wasn't thinking. I guess I get carried away with how I want things to be. Please, don't be mad at me."

I'll be mad at you if I feel like it! I want to retort. But for Mami's sake, for the sake of her relationship with her employers, I swallow the words. "I'm not mad. It's just that you don't get it. You and your dad . . . you can afford to 'speak out' without any real consequences. So maybe your dad takes a dip in the polls, or his opponent criticizes him. Big deal. You don't actually get hurt; you don't see the people who *are* getting hurt."

"I'm really sorry, Millie," he says, eyes wide, voice solemn. "I don't mean to trivialize what your family has gone through. I know I can't begin to understand."

I let out a long sigh. "Some of us just don't have it in us to fight. I'm not Rosa Parks. I'm not Corrie ten Boom. I'm just Millie, and I think I choose self-preservation over being a martyr."

"And there's nothing wrong with that. I never meant to say you shouldn't protect yourself and your family."

I don't want to continue this conversation. There's no point. Charlie means well, just like his dad. And I'm sick of explaining why meaning well isn't always enough. "I really need to go to bed, Charlie. Good night."

In the morning, Mami takes the kids to school. Oscar brings us all breakfast sandwiches, and we leave the house by nine. It's about a two-and-a-half-hour drive. One of Mr. Wheeler's campaign staffers drives, with Mr. Wheeler sitting in the front passenger seat, on his phone the entire time. Mami and I sit in the back with Mr. Zambrano, who's also on his phone, texting and checking various websites. The campaign staffer who's driving plays several episodes of a podcast that seems to be focused on Texas political commentary. According to the podcast hosts, Mr. Wheeler's bold stances are paying off, as his support base is growing.

The hosts also talk about the San Antonio mayor, Diego Gutierrez, who's running for governor. I've seen a few of his campaign posters in our old neighborhood. There's a lot of debate on this podcast about whether Texas is "ready" for a Latino governor. I wish we could just listen to some music.

Mami holds my hand and rubs my arm most of the way to Potrillo.

We park several blocks from the detention center and make our way through a group of protesters. Many people are holding signs: "Families Belong Together," "Don't Separate Children," "Close the Camps."

Oscar introduces us to a few people, including Sister Magdalena, who tells Mami about the ways her church organization is helping families once they've been released from detention. They match families up with immigration lawyers. They've also opened a resource center where asylum seekers can be reunited and can get clothes and a meal.

Eventually we meet up with Congresswoman Martinez, a

member of the U.S. House of Representatives who represents part of Potrillo and some of the adjacent areas. She seems to be in her mid-fifties, is barely five feet tall, and has a short gray bob. She's surrounded by news staffers and several news crews, who follow her and Mr. Wheeler and Oscar up to the main entrance of the detention center.

At the door, they're met by a staff member. I can't hear what is being said from where I'm standing. Congresswoman Martinez is doing most of the talking, and she's using her hands to emphasize her point. I can see that the staff member is not letting them go in; he's blocking the entrance and shaking his head. The three of them stand at the door for about five minutes more before the staff member closes it.

Representative Martinez turns back to the crowd of protesters and speaks into a megaphone that one of her staffers hands to her. "We are being denied entrance to the facility. And I suspect I know why." She points to the building behind her. "The children who are housed in this facility aren't receiving adequate care. The conditions are horrible. There isn't enough room for them to lie down, they don't have enough showers for proper hygiene, and the meals they're receiving are insufficient. There have been reports of abuse and neglect. And there's no way to know the full extent of these horrors, because the administration won't allow us inside. We must fight back. This separation policy is cruel and immoral. Children should be allowed to remain with their parents who are seeking asylum. It is their legal right to seek asylum, and as the process takes place, these parents should be able to have their children with them. This inhumane child separation policy must be reversed."

The protesters cheer, clap, wave their signs. Journalists press up against Congresswoman Martinez and Mr. Wheeler, calling out questions, shoving cameras and microphones at them. Mr. Wheeler seems to be soaking it all up, talking to as many people as he can. Oscar ushers Congresswoman Martinez over to Mami and me and makes introductions, while cameras track the congresswoman's every move.

"It is so nice to meet you, Millie," she says, taking my hand. "I've been following your story, and I'm so sorry about the fire." She takes Mami's hand. "How is your family?"

Mami thanks her. "We are doing okay. We were all safe, and that's what matters."

"Thank you both so much for being here," Congresswoman Martinez says. "We all have to stand up and speak out for these children. They have no voice right now. We are their voice." She gives me a hug before she moves on to speak to the cluster of nuns and the priests. The cameras follow her.

I'm grateful to just be in the background and not having to say anything on camera, but I know that the cameras caught footage of me speaking to her, and that will be shown somewhere. The thought terrifies me. Who could be watching? How many people are going to be angered, maybe even spurred to violence, when they see me here?

≈

You don't pass a Border Patrol checkpoint on the way into Potrillo, but you do on the way out. It seems so strange that there's a checkpoint to go from one part of Texas to another part of Texas. We aren't even crossing any borders, but because Potrillo is only about seventy miles from the U.S.-Mexico border, there are extra barriers to ensure that no undocumented person is going farther into the U.S.

Mr. Wheeler's campaign staffer comes to a stop at the checkpoint and rolls his window down. The Border Patrol agent asks him to open the back window, and he does with the button on the front door. "Is everyone an American citizen?" the agent asks.

"Yes, we are," Mr. Wheeler replies, leaning forward in the front passenger seat.

The agent shines his flashlight into the far back and looks inside. Another agent with a dog circles the car twice.

Uneasiness now overwhelms all my other feelings. But having Mr. Wheeler and his staffer in the car means the agents probably won't scrutinize us very closely. And after all, we *are* citizens. I shouldn't have to feel nervous.

My phone buzzes with a text. It's from Charlie: *Sorry for being insensitive yesterday. I hope things went okay in Potrillo. The kids have been terrific all afternoon.*

Maybe I'm just grateful for the distraction from this tense experience, but reading these words fills me with warmth. I type, *Thanks. We're on our way back now. Don't let Javi play your video games till his homework's done!*

He sends back a winky face, and I smile in spite of myself.

"Thank you," the first agent says. "You can be on your way now."

The stop has only taken a couple of minutes. But the discomfort stays with me long after we leave the checkpoint behind, until I drift off to sleep on Mami's shoulder.

CHAPTER NINETEEN

JUNE 2018

Graduation day somehow takes me by surprise. Everything about it feels unreal—the fact that this is the last time I'll be in the same building with all my classmates, the fact that Papi isn't here to see it, the fact that I've agreed to go to Charlie Wheeler's graduation party right afterward.

Back at the Wheelers' house, I tug on the strap of my sundress, pulling it into place to cover up the neckline of the new swimsuit Mami bought me. It's a purple-and-black one-piece that I've paired with short black board shorts. Mami has never let us wear bikinis, and I don't think I'd be comfortable wearing one anyway.

Chloe texts me, saying she's just parked. I'm glad she's here. I don't want to brave the backyard full of Charlie's friends by myself.

I slip on my flip-flops and take the steps two at a time. The hallway is full of people making their way out to Charlie's backyard, and I squeeze past them. As I reach the front door, Chloe comes bounding up the front walk.

"Hey," I say. "I like your wrap. Is it new?"

She spins around so I can get the full view of the flowered

wraparound skirt she's wearing over her black bathing suit. "Yes, a graduation present from my mom. She actually did well on this one." Chloe walks past me into the foyer, and we walk through the house toward the backyard. "This place is unbelievable. So does the party have normal people food or rich people food?"

I laugh and elbow her in the side. "Stop it. You're going to be nice today."

"I'm always nice," she says. She pulls open the sliding glass door, and we walk out into the scorching sun. She pulls her sunglasses down from where they've been resting on her head.

"You want to eat first or head over to the pool?" I ask as we walk down the wooden patio steps onto the grass.

"Pool. We have to show off our bods before we fill them with this rich-people food."

"Chloe!" I say, laughing. "People are going to hear you."

"I have no problem with that."

Charlie is across the pool, playing water basketball with his friends. He catches my eye and waves. I wave back as I make my way to the diving board. I feel his eyes following me as I walk the length of the diving board and jump in.

We spend an hour or so in the pool, floating on our backs and taking turns jumping off the diving board. We play a game of pool volleyball with Jen and three of our other friends from school.

"Want to go lay out?" Chloe asks eventually.

"Yeah, I could take a break from the water."

A minute later, we're stretched out on the pair of wooden deck chairs where we left our clothes. I sit back, drops of water dripping from my legs and hair onto the hot concrete. There's a game of chicken going on in the pool, and I'm so glad we got out in time. Dawson dives in, and I feel a faint spray of water tickle my feet.

Ivan and Jay emerge from the sliding glass door, and before I can tell her not to, Chloe bolts out of her lawn chair and skips over to them.

I don't want to look in their direction, for fear that Jay will think I'm looking at him. So I stay still, frozen in place, watching a gull dive lazily into the water below. A shadow moves to my left, and I know it's Jay before he even says, "Hi, Mil."

"Hi, Jay," I say, glancing over his shoulder to see Ivan pulling his T-shirt over his head as he and Chloe walk toward the diving board.

Jay slides into the chair that Chloe just vacated. "We did it. Graduated. Feels good, right?"

"Yeah. Do you feel ready to be an Islander?" He's going to TAMU-CC next year, like most of my friends. If I decide to stay in town instead of going to Stanford, I'll still be able to see them all the time.

"More than ready," he says. "I can surf in between classes."

I laugh and turn back to the gull, which has now been joined by another gull. They're circling each other, inching their way closer to the buffet table. The thought of Jay running to class with dripping wet hair amuses me now that I don't have to compete with his surfing obsession.

"Race me," Jay says, sitting up suddenly from his relaxed position.

"Nah, I'm good." I shake my head and sink deeper into the chair.

"Come on, Mil." Jay stands up, pulls his shirt up over his head and tosses it on the cement ground next to me.

I avert my eyes from his muscular arms, toned from

carrying a surfboard, from paddling against the strong waves. Those arms used to hold me, but I don't pine for them like I used to. I catch Charlie's eye across the pool where he and Dawson are playing pool basketball.

Jay reaches down for both my hands, and I let him pull me to my feet.

"No crying if I win," I say, remembering the last time we raced, the last time I won. It was about a year ago at the city pool. He'd underestimated my ability, forgotten how many hours I spent swimming against the tide to pass the time while he sat in the deep, waiting for a wave.

"Whatever." We stand at the edge of the pool, our feet inches apart. "Say when." Jay bends forward.

"Go!" I yell and dive into the cool water. I surface for air and launch myself forward. Jay's just ahead of me, and I urge my arms to move me faster. I see the other end of the pool and feel my hand crash against the cement just seconds after Jay surfaces, victorious and smiling.

"Almost had me," Jay says, breathing heavily. "It was close."

I'm panting, trying to catch my breath. I wipe my eyes and pull my hair from my face.

"Mil, I'm sorry," he says suddenly.

"No big deal," I say between each heavy breath. "You won fair and square."

"No." Jay wipes his face, shakes the water from his hair. "I don't mean that. I'm sorry for everything. For being a jerk, for messing up, for ruining everything."

"It's okay," I say, swimming toward the ladder. I climb up onto the concrete.

He climbs up behind me, and we stand there dripping in the afternoon sun.

"It's not okay. I was a terrible boyfriend. I wish . . . I wish I had done things differently. I wish we were still together."

Drops of water glisten on his chest, and the sun hits him directly in the face. He puts a hand up to shield his eyes and looks at me searchingly.

"Jay, it's best this way. It's in the past. I'm not mad anymore. I'm not hurt anymore."

"But is there a chance?"

I shake my head slowly. "I'm sorry, Jay."

His eyes fall to the ground; his hand shielding the sun falls too as a cloud moves over to cover it. "I deserve it."

"I'm not trying to punish you. I just don't feel that way about you anymore."

"Okay. Well, it was worth a shot. But you do deserve better, Mil. You deserve the best."

"Thanks, Jay."

"I'll, uh, see you around I guess," Jay says. He takes a step toward me. "Hug goodbye?"

I nod. Our wet bodies are against each other for only a second before I pull away.

"Bye, Jay." I look for Chloe, but she's in the pool by Ivan, and I figure that's where Jay is headed, so I turn around and walk in the other direction.

Mindy Stincil is at the buffet table. "Hi, Millie," she says as I approach. "Want a plate?"

"Sure." I reach for the plate Mindy holds out to me. "Thanks." I pick two slices of pizza, a fruit kabob, a handful of baby carrots, and a bag of chips. A quick look back tells me that Jay has joined Ivan and Chloe.

Mindy holds the ice chest open for me, and I take out a Coke. It's all soda. Charlie warned everyone that there would be absolutely no alcohol. A lawyer who's running for Senate can't risk getting caught serving to minors. That fact alone deterred half of our senior class from attending Charlie's party. People looking for a different kind of scene headed to Tim Condie's party down the street.

I follow Mindy over to a table on the patio, away from the pool. "You gave a great speech," I tell her. Mindy's our valedictorian, to nobody's surprise.

"Thanks. I was so nervous."

"I couldn't tell," I say. "And by the way, I never got a chance to thank you for the backpack, the calculator . . ."

"Oh, it was nothing."

"It was really thoughtful. It meant a lot." I open my Coke and take a drink.

"I wanted to do more. I felt terrible about what happened."

I smile and wish there was a way to magically change the subject now.

Mindy pulls a pineapple chunk off its wooden skewer and puts it in her mouth as she looks toward the pool. Dawson is on the diving board, doing a handstand. He walks on his hands off the diving board and falls headfirst into the water. The crowd around him erupts in laughter, and a smile creeps to Mindy's face.

"He's ridiculous, right?" she says turning to me.

"Dawson? Yeah." I take a bite of pizza and then set it down on my plate.

"Do you remember that time he rode his bike off the pier at Cole Park?"

"I heard about it, but I wasn't there."

Mindy laughs. "I was there. He just didn't stop—dove into the water, bike and all."

I look over at the diving board where Dawson is doing a belly flop. "That is pretty nuts."

"How nuts do you think a girl would have to be to really like him?"

I study Mindy's expression. "You like him?"

"Maybe. Is that really dumb?"

"No, it's not. But I always thought you and Charlie . . ."

"Oh, no. Charlie's like my brother. He's a great friend, has been since we were babies, but we've never liked each other like that. Besides, I prefer them kind of wild."

"Does Dawson know?" I ask her.

She shakes her head. "No. I was just too worried about what people might say. People kind of have this impression that he's stupid. He's actually pretty smart—near perfect score on his SATs. He does stupid stuff because he's always looking for the laugh."

I can't help thinking that it must be nice to have that luxury. Dawson's rich enough that he probably could've gotten into any Ivy League school as long as his parents made a big enough donation. His grades, his choices, won't hold him back from being successful. If I behaved as carelessly as he did, I never would've had a shot at Stanford.

But other than his privilege, I don't have anything against Dawson. "You should go for it," I say.

Her face lights up. "Do you really think so?"

"Yeah. School's done. Like you said in your speech today— the possibilities are endless. There's no reason not to try, if that's what you want."

She finishes off the last bit of pineapple on her kabob. "I think I might." She watches him as he climbs over the fence that borders the Wheelers' backyard. Once he reaches the other side he edges his way down to the crashing waves below.

Mindy and I both start laughing as Dawson jumps into the murky water. That water is really not for swimming, but such details don't seem to deter Dawson. He climbs back over the fence and dives into the pool.

She looks back at me. "Charlie's going to kill me for telling you this, but he really likes you."

My eyes immediately go to where Charlie is talking to Dawson in the pool. "No he doesn't."

"Yes. He does," Mindy says. "He talks about you all the time."

"Well, why hasn't he ever said anything?"

"Because he's so insecure about it. He thinks you still have a thing for Jay."

"I don't," I say automatically, trying to process what she's just told me. Charlie Wheeler likes me? Talks about me all the time?

"You should tell him that then. I mean, if you want him to know. But don't tell him I said anything. He would be so mad at me."

She pops the last grape from her skewer into her mouth. "Anyway, I'm going for it. You should too." She gets up, takes her plate over to the nearby garbage can, strides over to the pool and jumps in. I see her swimming over to where Dawson is now lying on a raft in the middle of the pool. His antics must have exhausted him. Mindy swims under the raft and topples him over.

I laugh and silently wish her luck. If it's Dawson she wants, I hope she gets him. I look over at Charlie, who is on the diving board. He looks over at me and smiles before making a perfect dive. I smile back and fiddle absentmindedly with the fruit kabob on my plate.

Charlie Wheeler likes me.

Do I like him back?

I used to like him for very simple reasons: he's good-looking and friendly.

But *friendly* is too surface-level a term to describe him. He is kind and giving, and he's never made me feel like I am beneath him. He listens, he's curious, he can admit when he's wrong.

My reasons have evolved, but my feelings are the same.

"Hey," Chloe says, sliding into the chair beside me. "Would you totally hate me if I leave now and head over to Tim Condie's party with Ivan and Jay?"

"Of course not. Go if you want. I don't mind."

"Are you sure? You should come."

"Nah. I'm going to stay here." I think about telling Chloe what Mindy has just told me, but it's too soon. I'm barely processing the idea in my head, and I don't feel like I can talk about it yet. Tomorrow. I will call Chloe tomorrow and tell her everything. Right now, I just have to figure out what I'm going to do.

"Okay, love you, Mil." Chloe pulls her wraparound on over her bathing suit and gives me a quick hug before heading over to Ivan and Jay. Together, the three of them exit the patio. I briefly think of all the wet footprints that my classmates are tracking in and out of the Wheelers' house, which my mom will have to mop up later.

I'm starting to get cold; the Corpus wind intensified as the sun went down. I walk across the yard where I left my sundress and towel. I slip the dress over my still wet bathing suit, grab another plate of food, and sit down on a lawn chair to people-watch. The party started with more than fifty people from our graduating class, but as the evening progressed, it's whittled down to about twenty. I guess most of the others have headed to Tim Condie's party, with his ice chest full of beer and whatever else he's managed to sneak into his house.

I look back at the pool, where Mindy and Dawson are both lying on a double raft. He's saying something with wildly gesturing hands, and she's laughing.

"Hey," Charlie says as he approaches me. He's wiping his face with a beach towel, and water's dripping off his hair, down to his chest. "Hope you're having a good time."

"Yeah. It's great." I'm not even lying. I appreciate how low-key this party has been.

He looks around the yard, at the pool. "Is Chloe still here?"

"No, she went to Tim's with Jay and Ivan."

He laughs. "I guess a lot of people have headed over there. It's okay. Most of the people I really care about are still here." He does a double take. "Unless you're going to Tim's too?"

"No. Have you met my mom? She would kill me."

Charlie puts his towel down on the table and starts twisting one end of it. "Are you upset that Jay left?" he asks.

"No. Why would I be upset?"

He keeps his eyes down on the towel in front of him. "It looked like you guys were having fun together."

"Not really. He's . . . we've just been hanging out a bit because Chloe and Ivan are about to get together, I think. So, you know. Jay and Ivan are like joined at the hip."

"Oh. It looked like maybe he wants to get back together with you."

I look down at the twisted-up towel in Charlie's hand. "He does, but I told him no. I just don't like him like that anymore."

Charlie smiles. "I don't blame the guy for trying. But . . . I'm glad he didn't succeed."

His words summon a host of butterflies to my stomach. I don't know what to say in return and am saved from having to think of something when Dawson and Mindy come up to us. Dawson has his arm around Mindy, who's beaming.

"Hey, man," Dawson says. He starts shaking his head, tossing drops of water at all of us and onto the table.

Charlie laughs and wipes his face with the towel. "Don't tell me. You guys are bailing on me for Tim's party."

"No way," Dawson says. "I'm going to take Mindy on my dad's boat. You guys want to come?"

I smile at Mindy, happy that she went for it.

"I'm not going to leave my own party, Daws. There are still people here," Charlie says.

Dawson looks around, as if noticing for the first time that the yard isn't empty. "Well, sorry to bail, but I want to get the boat out before midnight. Otherwise, I can't call it a midnight cruise."

"Don't worry about it," Charlie says. "The party's winding down anyway, but I have to stay and clean up."

"We should stay and help him clean up!" Mindy says, turning to Dawson.

"Don't worry about it," Charlie says. "You guys go."

"I'll help him clean up," I say.

"No," he says, turning to me. "I can handle it. It's not a big deal. Just a few soda cans." He looks back at Dawson and Mindy. "You two enjoy your midnight cruise."

Once they've disappeared into the house, Charlie says, "Wow. When did that happen?"

"Mindy and Dawson? Like, ten minutes ago, I think."

Charlie smiles in a sort of baffled way. "Huh. How did I miss that?"

"You were busy hosting a party."

"Yeah, that's a good excuse. Let's go with that."

It's after eleven. The last few guests emerge from the pool, stopping to thank and hug Charlie on their way out.

I know he said he didn't want me to help clean up, but there's no way I'm leaving the entire mess for him. Without saying anything, I get up from the table and pick up the garbage can behind me. I take out the half-filled bag and start walking around the patio, picking up stray cups, plates.

"Don't, Millie," Charlie says, jumping to his feet. "You shouldn't have to clean up."

I push the garbage bag behind my back before he can reach for it. "I want to, Charlie. Let me help you. As a friend."

"But you're my guest."

"I live here too." I pick up a half-empty can of Sprite. "Besides, it's a beautiful night. I'd rather hang out here than go to bed. And if I stay out here, I'm not just going to sit on my butt and watch you clean up the whole yard."

We spend the next fifteen minutes scouring the yard for balled-up napkins and empty soda cans, and then walk the garbage out to the bins by the side of the house. Charlie fishes out aluminum cans and puts them into the recycling bin.

I walk around to the back again and make my way to the edge of the yard, by the fence.

Charlie joins me, whistling the commencement tune that played at our graduation. He leans his back against the fence, facing away from the bay. I smile at him, feeling a rare confidence.

"I used to have a crush on you, you know," I say.

I see his eyes widen slightly in the dark. "When?"

"When we were twelve. We came here for Caroline's first birthday party. Your mom had been so nice to invite our family; it was the first time I'd ever come to your house. And I thought you were pretty cool." I say the word *cool* in a playful voice, letting it roll off my tongue.

"Why didn't you tell me?"

"Yeah right," I say, laughing. "Like a twelve-year-old girl would ever tell a twelve-year-old boy who is way out of her league that she likes him."

"Out of your league? If anything, you're way out of *my* league. Or maybe we're in the exact same league."

He takes a step closer to me, his back sliding along the fence, his face turned toward me. "I've liked you too, Millie, but I felt like everything I did annoyed you. I felt like you were uncomfortable with how we knew each other, that your mom works here, and figured it was just easier if we didn't really talk to each other."

"That's all true," I say, finally admitting it to myself. It's always been easier not to talk to Charlie, not to be his friend, because time spent with him reminds me that he's privileged in ways I will never be, that his family has power over mine, even if he doesn't see it that way. "That's why I crushed my crush."

"I can't believe you had a crush on twelve-year-old me. I was a skinny dork with buck teeth."

I laugh, remembering his slight overbite prior to his stint with braces. "I thought you were cute."

"Past tense?"

"Well . . . would I be standing here next to you if I didn't still think so?"

"I mean, maybe you're standing right here for the view."

I look out past his shoulder at the view of the bay, the rising waves that crash and fall over and over again. "I've seen that view a thousand times," I say, turning back to him.

He stands up straight and turns his whole body toward me.

"I'm not here for the view either." He softly traces his fingers up and down my arms. I feel a slight shiver shoot up my arms and neck. The Corpus wind does nothing like this to me.

His hands come to rest on my elbows, and he very gently pulls me toward him. My hands wrap around his waist, and his fingers move from my elbows to my back. I'm about to kiss Charlie Wheeler. Twelve-year-old me never thought this could happen.

His lips press against mine, firm and fast. He turns his head to the side, and his kiss softens, slows down as his hand moves up to my neck, and he gently wraps his fingers around the back of it.

"Millie!" Mami shouts my name from the steps of the patio, and I hear the door slam closed behind her.

I pull away from Charlie and pry my hands from his waist. His hand falls from my neck.

"I'd better go in," I say.

He nods and avoids looking toward Mami, who is waiting for me on the patio. I don't know why she sounds so mad. It's not like I've never kissed a boy. And Mami trusts me; she knows I'm a Catholic girl at heart, and that her teachings about waiting to have sex weren't lost on me.

Still, she's practically glaring at me as I walk past her into the house. She signals for me to follow her through the house and out the front door. We walk to her car parked out front and silently, we slide into the front seats.

"No se ve bien, mija," she starts. *It doesn't look right.* It's a statement I've heard my entire life. Before Papi died, when we could afford to occasionally go out to a restaurant, Mami would never send back food, always eating the meal without complaint no matter how badly the cook or the server messed it up. Because sending it back would give the appearance of angling for a discount or a freebie.

"Que pasó, Mami?" I ask her, turning in my seat to look at her. It's stifling in the car because she hasn't turned it on.

"It doesn't look right for you and Charlie to be kissing while we're guests in his parents' house."

"This was the first time, Mami. It's not like we've *been* kissing."

She ignores this. "You know I like Charlie. Of course I do, and I can't think of a nicer boy for you, but Millie, not while we're living in the Wheelers' house. How would that look? If people think that you and Charlie are dating, and they know you live in his house. What would they say? What would they think?"

I want to tell her that I don't care what they think, but that's not the kind of thing you tell Mami. "I don't know."

"I don't want anyone thinking that about you, mija. Or about Charlie. There are so many people looking at the Wheelers right now with the Senate race. Charlie needs to be careful too. It's better if you just stay friends for now. No dating, no kissing, while we're living here."

I know there's no arguing with Mami. Once she's made up her mind about something, once she's given me a directive, I obey without question or hesitation. On one level, her concerns make sense to me, but on another level, I feel that as long as I know I'm not doing anything wrong, it shouldn't matter what anyone else thinks.

"Sorry, mija, but that's the way it has to be. I'm hoping it won't be much longer, but as long as we are guests in this home, you and Charlie cannot date each other."

I nod. "Can I go talk to Charlie? Explain everything to him?"

"Está bien, mija," she says. She stays put as I get out of the car and walk back to the house. She's not going to chaperone me. That's a sign that she trusts me, knows I will make good choices. Which of course has always guaranteed my absolute obedience—after all, how could I disobey her when she's placed so much faith in me?

≈

Charlie is still in the yard, almost exactly where I left him. He searches my face as I approach.

"Is she upset?" he asks.

"No. She just thinks it doesn't look right for us to be kissing while my family is staying here. She just wants to protect my reputation. And yours. Reputation is a huge thing to Latina mothers, especially Catholic Latina mothers."

He crosses his arms, leans back against the fence again. "So, I'm not allowed to ask you on a date or kiss you until your family has moved out? That, Millie, is a double-edged sword. If I want to date you, I have to want you to move out, which I don't. At all. But if I want you to stay, so that I get to see your beautiful face first thing each morning, I won't be able to date you. Which one do I wish for? Because I want them both."

"Charlie," I say firmly, "my family has to move out at some point. The sooner the better. So it's not really a question."

This seems to take him aback. I wonder if he actually thought that we were just going to stay here forever, that Mami would become the live-in housekeeper and nanny, that Caroline would have a permanent playmate in Ceci. A rich person's version of a happy family, where the devoted help is always available.

"Well, I guess in a way this is a positive development then," he says, and his smile has a hint of mischief in it. "Now that your mom's said we can't date, I feel pretty confident that you do want to date me."

I smile in spite of myself, knowing that my smile borders on flirtation, but I can't smile any other way at the moment. It's hard to keep my resolve when I can see that he wants to kiss me again, when I know that I want to kiss him again. But I am Sandra Vargas's daughter, and I don't go back on my word to my mother.

"You know my mother almost as well as I do . . ."

"Yes, and that is why I will not cross her." He's still smiling. I'm relieved that he's being understanding, that he doesn't seem resentful. "Your mom is such a good mom, and you're such a good daughter."

"I am a good daughter. It's one of my biggest flaws."

Charlie laughs. "The minute you move out, though, I'm asking you out on a date. Will you say yes?"

His announcement comes barreling toward my stomach and sends the butterflies that have been fluttering around down there into high speed.

"Yeah."

He grabs the fence in front of us with both hands and leans forward against it, his eyes still on me. "How can I say good night right now without kissing you good night?"

I look up toward the house and see the dimly lit window where Mami sleeps; a shadow passes slowly across it. "Save the good-night kiss for the doorstep of my new home."

"Can I at least walk you inside, to your door?"

"Yeah, but no hand-holding," I say, turning to walk toward the house.

"How did you know I wanted to hold your hand?"

"Lucky guess."

CHAPTER TWENTY

When I walk into the kitchen the next morning, Charlie's at the table, eating cereal with Javi. His blue eyes light up the moment he sees me, and it makes me blush because Sele is in here too, rinsing her bowl in the sink.

"Good morning," Charlie says to me, his eyes following me from the entryway all the way into the kitchen and to the chair across from him.

"Good morning," I reply, meeting his eyes for just a minute before I reach over to get a bowl. "Where's Mami?" I ask Sele.

"She went to get groceries. She'll be back in a few hours." Sele wipes her hand on a kitchen towel. "I'm about to watch a movie in the family room with the girls."

As she heads out of the kitchen, Javi takes this opportunity to ask, "Charlie, can I borrow your Xbox again?"

"Sure thing, bud. It's in its usual spot in my room."

"Thanks!" Javi bolts from his chair without finishing his cereal.

"Just don't mind the unmade bed," Charlie says.

"Maybe you can make his bed for him in exchange for him letting you play," I say to Javi.

"Oh, Millie. You have to ruin everything!" Javi shoves his chair in and looks at Charlie.

Charlie makes a face and shakes his head, mouthing the word *no*.

Javi grins at Charlie before racing out of the kitchen.

"Why do you have to ruin everything?" Charlie says playfully, looking at me.

I wipe my mouth with a napkin and set it down next to my plate. "You can't be too nice to him. He'll take advantage." It's the kind of thing Mami would say. I haven't been able to be a fun sister in a long time; I've had to be the substitute mom.

"Hey, I would've said anything just so I could be alone with you for a few minutes," says Charlie.

I do my best at giving him a harsh look, but it doesn't last more than a second before a smile sneaks out.

"Can I ask you something?" he says, lowering his voice even though we're alone in the kitchen now.

I'm hoping he doesn't want to revisit last night's conversation because it's already so hard for me to say no to him. I want to say yes. I want to kiss him. I want to date him. But my mind is made up. If Charlie and I are meant to be together, then we can wait a few weeks, or however long it's going to take for us to find a new place to live.

"Yes," I say.

"I noticed that Chloe and Jay and Selena and anyone really close to you calls you Mil. Can I also call you that?"

The question surprised me; it's a trivial thing to ask, but it seems to really mean a lot to him. "Yeah, I think I'd really like it if you called me that." I look down at my bowl of cereal. It's getting soggy, but I don't feel like eating. All I want to do is watch Charlie across the table.

Caroline's voice comes from the other room. "Charlie, come help us. I can't get this thing to turn on."

Charlie shakes his head and looks at me. "Guess I'd better go help them get the movie started." He walks over to the sink and rinses his bowl and spoon. "Are you coming to watch?"

"I think so, in a little bit."

"Okay." After drying his hands on a dish towel, he turns to grin at me. "I'll be waiting for you."

≈

Five minutes later I'm sitting on the back patio, talking to Chloe on the phone.

" . . . So then Jay decided he didn't want to go to Tim Condie's party after all," she says, "so he just walked home. I think he was really bummed out, Mil. You like crushed him or something."

"Ugh, now I feel bad."

"Well, you shouldn't. I'm only mentioning it because after Jay left, Ivan held my hand as we walked the rest of the way to Tim's house. And then when we were out in Tim's backyard, there weren't that many places to sit, so Ivan pulled me down on his lap, and we sat like that for a long time."

"Chloe, oh my gosh. He definitely likes you."

"Yeah, he does. We talked for like two hours straight. Then when we walked back to our cars, he kissed me, for like a really long time. I mean, my lips are still numb. But it was really nice, and he was a real gentleman. And then he asked me if I wanted to hang out today. He's picking me up for lunch and then we're going to a movie or something."

"Aw, I'm so happy for you. And, not to change the subject, but I kissed someone last night too."

"What?" Chloe's voice gets louder. "Did Jay come back after he left us?"

"No, no. It wasn't Jay." I pause for a moment to give her a chance to guess, but she doesn't. Silence hangs between us. "It was Charlie Wheeler."

"You kissed Charlie Wheeler?"

"Well, technically he kissed me. I think."

"Wait, stop. Details. Start from the beginning and don't leave out a thing."

I tell her everything, starting with my conversation with Mindy and concluding with Mami's insistence that I steer clear of Charlie until we move out.

"Man, your mom is harsh, Mil. I can't believe that. What if you move in with me? Then you can date Charlie right away."

I think about the possibility for a moment. "No, she wouldn't go for that. And I can't ditch the rest of my family. Mami still needs my help with the kids."

"But you really like him?"

"Yeah, I think I've always liked him. It's just weird, you know, because my mom is their housekeeper. It just feels too much like a telenovela. But he's a really good guy. He doesn't act like he's better than other people. He's very down to earth."

"He is. And, Mil, you're eighteen. You just graduated high school. Your mom can't run your life like that."

"Chloe, don't start, okay? You don't understand. I respect her opinion, and I know that she's doing it to protect me. Besides, it won't be forever. I just have to be patient." I get up from the patio chair and head back to the sliding glass door that leads into the kitchen.

"I just want you to be happy, Mil."

"And so does she."

"Well, at least you got to kiss your boy before she caught you. I think it's great. And I hope you guys find a place soon."

"Me too." I reach out to grab the handle of the sliding glass door. "Well, I better go. And please don't tell Ivan about any of this. I don't want Jay or anyone else knowing right now. I don't want anyone jumping to conclusions. You know, the whole reputation thing."

A horrible thought flashes through my mind: Michael Winter posting another video, telling the whole internet that the *little illegal girl* is dating the Senate candidate's son.

"No problem," Chloe says. "My lips are sealed. And, hopefully, my lips will be busy doing things other than talking."

I laugh, forcing the trolls out of my mind. "Thanks, Chlo. Have fun with Ivan. Text me later to tell me how it went."

"Okay. I'd better go shower and get ready."

I hang up and go to the kitchen to clean up my bowl of mushy cereal before going to the family room. The curtains are drawn and the lights have been turned off. Caroline and Ceci are lying down on their stomachs on a big quilt right in front of the TV. Sele is curled up in an armchair, absorbed in her quilting. Charlie is sitting on the large couch with his feet up on the coffee table, scrolling through his phone.

"How's the movie?" I whisper as I sit down next to him. I make sure to not sit too close and he seems to notice.

"It's good," he whispers back.

"I can tell by the way you're on your phone right now."

He laughs and slides the phone into the pocket of his cargo shorts. "Dawson texted me. He and Mindy had their first kiss last night."

"I guess it was a night for first kisses. Chloe told me she and Ivan had one too."

Charlie straightens up in his seat. "Did you tell Chloe about us?"

"Yeah. She thinks you're cool."

"Good. I'd like to have your best friend's approval."

I smile, scooting in just a centimeter or so. "What about *your* best friend's approval?" I ask, my voice still low.

"Dawson? Oh, yeah. His approval was solidified about two years ago when I told him I liked you."

I lean in closer. "Two years ago?"

"Yeah, but you were with Jay at the time, so I couldn't do anything about it. And then when you broke up, I wasn't sure you were over him. I didn't want to be a rebound guy, so I just waited."

"I'm completely over Jay. Not even a tiny bit of feelings left for him."

His leg edges a little closer to mine. "Well, then it's the perfect time for us."

"Or at least very close to the perfect time." Thoughts of Mami's directive are still fresh in my mind. But she didn't forbid me from sitting next to Charlie on the couch, nor did she say exactly how far I was to sit from him. So I scoot a few inches closer, though I keep my hands clasped in my lap.

His leg relaxes against mine. His hands are on his knees, and I know he wants to hold mine, but this is as far as my conscience will allow. Our shoulders are touching. Our legs from thigh to knee are touching. And the butterflies in my stomach are in overdrive. We sit like that for the duration of the movie. Occasionally, I turn to look at Charlie, and he smiles at me.

≈

As we settle into summer, I'm helping Mami watch the kids more often. This afternoon Caroline and Ceci have decided their new spot for reading is Caroline's little house. Each time I've checked on them, they've been sitting at the little pink wooden table in tiny pink chairs reading Beverly Cleary books.

Sele comes bursting through the glass door onto the patio where I'm sitting. "Millie! I was watching TV, flipping through the channels, and they just said that the government's stopping the child separations. ICE is going to house families together in the detention centers and try to reunify the kids and the parents." She drops down onto the patio seat next to me, eyes shining. She looks completely overwhelmed with relief.

"That's good news!" I say, reaching over to squeeze her hand. "I wonder why they changed it . . ."

"Apparently it was all the media attention, all the people speaking out against the policy, all the lawsuits. It made the administration look really bad."

"So they're going to be reuniting the kids with their parents?" I ask her.

"That's what they're saying. A lot of parents still don't know where their kids are, and ICE hasn't even kept good track of where they've all been sent. So it's not going to be easy. It's a start though." Sele jumps back to her feet. "I'm going to go tell Mami. She's upstairs."

She dashes back inside, leaving me to stare across the lawn at the playhouse. I can't help imagining Ceci being separated from Mami, Mami not knowing where she was. I picture Ceci and Caroline playing in the playhouse, oblivious to the pain that other children their ages might be suffering at this very moment. Circumstances not too different than ours could have put Ceci and the rest of us in that position, but not Caroline.

Her life is so removed from those realities.

I'm still thinking about this when Charlie comes through the sliding glass and takes a seat next to me on the patio. "Hey, Mil."

"Hi, Charlie," I say, finding that I like it when he calls me that.

"I promised Javi that if he finished all the chores your mom gave him, I would take him down to the skate park and teach him a trick."

I smile. "Well, I bet he'll finish quickly then. That sounds like a great offer." The skate park is part of Cole Park. We've been there dozens of times, but mostly, we've stayed at the playground, with Javi skating on the sidewalks and perimeter of the park. Javi has watched the skaters longingly, always too intimidated to join them.

"Do you want to come too?" Charlie asks.

"Sure," I say. "I could use some exercise." And a distraction from thinking about children being torn from their parents, disappearing without a trace.

"I can loan you one of my boards so you can keep up with us."

One of his boards. It's when he says this sort of thing so casually that I remember how different our lives are. He has multiples of everything he wants.

He sees the hesitant look on his face and misinterprets it. "Or you can borrow my bike, if you'd rather."

"The bike sounds good," I say.

His proximity to me is unnerving. His arm is inches away from mine, causing the tiny dark hairs to rise as the energy between us increases. I'm afraid to look up at him, wondering if he's feeling it too.

His hand is between us on the bench, and I see his fingers moving slowly toward my hand. I keep my eyes on my lap, refusing to acknowledge his hand, its closeness, and the heat it's sparking on my arm. I feel his fingers brushing against mine, and I quickly pull my hand away.

"Charlie, don't."

"I'm sorry, Mil. It's so hard."

"I know. It's hard for me too, but I promised my mom."

"I just want to hold your hand. Why is that so bad?"

I move over to the end of the seat. "It's not bad, Charlie. It's just that my mom specifically asked me not to, and we just have to wait."

"I know." He sighs. "I guess we can go check to see if Javi is ready to go."

In the kitchen, Mami is chopping vegetables for stew, and Javi is putting a new garbage bag into the newly emptied garbage can. I wish I had known it only took a promise of the skate park to get such productivity out of him.

The sight gives me pause, though. Javi's only doing his usual chores, but he's doing them in someone else's house. In a way, by helping Mami out the way we always do, we've been helping the Wheelers out. Five housekeepers for the price of one.

I shove the thought away. The Wheelers would be mortified if they knew we felt obligated to do household tasks. But it's an inevitable byproduct of us living here.

"Mami, you need any help?" I ask.

"No, mija, gracias. Sele already offered, she'll be back in a minute."

"Millie, Charlie said he'd take me to the skate park when I'm done!" says Javi exultantly.

"I know. He told me."

The mention of Charlie's name stops Mami's chopping.

"I'm going to walk down with them," I say to her. "Is that okay?"

She resumes chopping and quietly says, "Está bien, mija."

I expect Mami to restate her expectations, but she doesn't. She knows it need only be said once.

"Before you go, though," she says, nodding at an envelope on the table, "Mr. Zambrano sent a letter for you."

I sit down at the table and open the envelope just as Sele walks in. She hovers behind me, reading over my shoulder.

Hello. My name is Susana Vaquero. I think Oscar Zambrano may have told you about me. He has told me all about you! I live in Victoria, Texas, and I was set to graduate from Victoria East High School this month. But a few weeks before graduation, my family had to move because we were in danger of being deported. There was a lot of media attention on my family and my high school. I'm sure you know about that. I saw your segment on Sebastian Smith's show, and I heard about the fire. I'm so sorry that happened to your family. It is so hard to have my name out there with articles on the internet about me. I've read so many nasty comments about myself. It makes me want to go away and have no one ever say my name in public again. But I won't let them win. Next Wednesday, we are having a rally at the fairgrounds in Victoria at 6 p.m. I'm going to be speaking in support of undocumented immigrants. They can come and get me if they want, but I'm not going to hide anymore. I'm going to speak out. I hope you will come. I'd love to finally get to meet you. Oscar said to text him if you can go.

Susana

I fold up Susana's letter and put it back in the envelope. Susana's predicament is really sad; I can't imagine facing her circumstances—fearing the possibility of being deported. I want to help her, to be at the rally for her, but I really don't see how my presence could do any good.

"You're going, right?" Sele asks eagerly.

I put the envelope on the table without answering her. The last time I was at a rally, my identity ended up being exposed to the entire state of Texas. And now, thanks to Michael Winter—and my trip to Potrillo—people know my face. I could be recognized.

Besides, protests can be dangerous. Police can get involved. People can get arrested just for being in the wrong place at the wrong time, just for looking like I do.

I want to help Susana, but I don't want to expose myself further. I want to put the whole immigration debate and my involvement with it behind me. Besides, if the family separation policy at the border is ending, maybe other immigration policies will change for the better too. Maybe the worst is behind us.

"Did Mr. Zambrano tell you what the letter says?" I ask Mami.

She's still chopping. "Si, he called me. Mr. Wheeler is going to be there. Charlie too. You would have to drive down separately from them, but . . ."

"I can't go, Mami," I say. Behind me, Sele draws in a sharp breath.

I get up, push the chair in, and walk out of the kitchen before they can guilt-trip me.

≈

I pedal Charlie's mountain bike slowly down Ocean Drive toward Cole Park. Javi is already half a block away, balancing on one of Charlie's spare skateboards. Charlie goes zooming past me with a wave, catching up to Javi.

I take my time, feeling the strong breeze against my face, my hair waving wildly behind me. There isn't a more beautiful bike ride in all of Corpus, except maybe the rides on the beach Chloe and I have taken on the Island. Looking at all these beautiful homes, with the expansive sea as a backdrop and the horizon spreading out behind, almost makes me think I could live in Charlie Wheeler's house forever, were it not for the fact that I would never get to kiss him again.

The skate park is full of people taking advantage of the nice weather—people who could easily be from our neighborhood. Charlie's the one who sticks out here, though he doesn't seem to mind at all. Several spectators are crowded around the edge of the concrete skating area. I'm content to remain outside the fence, where I sit down on a bench to watch.

Charlie skates down a ramp and comes to a quick stop at the bottom. Javi stands at the top of the ramp, hesitant at first, and follows down to where Charlie is standing. I wince as I watch his too-quick descent. Most of the other skaters here are older teens and young men. Javi is probably the youngest, and I'm so glad that Charlie is here with him.

They start out with some simple moves; Javi shows off what he can do and then starts copying Charlie. I notice that Charlie watches Javi carefully and offers him pointers but still gives him plenty of space to try things on his own. Not for the first time, I reflect that this is one silver lining of our current living arrangement. Instead of hanging out with our troublemaking neighbor all summer, Javi is spending time with a guy like

Charlie—someone who's responsible and kind, someone who's actually a worthy role model for a younger boy.

Eventually Javi follows Charlie to a metal bar that skaters have been sliding along. I can't imagine that either Charlie or Javi can do what I've just seen a few other skaters do.

Charlie skates across the base of the park and jumps onto a metal bar, sliding across it, only stumbling a bit as he dismounts. I stand up and walk over to the fenced partition, scared that Javi will attempt the same thing. There's no way he can make it.

I hold my breath as I watch Javi skate the same path, but as he reaches the metal bar, his skateboard falls right off and he tumbles onto his feet. Charlie, who's stayed nearby, says something I can't hear and Javi nods.

Javi picks up the board, jumps back on and skates over for another attempt. I grip the fence in front of me, wondering what Mami would say if she could see this. First, she would yell at me for not stopping him. Then she would yell at Charlie, and finally she would save the biggest scolding for Javi himself.

Javi tries again, this time falling right to his knees. Part of me wants to go in and stop him, but the other part of me wants to see him succeed.

Javi tries several more times, each time falling down on his knees.

He gives up. Charlie teaches him a few easier tricks, going down the ramp and skating around the base of the park, but Javi stays away from the metal bar.

I let out the breath I've been holding. And I try not to think of those families at the border, still not sure if their kids are safe, still feeling helpless to protect them.

≈

When we get home, Mami is at the kitchen table, talking on her phone. I wave to her on my way past, but freeze when I see her face. She's tapping on the table with her fist and nodding as she listens to whoever is on the other end. She says little beyond an occasional "okay."

I wait until she disconnects the call.

"Que pasó?" I ask her.

She lets out a long breath and stares at the blank screen of her phone. "That was Detective Blake."

I sink down into the chair next to her. "What did she say?"

"There's been no progress on the case." She sets her phone down in front of her and cleans the screen with the hem of her shirt. "She said the majority of arson cases go unsolved. There are no fingerprints, no witnesses. They have nothing to go by."

"But they have to find out who did this," I say. I try to meet Mami's eyes, but her head is hanging low, resting on her palm.

Mami always has answers, can usually offer me some kind of comfort, but not today. "Detective Blake said they're still looking up IP addresses from some of the online comments. But I think we have to be at peace with the possibility that we'll never know who set the fire."

I cross my arms in front of me on the table and lay my head on them.

"God will look out for us." She reaches over to me and squeezes my arm. "We'll find a new home."

"This is my fault," I burst out, my head still buried in my arms. "I shouldn't have done that interview with Mr. Zambrano. These people came after us because of me. They found us because of me."

"Mija, you can't blame yourself for this. You did the interview because I asked you to. And do you know why?"

I shake my head.

"Because we were never safe. Not really. Even as citizens, we aren't safe here. People will hate us no matter what we do, no matter how much we keep our heads down, no matter how silent we are. Hiding would not have protected us."

I look up at her, shocked that she can say this so calmly.

"We can't be scared, Millie. It's not living if you live in fear."

CHAPTER TWENTY-ONE

A couple days later, Mami asks me to take the kids to the beach so she can do some errands. Dr. Wheeler and Charlie have swapped cars for the day so that Charlie can drive us all in his mom's Land Cruiser. Mami and I have packed a cooler full of drinks and snacks. Caroline is bringing every beach toy she owns. She and Ceci are wearing matching swimsuits that Dr. Wheeler bought them as end-of-year presents. The only shadow over the day is the fact that Sele hasn't been saying much to me. She's not giving me a full silent treatment, but she's seemed unhappy with me ever since I said I wouldn't go to next week's rally in Victoria.

We drive to North Padre Island, which is twelve miles closer than the National Seashore where Charlie and I went to see the hatchlings released. As we walk down the ramp to the sand, Charlie says to me, "You really love this, don't you? I can just tell by the way you look out there."

"Yeah, there's no place quite like it, right?"

Charlie sets down the cooler. "There's no place quite like it when you're here with me."

I spread out our towels while Sele and Javi bolt for the water with Charlie's boogie boards under their arms, and Caroline and Ceci start digging into the sand. They insist that Charlie help them build a sandcastle for their Hello Kitty miniatures. I know Sele will stay close to Javi, but I keep an eye on them as they plow through the waves.

Sele catches me watching, and her brows knit together in a frown before she turns away. I can't remember the last time we weren't getting along. And even now, it's not like we've had a fight—I can just sense that she's upset. Or maybe . . . disappointed.

Charlie is already on his knees filling a large blue bucket with moist sand. He pats it down with his hand and skims the excess sand off the top. "Ready, girls?" he asks as he turns it over to make the first part of the castle.

"Okay, we need another one," Caroline demands. "And we need some water." She gets up and skips down toward the water's edge.

Ceci is filling her own bucket, and I help her scoop sand into it for a minute, until I realize I've forgotten about the sunblock. I retrieve it from my beach bag and bring it over to where the girls are busily filling small plastic molds that will shape their castle. "Come here, Ceci. I need to put sunblock on."

"I don't need it," she says.

"Come here."

She sighs and gets off her knees to come over to me. I squirt the cool, white cream onto my hand and rub it on her shoulders and back. "You're next, Caroline," I say as I continue to do Ceci's back, arms, and face.

Caroline takes her place, and I squirt more cream on my hands, rubbing them together. I begin on her pale shoulders, applying nearly double the amount that I used on Ceci.

Caroline's pale skin tone worries me, and I fear she'll burn within minutes. I do her neck, arms, and face with an extra dab on her nose.

Charlie is nearly finished with the girls' Hello Kitty sandcastle, and Ceci and Caroline are taking turns running back and forth to the shore. They're filling buckets and pouring water into a small moat that surrounds their castle. The water sinks into the wet sand, vanishing almost as quickly as they fill it, but that only hastens their work.

By the time I've rubbed sunblock on my own arms and neck, Charlie finishes his sculpting and cleans his hands of sand in the water that Caroline is pouring into the moat. He joins me on the blanket, lying down with his arms stretched out behind him.

"Very nice work on the castle," I say.

"I think so. Should keep them occupied for a while."

"Aren't you going to put on any sunblock?" I ask him. Mami ingrained in me a great fear of skin cancer.

"Will you help me?" Charlie asks.

"No," I say, handing over the tube. "You're a big boy; you can handle it."

He puts some on his face and arms, and I immediately worry about the little part of the back of his neck exposed to the hot sun, but I don't do anything about it.

"Javi's doing pretty good on the boogie board," Charlie says. "You think he'd want me to go out and help him a bit more?"

"He'd love it. He really looks up to you, Charlie. He thinks you're pretty awesome."

"How about his big sister? Does she think I'm awesome too?"

"Selena? Yeah, I'm sure she does." I smile without looking at him, without taking my eyes off the ocean in front of me.

He laughs. "That's good, but that wasn't the big sister I was referring to."

I peel my eyes off the cresting waves that I find so mesmerizing. I turn to look at him and lean my head down on my bent knees in front of me. "Pretty awesome."

He reaches over to me, bridging the five-inch gap between us, running his fingers up and down my arm. The effect of his touch on that small space reaches up to my neck and shoulders, and I shiver despite the scorching sun on my back. "I love your skin," he says, his fingers grazing my forearm.

I watch as his fingers move up and down my arm, across the width of it, in circles, and then up and down again. I turn to look at the girls, so focused on making a home for their Hello Kitties that they're oblivious to Charlie and me. "Maybe you should stop," I say, thoughts of Mami never far away.

His fingers freeze. "If you want me to stop, I will," he says.

"I don't want you to," I say. For a moment I shut out thoughts of Mami, of the girls just a few feet away from us, of Javi and Sele swimming. All I focus on is the sound of the waves, constant and powerful, and on Charlie's touch on my arm, prompting feelings I've never felt before, not even with Jay.

I pull myself up, grabbing his hand as I stand. "Last one in the water's a rotten egg." I release his hand and run toward the water's edge.

≈

When we get back from the beach, Javi helps Charlie clean out the Land Cruiser while Caroline and Ceci head off to shower. Sele and I bring the cooler into the kitchen to empty it of leftover drinks. I try to catch her eye, but she's still acting withdrawn.

Mami is seated at the table with some paperwork in front of her. "Hola, niñas. How was the beach?"

"Good, Mami," Sele says sitting down beside her.

I look over Mami's shoulder. "What's that, Mami?"

"This is a copy of the lease I just signed. I rented a house for us, not too far from the elementary school. We move in on Saturday."

Two thoughts pop into my mind simultaneously. One: We will finally be in our own place and not have to feel like houseguests anymore. That is the ultimate relief. And two: I will finally be able to kiss Charlie Wheeler again.

I ask Mami for more details about the rental house. It's pretty close to our old neighborhood, and it's small, similar to our old one. That doesn't matter—it will be ours.

CHAPTER TWENTY-TWO

Tomorrow is moving day, so Mami told us to wash and fold our clothes and she would bring us boxes to pack them in. Sele and I are on the floor in our guest room folding shorts and T-shirts. In the flurry of preparations, Sele is acting more normal around me. We're not saying much as we pack, but the silence feels companionable. Part of me hopes that she understands why I decided not to go to that immigration rally. A bigger part of me just wants to focus on the task in front of us.

There's a knock on the door, and when Sele answers it, Dr. Wheeler walks in.

"Hi, girls. How's it going?" She walks slowly into the room as if she's entering someone else's space and not her own.

"Good," Sele says. "We're almost done packing."

"Oh, good. Good. Well, I sure am going to miss you girls. Your whole family will be missed. We've loved having you here. And Caroline, her little heart is just breaking. She's going to miss Cecilia so much. So, make sure to come with your mom during the summer and hang out. Caroline would love that. And Charlie too, I'm sure," Dr. Wheeler says with a wink in my direction.

Immediately, I wonder what Charlie has said to his mother about me.

"Anyway, I have a little parting gift for you two. I already gave Javi and Cecilia theirs." She walks out into the hallway and comes back in holding a wheeled suitcase in each hand. "These are for your clothes."

"Wow, thanks," Sele says.

"This one is for you, Selena. A little birdie told me that green is your favorite color." Dr. Wheeler hands Sele a large hunter-green suitcase. "And purple for Millie." It's a dark purple suitcase with black trim.

"Thank you, Dr. Wheeler," I say, taking the suitcase from her. "This is really nice. You didn't have to do that." I think of the cardboard boxes Mami was going to get for us.

"Of course I did. We just love your family. You mean the world to us. And if there's anything else you need, please let me know."

"Thanks," I say, looking around the room at all she and her family have done for us already. I think there isn't anything we could possibly do to ever repay them. It's humbling, this charity, and it's hard to accept, but I try to push the prideful feelings aside because I know Mami has. It scares me, though, to think that I'm about to embark on a relationship with Charlie Wheeler, knowing we're not on equal footing.

Dr. Wheeler squeezes her lips together in a tight smile. "I know what you girls are thinking, and you're wrong. Do you know my friend Sarah Campbellton? She's one of the doctors I work with?"

Sele and I nod. I don't know Dr. Campbellton, but I've heard Mami mention her.

"Well, she's had four nannies over the last six years.

Caroline's only had one person taking care of her in her life, and that is your mom. The day I went back to work, I handed Caroline over to your mom with tears in my heart, but also with a feeling of complete trust and peace. I trust your mother in everything. You can't buy that kind of trust. My family is so blessed."

Her frank words enter my heart and sting my eyes.

"So, you may think that you owe us for what we've done to help you, but the truth is that we owe you and your family far, far more." She smiles, and it lightens the mood a bit. "And I always say that if your mother ever stops working for us, I'm quitting my job because there's no one else I could trust with my little girl."

She laughs, but I feel a pain in my gut. Caroline is only seven. I imagine Mami working for the Wheelers for another ten years, until Caroline is practically my age. I picture Mr. Wheeler becoming a senator, flying back and forth from D.C. multiple times a year, mounting a reelection campaign six years from now. Charlie and I will be twenty-four by then, out of college, full-fledged adults. But Mami will still be here, at the Wheelers' house, as if frozen in time.

"So, I'll leave you to your packing," Mrs. Wheeler says. She gives each of us a hug before she leaves. I wonder if she's thinking of me as her son's potential girlfriend . . . or just as her housekeeper's daughter, who's made her own life so easy.

≈

I zip up my new suitcase, pull it off the bed, and reach over to pick up my backpack, which now holds my makeup and other bathroom stuff. Mami has gone in the moving truck to the new house, and Charlie and I are supposed to take the kids and the suitcases over there in Dr. Wheeler's Land Cruiser.

"Hey," Charlie says behind me, and I turn around. He's standing in the doorway, but his smile reaches me from across the room. "Need some help?"

"Yeah, maybe," I say, pointing down to my suitcase.

He looks down at the suitcase and then back up at me. He takes a step closer and reaches out for one of my hands. His touch is warm and soft, and I want him to never let go. "So, this is it, right?" He smiles nervously, his warm fingers playing with mine. "I can finally kiss you?" He says it in question form, like he's not sure yet.

Before I can think too much about it, I shoot my arms around his neck, pull myself against him, and press my lips to his. His hands quickly jump to my hips and his lips respond to mine. Slowly, he kisses my bottom lip, then my top lip, and then he presses his mouth to mine more eagerly.

"Millie!" I hear Javi's voice from the hallway, and I start laughing.

Charlie laughs too and pulls away. "Nice timing, Javi," he says under his breath with a smile. He picks up my suitcase and steps back a few feet just as Javi comes into the room.

"Millie, I can't find my shoes!"

"They're probably right where you put them last. Did you check downstairs?"

"Yes, and I can't find them."

"Look outside, in the backyard."

"Oh yeah!" Javi says, disappearing down the hallway. "I left them outside last night!" I hear him bounding down the stairs, and the sliding glass door slams open a minute later.

"Sorry for the interruption," I say to Charlie, who's still smiling at me.

"To be continued?" he asks.

"Yeah." My lips are still throbbing and moist, and I can almost still feel his hands on my hips.

"Can we go out on a date tomorrow?" he asks, still holding my suitcase. "Like a real date?"

I pick up my backpack and follow him toward the door. "I'd like that."

"Okay, I'll text you tonight." He leans in and kisses me once more on the lips, a quick, soft kiss that leaves me with goose bumps from my shoulders to my fingertips.

≈

Charlie drives the twelve minutes to our new house, and when we arrive, the small moving truck is already there. A bunch of our old neighbors are helping Mami unload boxes and furniture from the moving truck. Mrs. Rosario has given us her kitchen table, claiming she was going to buy a new one anyway. There are also boxes of dishes and plates from Mrs. Rosario's kitchen. Chloe's dad has brought his pickup with twin beds that used to belong to Chloe's older sister and brother. Charlie parks the Land Cruiser across the street and carries our suitcases to the front door.

It's our new house, but there isn't anything new about it. Walking up to the house carrying Ceci's Hello Kitty suitcase and Mindy Stincil's red backpack doesn't bring me the immense joy I'd thought it would. The searing rays of the sun scorch the patchy brown grass of the lawn. We walk across a cracked sidewalk and up a cement path filled with weeds.

I take in every detail: the torn screen on the front door, the graying paint that once was white, the flower beds laden with old leaves, the cinder blocks that hold the house in place above the ground. It has no foundation, but rather a crawl space where stray cats make their home and brown beetles go to find shelter from the sun.

I hate the feelings of ingratitude and disappointment that invade this moment. I know perfectly well that this is all Mami can afford and that as hard as she works, it will always be all she can afford.

Charlie helps us move the rest of the boxes and small items inside. I'm in the kitchen setting down a box of plates when he comes in behind me with a box of small appliances, which he puts on one of the undersized counters. He takes his maroon A&M hat off and wipes the small beads of sweat off his forehead. "I think we got it all. It wasn't too bad, right?"

"Yeah, not bad," I say, thinking it's a statement of how little we have.

Charlie leans back against one of the counters and picks at the edge of a half-open box of kitchen utensils. "So, for our first date tomorrow, I'd like to take you to San Antonio, maybe go to the Riverwalk."

I can't remember the last time I went to San Antonio. We went to SeaWorld once when Papi was alive.

"Yeah, that sounds like fun." I push the cardboard box aside. "And thanks for being so good about this. Following my mom's rules—it's really important to me."

"That's one of the things that makes me like you so much. Just one of them. There are a lot of other things too." Charlie reaches over to touch a strand of my hair, and he holds it between his fingers for a moment before letting it fall. "Tomorrow. San Antonio. All alone. I can't wait."

CHAPTER TWENTY-THREE

It's my first date with Charlie Wheeler—a day that seemed like it would never come.

"Did you just wash your car?" I ask him as I slide in next to him.

"Yeah. I can't show up with a dirty car on our first date."

"It looks good," I say, taking in how clean it is on the inside too.

"So, I know the kiss usually comes at the end of the night, but since our whole relationship has been nontraditional, maybe we can start with the kiss?" He looks over at me hopefully.

I glance toward my front door, half-expecting Mami or one of my siblings to be standing there watching us, but I don't see anyone. "I just hope we don't get interrupted again."

"How about I drive a few blocks first?" he asks.

I laugh. "Okay."

He drives around the corner to a quiet street. After he puts the car in park, he turns to me and takes a strand of my hair and rubs it between his fingers just as he did yesterday in the kitchen. His hand moves slowly to my face, and he cups both his hands around it. I pull myself up onto my knees, lean forward, and adjust my arm in the space between us. He leans in and kisses me; gently at first, soon more intensely. I wrap my arms around his neck and pull him closer. One of his hands slides off my face and it falls to my waist. Slowly, he runs his fingers up my back, pressing me closer to him.

We pull away and look at each other, smiling. I unwrap my arms from his neck, and he leans back.

"I guess we'd better go," he says.

"Yeah, but I'm glad we did the kiss first," I say. I readjust my legs and stretch them out in front of me as I rebuckle my seat belt.

He starts the car and pulls away from the curb. "Now I guess we can get on with our date."

It's a two-hour drive to San Antonio, and I can't think of a better way to spend it than sitting next to Charlie.

"So, the other day when my dad was home for a few hours I sat down with him to start looking at classes for fall semester. He was almost cool about it. It's the first time we've talked about it when he hasn't made me feel like a complete traitor."

"That's good! How's your mom been about it all?"

"It's hard for her. She's caught in between, like with almost every decision I've ever tried to make on my own. She wants to support me, but doesn't want Dad to feel like she's picking sides. And have you told your mom about Stanford yet?"

"Not yet. Soon."

He reaches for my hand and gives it a little squeeze. "Thanks for trusting me with it. I'm just beyond happy that we'll be there together."

I smile and turn to look at him, his profile. "Me too. It actually makes me feel so much better about my decision. I'll tell everyone soon. Things are better now that we have a place, and everyone seems happier."

We drop the subject of Stanford and talk about our plans for the summer. Charlie's got a job teaching tennis at his dad's country club, and he's going to volunteer at his dad's campaign office too. Mindy and Dawson are officially a couple, and they're already planning an end-of-summer party on Dawson's dad's boat, but Charlie isn't sure if he'll be able to go, since there will probably be alcohol. My plans are less exciting: babysit my siblings and help settle into the new house. But Charlie asks me all kinds of questions to pass the time on the long drive: my favorite movies, my favorite books, my happiest memories . . . and I can tell he's listening carefully, filing everything away in his mind, the same way I once put my most cherished trinkets into my jewelry box.

≈

Charlie parks at the Rivercenter Mall parking lot, and we take the elevator down to the ground floor. We came here once when I was a little girl. Papi took Sele and me to see the Alamo and brought us here for ice cream.

Charlie grabs my hand as we make it onto the pathway that follows the river. "What sounds good for lunch?" he asks.

"Everything sounds good," I say, looking around, wondering about the place where we had ice cream. I don't even remember what it was called, and that was so long ago, it may not even be here anymore.

We walk on a cobbled path along the river. Large barges flow slowly past us. I stare at one boat named *Dolly* as it glides through the water.

Charlie tugs on my hand. "Want to ride one?" he asks. "It kind of looks like fun."

"It is a lot of fun. Let's do that after we eat."

My instinct is to ask how much it will cost, but of course that won't be an issue for Charlie.

≈

As we disembark from the boat, Charlie holds my hand, our fingers intertwined. "That was so fun," I say. "As long as I've lived in Texas, I've never done a boat tour."

"Glad to initiate you. I like that guide. He's always funny."

We turn the corner and walk along the outdoor path that leads toward the Alamo. The plaza surrounding the Alamo is filled with people. We're strolling toward a large crowd, and it looks like there might be a news crew there.

"I wonder what's going on," I say.

Charlie squints his eyes, trying to get a better view. "Oh, I think I heard something about Mayor Gutierrez having a campaign rally today."

"That must be it." Diego Gutierrez is running for governor.

"Yeah, I wish I had remembered earlier. We could've come to listen. It looks like it's over. Wouldn't that be great, though? Diego Gutierrez has done a lot here in San Antonio. I would love to see him be governor—maybe even president one day. He could be the first Latino president of the United States!"

"I don't think I know too much about him," I say, not liking where the conversation is headed. I don't want to talk about politics or campaigns. I stop walking, and Charlie stops with me. "Let's go back around the other way."

"Why? I want to see if we can get a look at Gutierrez. Maybe he's still here."

I look toward the crowd and then in the direction we just came from. Behind us, people are fanned in different directions, some headed to the gardens behind the Alamo, some to Rivercenter Mall, and others across the street to the little museums and shops. As I turn back to face the front of the Alamo, I see a familiar-looking man watching me. He's dressed in black slacks, a charcoal button-down shirt, and a blue tie. He has dark hair peppered with gray. I'm not sure where I know him from, but I know him. And he seems to know me.

"Let's go, Charlie," I say, pulling him back toward Rivercenter Mall.

The man in the blue tie is now walking toward us. Finally, Charlie sees him too and recognition sets in.

"Hey, I think that's Sebastian Smith," Charlie says.

Sebastian Smith. The host who interviewed Oscar. I wonder why he's walking toward us, and I really don't want to find out. "Come on, Charlie, let's go." I begin pulling on his hand, but he won't move.

"Excuse me," Mr. Smith calls out, his pace quickening. "Excuse me. You're Milagros Vargas, right?"

"Yes," I say cautiously, dropping Charlie's hand.

He's caught up to us now. "I'm Sebastian Smith. Oscar Zambrano did a segment on my show about you." He extends his hand, and I reluctantly shake it.

Mr. Smith turns toward Charlie to introduce himself and shakes his hand. "You look familiar too. Why?"

"I'm Charlie Wheeler, sir."

"Ah, Charles Wheeler's son?" Sebastian says, still shaking his hand.

"Yes, sir."

"Well, it is a pleasure to meet you both." He looks between Charlie and me. "Milagros, would you mind . . ."

"Millie. I go by Millie," I say instinctively.

"Millie, sorry. Millie, would it be okay if I taped a quick interview with you? My camera crew is just down there . . ."

"No. Sorry, but no."

Mr. Smith nods. "I understand. It's just that with Diego Gutierrez running for governor, I'd love to get a reaction. Just a few questions. I think it would be great for viewers to hear from you. You're eighteen, right? So, you can vote. I just think it would be great."

"No," I say, shaking my head, meeting his eyes to let him know that I'm serious.

"Millie," Charlie starts to say, but I put my hand out toward him, and he stops.

"Mr. Smith, do you know what happened to me after you profiled me on your show?"

Mr. Smith's face grows somber. "Actually, I do. We had a follow-up story about it."

"Well, I didn't watch it," I say. "I didn't have a TV at the time."

"Millie, I'm sorry," Mr. Smith begins.

"Stop. I got nasty notes put in my locker, I got trolled online, and my house burned down. To the ground. My family could have been hurt. And now you have the nerve to ask me for an interview."

"Millie," Charlie says, putting a hand on my arm.

I wave him off. My heart is beating violently against my chest. All my life, I've trained myself to keep my harshest thoughts inside, to squash them before they materialize. "No,

Charlie. You stop." I turn back to Mr. Smith. "This is just a story to you. That's all you care about—another story to feed your news cycle for five or ten more minutes. Well, this is my life. My little brother and sisters had to run out of a burning house. Because I did your story. And if I do another story? What's going to happen then? You don't have to worry about it because you're safe."

Mr. Smith's demeanor doesn't change, almost as if people speak to him like that on a daily basis. "You're right, Millie, I haven't had anyone burn down my house. But I'm no stranger to death threats. In fact, I am probably the leading recipient of hate mail at my entire network. And it's because I report on things that some people don't want to hear. But I'm not going to stop reporting on those things, and I don't think you should stop telling your story."

"Mr. Smith, can you give us a minute?" Charlie says.

"Of course. Of course." Mr. Smith takes a few steps away and turns around.

"Charlie, let's go," I say, glaring at him.

"Please think about it, Millie."

Charlie's statement pricks the thin exterior that is keeping my tears in check. "*What?*"

"Think about doing an interview. I know you're scared, but I think it's important. Mr. Smith is on your side. He wants to change perceptions about immigrants. Isn't that what you want too?"

"What I want?" I laugh away the first tear that emerges. "What I want is never the issue. What I want never matters. Do I want to get my siblings ready in the morning and walk them to school? No, but I do it because that's what my family needs. My mom needs to be at *your* house to get *your* sister ready for school. Do I want to come home after school and make them do their homework and cook dinner for them? No, I don't want to, but I need to because my mom is at *your* house, taking care of *your* sister and making dinner for *your* family."

"Millie, I'm sorry." Charlie reaches out for me, but I push him away.

Everything I've always felt about the Wheelers bubbles to the surface, and for once I don't bite back my words. "What I want is always put on hold for what my family needs. And what my family needs is inextricably tied to what the Wheelers want. The Wheelers want my mom to work more hours. Done. The Wheelers need my mom to serve at a dinner party. Done. The Wheelers need my mom to babysit Caroline at night. Done. And done. And done. Every time. Because we need the money." The tears I was trying to hold at bay are now streaming down my face, but I do nothing to stop them because I can't anymore.

"Millie, please . . ."

"I want to go to Stanford, but I'm afraid that I can't—that I won't be able to look my mom in the eye and tell her I'm leaving, because she needs me to take care of her kids so she can do whatever the hell the Wheelers will want next."

Charlie stares at me, his expression full of distress. "Millie, I'm so sorry. I didn't know you felt that way."

"Did I want your dad to use me as a symbol, as an inspiring story? No, but because he did, people know who I am. And if those people find out we're dating, things will get a thousand times worse for me and for my family. So I can't talk to Mr. Smith, because I need to keep my family safe. And you don't get that."

"Okay, Millie. I'm sorry I said anything. Just please stop crying." He reaches out to take my hand, but I don't let him.

"Oh, sure. Tears stop at the Wheelers' command. Everything stops or goes at the Wheelers' command, including my family. Well, I won't stop crying just because you want me to. I should have known this would never work out."

Without even looking back at Sebastian Smith, I take off in the opposite direction and wipe at my eyes furiously. But the tears don't stop. I don't even know where I'm walking to, as long as it's away from where I am.

From the corner of my eye, I see Charlie walk over to Sebastian Smith for a minute before he races to catch up with me. "Millie, wait," he says.

I slow my pace, but I don't wait for him.

"Can we please talk?" he asks. This time he doesn't reach out to touch me.

I wipe at my face one more time before facing him. "I'm sorry, Charlie. I really like you, but I don't think we can be together."

"Because I suggested that you talk to Mr. Smith?" Charlie asks, sounding baffled.

"No. It's not even about that," I say as I keep walking. I know where I'm going now: toward the parking garage where Charlie left his car. "It's just that I don't think we can get past our differences."

"We're not that different."

"Charlie, yes we are. How can you say that?"

"Because you and I, if you set aside our backgrounds and family situations, have a lot in common."

"We *can't* separate ourselves from our background and our families. And I wouldn't want to. That's a huge part of who I am, who I'll always be." I reach the elevator that takes us to the parking garage and press the button to go up. I press it two more times.

"I didn't mean it like that," Charlie insists. "I just meant, none of our differences change how I feel about you. What's important are our feelings for each other."

"It's just not that simple. Not for me."

Charlie sighs behind me. "Millie, I wish you weren't so mad right now."

"Well, you won't get your wish tonight because I *am* mad. I'm mad that you and your family have kept pushing me on this all along. It's like you don't even care how I feel about it. You wanted me to agree to more publicity, and you wouldn't listen to me saying no. Your dad wants to force people into doing what he wants, and I don't know if you're any different."

"I'm not my dad," Charlie says.

"No, but you'll always be connected to him. And he's going to win his election, and become a senator, and then even more people will know about him and you and me and my family. Including people who hate us. Us, Charlie, not you. People will never hate you the same way they hate me, which means I will always have to live in fear in a way you don't, and that's just the ugly truth."

The elevator doors finally open, and we both walk inside.

"It's just better this way. At least we had the summer, but it's better if we end it now before we get in too deep."

Charlie leans against the back of the elevator. "So you would reduce us to some summer fling? Like I don't even matter that much to you?"

"You do, Charlie. And that's why I think it's best if we just end it now before these feelings intensify."

The elevator doors open, and we walk past several rows of cars to Charlie's Volvo. He opens the door for me, and I wish we didn't have a two-hour drive ahead of us.

≈

Charlie pulls into the busy downtown traffic, his hands gripping the wheel tightly. "Help me understand how we got exactly to this point. We're finally able to be together, we had a great time, and one misstep, and we're what? Broken up? Did we just break up?"

I turn toward the window and lean my forehead against the cool glass. "I don't think we were officially together yet."

We come to a stoplight, and the car jerks back. Charlie lets out a long, quiet breath. I stare at his hands, his kind, gentle hands. Those hands made me a half panini. Those hands bought me three shirts just because he knew purple was my favorite color. Those hands wrapped around my fingers tonight and made me feel loved, secure, and happy.

"I want to be with you, Charlie, but this isn't about one misstep. This is about you being the son of a high-profile rich white guy, and me being a working-class Latina who doesn't want her every move to get turned into a political debate."

Charlie pulls onto the expressway. "You can't just reduce us to our demographics . . ."

"Other people will. And before you say you don't care— you have the luxury of not caring. It's safe for you to not care. Besides, I bet if your dad wins this Senate seat, a lot of people around you will care too."

"Nobody who matters to me."

"What about your parents? I'm sure I'm not who they have in mind for you."

"Are you kidding? They love you."

"The housekeeper's daughter?"

Charlie squeezes the steering wheel and shakes his head.

"Is that what you think? My parents don't think of your mom as the housekeeper. She's like a part of our family. And—"

"She is NOT LIKE A PART OF YOUR FAMILY," I explode. "Your parents pay her, Charlie. They pay her just enough that she can afford to rent a dilapidated house in a sketchy part of town. The fact that you occasionally also give her your charity doesn't make her *family.*"

There's a long pause. "Okay," he says at last, "okay, that's fair. But they do care about your mom. They genuinely care about all of you, and they think the world of you, Millie. They would never object to us dating. My parents aren't bad people."

"I'm not saying they are. I know they're great people; they're just not my people."

"So you just want to give up, before we've even really tried to make it work?"

"I think we have tried."

Silence fills the car. For the next two hours, Charlie doesn't say anything to me except "Is it cool enough?" and "Want me to turn on the radio?" and "Are you hungry?" I say fine to the temperature, yes to the radio to dispel the silence, and no to being hungry.

Finally, Charlie pulls up in front of my house, sits back, and rubs his hands up and down the steering wheel. "This did not go how I thought it would, how I hoped it would."

"I'm sorry," I say, because I am. Not for speaking my mind, but for shattering the dream of us being together, a dream I desperately wish we could've held on to for at least a little longer.

"This can't be it, Millie." He turns over to look at me. Shadows play on his face and only half-hide his downturned mouth. It is very rare that Charlie Wheeler doesn't smile, but this is one of those times, and I'm the cause of it.

"Maybe we just need some time to figure things out," he says. "Can we talk in a few days?"

"Charlie, I don't want to keep rehashing this. If you care about me, you'll respect my decision."

Charlie pulls his eyes away from me and turns to look out of the window. "Okay. I will. Just . . . know that I love you, Mil."

I want to say that I love him too, but that will only leave the door open for him to hope. And there's no point in hoping.

"Thanks for tonight. I wish it had ended differently too," I manage to say. "Good night, Charlie."

"Good night, Mil."

Earlier today, when I pictured the end of our date, I imagined him walking me up to my front door, giving me a parting kiss. Instead, I get out of the car and go inside alone.

"Millie." Mami's loud whisper from the living room startles me. It's after ten, and I'm surprised she's still awake.

I walk the few steps to the couch where she's sitting. "Hi, Mami."

"How did it go?" she asks me.

I don't sit down next to her because if I do, my already shaken composure will disintegrate, and I don't want to divulge the details of my terrible evening. "It was okay. I feel pretty tired, so I better go to bed."

"Está bien, mija. Buenas noches."

As I crawl into bed, all the night's events come tumbling back into my mind and make the small, hollow gap in my heart expand until all I feel is an emptiness that hurts so much. I love Charlie Wheeler. I've loved him for a long time, but I will also always resent his family—for taking Mami away from us so much, for exposing us to danger, for thinking their charity is enough to compensate for everything we will never have.

≈

The next morning, Mami asks me if I want to go to the Wheelers' with her. She's taking Javi, Sele, and Ceci to spend the day there. I tell her that I'd rather stay home and finish unpacking my room. I can't bear to tell her that I don't want to see Charlie, that we had a fight.

So after they all leave, I spend most of the morning in my room cleaning cobwebs and dead insects out of the closet. I put away some of my clothes in the donated dresser and hang up the rest of them. I also scrub the bathtub and mop the linoleum floor in the bathroom, which looks like it hasn't seen a mop in its thirty years.

I think about Charlie all morning. I wonder if he'll say something to Mami about the date. I wonder if he's even home or if he's spending the day with his friends or at his country club job. I keep expecting him to text me, to ask if he can come by and talk, but he doesn't. He promised to respect my decision. I don't know why I expected him to do otherwise.

Chloe comes by with tacos around lunchtime. We sit at the Rosarios' old table in the kitchen. She takes a bite of a carne guisada taco, her favorite, and I savor my carne asada, which reminds me of the carne asada Papi used to make every time we'd go to the park. He'd bring charcoal, starter fluid, and a tub of his marinated steak, which he'd grill on one of the park grills.

"So, I think I've seen Ivan every day since graduation," Chloe says.

"Does that mean it's getting serious?"

"Yeah, things are really good. I think he's matured. Seriously. He's all ready for college. We're even talking about taking some classes together. But what about you? How was the big date last night?" Chloe scoots her chair in, her full attention on me.

I put my taco down and turn my eyes downward. "Not so good actually."

"What?" She slaps the table with her hand. "Tell me what happened."

I explain as best I can. "We're just too different, Chloe. It would never work out. It's just better that we end it before it even really begins."

Chloe finishes the bite she has in her mouth and shakes her head. "Are you serious, girl? Charlie is a really great guy. I think you need to call him right now."

"No, Chloe. I think I did the right thing. I like Charlie a lot, but the reality is that he doesn't get where I'm coming from, and that will always get between us."

She ponders this for a moment. "Well, it's your call. And I mean, you said it yourself: college boys. Pretty soon you'll probably meet some other great guy who's got more in common with you. Some super-hot Latino from, like, Oakland or wherever."

"Wow, brilliant stereotyping, Chlo."

"I'm just saying, the world is full of people to date if you really don't want to date Charlie Wheeler."

The thought should cheer me up, but it doesn't.

When Mami brings the kids home, they disperse to do the chores she's assigned them. Sele and I go into our room to finish cleaning and unpacking.

About ten minutes in, Sele puts down a rag she's been using to clean the baseboards and plops down on the floor. "Charlie told me what happened."

"Does Mami know?" I ask.

"No, he didn't tell her, and I didn't either."

"What exactly did he say?"

"That you ran into Sebastian Smith and he wanted an interview. Charlie said you got mad at him because he tried to push you into doing it and that you're still mad at him."

"That's all he said?"

"Oh and also that you think you're too different because he's rich and white and his dad's about to be senator or whatever."

"What do you mean, *whatever*? That stuff is all a pretty big deal, Sele."

She shrugs. "I mean, sure. I'm not saying it doesn't matter. But it's not the only thing that matters."

Sele stands up. "I just think, if you're going to let people convince you that dating someone who's different from you is too hard, you're kind of letting them win." With that, she picks up an empty cardboard box and goes out into the hall.

CHAPTER TWENTY-FOUR

I look at my watch as I sit on the floor of my new room sorting socks. It's Wednesday afternoon. The rally in Victoria is going to start in a couple of hours. I already texted Oscar that I can't go. I thought about it carefully, weighed the consequences of going and skipping. But I keep thinking about Susana's letter. *They can come and get me if they want, but I'm not going to hide anymore. I'm going to speak out.*

Her fearlessness won't leave my head. The consequence of Susana going could be deportation. If she shows up at the rally, speaks her mind, she could be picked up by the authorities and sent to a country she doesn't even remember. She's going into the situation knowing this, knowing how much she has to lose, but doing it anyway.

What do I have to lose if I go? Will I be deported? No. My standing in this country is far more secure than hers. Yet I am here, and she is there.

I toss the last few pairs of socks into the basket, and put the basket on the bed, where Sele sits sewing.

She looks up at me. "What?"

"I think I might go to Victoria after all."

Her eyes widen. "Can I go with you?"

I hesitate for a moment. "I don't know what it's going to be like. There might be police there. It could get dangerous or . . ."

"I want to go." She gets off the bed and walks over to her dresser, where she pulls a folded piece of paper out of her top drawer. "I printed out the directions, in case you changed your mind." She unfolds the paper and hands it to me.

I look over the driving directions, feeling grateful and ashamed at the same time.

"I'll go tell Mami," she says.

While she's gone, I wonder what on earth I should wear to a rally. Definitely not the short-shorts, tee, and flip-flops I'm wearing now. I pull out a pair of black dress pants and the white blouse with tiny purple polka dots that Charlie gave me.

When I walk into the kitchen, Mami and Sele are standing by the door. Mami hands me the keys with a smile. "Go, mija."

I nod and take the keys. I know if I open my mouth to speak, I will probably cry. I can't start this with tears. Sele follows me out the door and we get into Mami's Tercel.

Sele looks at the driving directions as I head toward the expressway. "Get on 77," she says.

I nod and drive in silence for a while. Finally I say, "Remember when Papi died, and Mami would come lie in bed with you every night?"

"Yeah," Sele says. She folds and refolds the sheet of paper on her lap.

"I used to think it was because she wanted to comfort you because you were so sad. And you *were* sad, but I think you were also comforting her. She needed you. You're like this quiet, calming force in our family. I don't know what we'd do without you."

"We all do our part," she says. "And our parts change a little as we grow, you know."

"Yeah, I know. Like I think Javi can do the dishes next year, right? He's getting old enough."

Sele nods. "Yeah, he'll do the dishes. I'll do the cooking."

"You *want* to do the cooking?"

"I can do the cooking, sure."

"I might be very busy with college," I say.

"I understand. We'll be okay when you're not around, Mil."

"Sele, I wasn't sure how to tell you this, how I would tell any of you this." I pause for a second. "I have a scholarship to Stanford; I'm not going to stay here. I'm sorry I didn't tell you before."

I can feel Sele staring at me, though I keep my eyes on the road. "Wow. I can't believe you wouldn't tell me. Don't you trust me? You don't think I can handle things without you?"

I let out a long breath and let silence hang in the air between us. "Of course I trust you," I say slowly. "And I know you can handle it, but I was waiting for the right moment to tell you."

"You should've told me right away. You should've told all of us. We would've been so happy for you."

"But I feel bad just leaving you guys to deal with everything on your own."

Sele leans forward in her seat. "But it's *Stanford*. It's why Mami and Papi came here—so that we could have the best. The Island University is good, but Stanford is the best. Mami will be happy for you too. You shouldn't keep this from her anymore."

I nod, but I can't say anything. I focus on the drive; look for the place where I'll have to turn. Sele directs me the rest of the way to Victoria and to the fairgrounds where the rally is being held. Most of the parking area is filled, with only a few open spaces scattered along the far edge.

I hear a booming voice as we enter the spacious fairgrounds. A large crowd is gathered around a platform stage. Sele and I make our way through the crowd. A lot of young people are wearing Victoria East High School shirts. Two young men are wearing Titans football jerseys and holding a banner. Sele and I walk around them, passing several older white people carrying signs.

Toward the front, I see Mr. Wheeler, Charlie, and a few other people standing at the bottom of a small stage. A young woman with long, curly dark hair is at the top of the stage behind a flimsy makeshift podium. This must be Susana, and I'm amazed at how poised she is in front of this huge crowd—like that's where she belongs.

She speaks animatedly into a microphone. "We are here to do no harm. I am here to harm no one. I love this country, and it is my home. I want to help build up this country just as millions of immigrants before me have done. I am just one of many who are here to work, who are here to help, who are here to succeed, who are here to dream."

The people start to cheer, and the movement of signs and banners ripples through the crowd. I don't read them. My focus is on Susana. As she scans her audience, her eyes come to rest on me and recognition sets in. She waves at me, and I find myself moving closer to the platform.

"Thank you so much for coming out today," she continues. "Our crowd is full of dreamers, full of supporters who have come a long way to show Texas that we stand in solidarity with those who dare to dream."

Susana starts to wave her hands more eagerly to me as I

keep walking forward. Eyes begin to turn toward me a few at a time. Most people here don't know me and perhaps are wondering why she is signaling to me. Charlie soon spots me, and I've never seen him look happier. The sight of him makes my heart constrict.

"A new friend is here today. She has come all the way from Corpus Christi, and I hope that she will come up and join me on the stage." Susana steps to the side as I reach the small set of steps that leads up to the platform.

I climb the steps, heart hammering in my chest. Once I reach the podium, Susana squeezes my hand and points to the microphone.

I'm not prepared for this. I was coming to show my support, but I hadn't planned on speaking. I look out at the expectant faces before me. As the seconds elapse, they quiet, wait for me to say something, but I don't know what they want to hear, what Susana wants me to say.

So, I just talk. "My name is Milagros Vargas. I was just a few months old when I came to Texas. I didn't ask to come here, didn't make that choice." My voice catches, and I pause, trying to calm my frantically beating heart. "It was made for me by loving parents who risked everything, gave up everything to bring me here. They came here seeking asylum. And they didn't do it for themselves. They did it for us."

A few people let out approving cheers. I stop for a moment, finally taking in the crowd before me. Everyone is watching me. I see the signs clearly for the first time: "Immigrants are Welcome Here," "No one is Illegal," and "Keep Families Together." I look at Sele, and she nods at me.

"Some people may say, 'You don't belong here,' but I don't know anywhere else but here. This is my home. And I may not have been born here, but I know citizenship. My parents taught me this. My mother will drive back to a store to pay for something they forgot to charge her for. She's taught me what is right. And she's taught me to be proud of who I am. I do belong here."

There is more cheering and enthusiastic sign-waving from the crowd. I wonder if I'm done speaking. I think I'm done. I'm not sure if there's anything more to say, or if I'm supposed to move out of the way to let others speak.

I lean into the microphone again. "People like Susana deserve to be here as much as I do, as much as anyone does. She has a kind of courage that I'm only beginning to understand. I was scared to come here today; scared of what people would think of me, would say about me. But I don't want to be scared anymore. I want to do all I can to help in this fight." Applause erupts, cutting off my last word.

There. Now I'm really done. I look around, hoping someone will come up to take the microphone. A man I don't know climbs the steps to the platform, clapping as he walks toward me. I hand over the mic and he begins talking. Susana embraces me and then we stand together off to the side as the man at the microphone concludes the rally with some closing remarks. Applause follows his speech, and Susana turns to me.

"Thank you so much for coming, Millie. I'm so happy to meet you."

"I'm so happy to meet *you*," I say. "I think you're so brave."

Oscar Zambrano comes over to greet us. "It's good to see you, Millie. I'm glad you two finally get to meet."

I look at Oscar, at the small beads of sweat accumulating on his forehead. I think about all the unkind thoughts I've had toward him for pushing me to do that interview. As I watch him wipe the sweat from his brow, see his rolled-up sleeves, the underarms of his shirt soaked in this June heat, all I can feel is gratitude. It was his prodding that propelled me to the spotlight—the last place I ever wanted to be. But it is being in that spotlight that's helped me realize there *is* something—a very small something—that I can give others.

The concluding speaker comes over and whisks Oscar away. That's when Charlie comes up to me, looking hesitant. "Hey, Mil," he says softly. "I didn't know you were coming to this."

I look down at my feet as I close the small gap between us. "It was kind of a last-minute decision."

"I'm so proud of you. You were amazing."

"Thanks."

Mr. Wheeler reaches us, and he slaps a hand on Charlie's shoulder. "Millie, I'm so glad you came. So glad. Your words were inspiring," he says.

I still don't like that word: *inspiring*. I don't want to be anyone's inspiration. I don't want any of this to be about me. But I say, "Thanks, Mr. Wheeler," and leave it at that for now.

"Thank *you*," he says, "for saying what our lawmakers and our fellow citizens need to hear." He shakes my hand before wading into the crowd on his own.

I sigh. As a person, as my mother's employer, as the father of the boy I briefly hoped to date, I still find Mr. Wheeler deeply frustrating. But I can't deny that as a politician, he's fighting for the right things—for policies and ideas that I would want my senator to champion. I will at least give him credit for that.

I look around and see expectant faces watching me. Some are young, including a lot of Latinas about the same age as Susana and me—perhaps activist students. There are scattered groups of middle-aged white people, and I can't help feeling surprised that they're here, that this cause is important to them. And of course there's Sele, weaving her way over to me, beaming with pride.

Charlie's hand sways toward me, and I know he wants to touch me, but he doesn't. Abruptly, he puts both hands deep into the pockets of his jeans. I want to talk to him, but I don't know what to say.

Susana gives me a hug. "Thank you for coming, Millie. It means so much."

"Thanks for inviting me. Do you know Charlie?"

She smiles. "Yes, I met Charlie and his dad earlier. I hope Charles Wheeler will be our senator one day soon. It stinks that I can't vote for him."

Of course, because she's not a citizen, she can't vote. Once again, I think about the unfairness of it all.

Charlie's dad calls to him and waves him over to where he's standing. Charlie excuses himself and, with a last look at me, walks away.

Susana is still focused on me. "There's something else you can help me with, if you have some time this summer."

"What is it?"

"Well, now that families are being reunited and released from the detention centers, there is a lot they need help with. There's a resource center in Potrillo where they can go once they're released—where they can have a shower, get clean clothes, and get help with transportation. The organization that runs it needs volunteers to help pass out the clothes and shoes and toiletries, and to help serve the meals. I've been collecting shoes to take down there. But I can't go," she says, looking down at the ground. "There's a Border Patrol checkpoint on the way back, and they'll ask if I'm a citizen. I could get detained there. I can't risk it right now."

I remember that checkpoint. I remember how much it intimidated me, even though I'm a citizen.

"So you want me to take supplies down?" I ask.

She nods. "Yes, if you're willing. I've collected about two hundred pairs of shoes. Can I get your contact info so I can drop them off?"

I look at her, and I see my parents. I see my younger sister. I see people who are brave because they have to be. I see people who will give of themselves because the alternative is to live in fear, closed off from everyone who tries to love them. I see people who have so little, yet are willing to fight for those with less.

I nod. "Absolutely."

CHAPTER TWENTY-FIVE

I wake up at six because that's when Mami wakes up to make coffee. The kids are still sleeping, and she's sitting in the kitchen in her bathrobe, waiting for the coffee to percolate.

"Buenos días, Mami," I say, coming into the kitchen. I sit across from her, stifling a yawn.

"Buenos días, mija. Why are you up so early?"

I plunge right in. "Stanford offered me a full scholarship. They want to pay for everything, Mami. Tuition, books, room and board."

"What? Stanford, mija? Really?" She grabs me by the shoulders and pulls me into a long embrace.

When she lets go of me, she takes a deep breath, and a few short sobs accompany her exhale. "When did you find out?"

"I've known for a while, but I wasn't ready to tell you."

"Well, you're going, right?"

"Yes, I already accepted. I'm sorry I didn't tell you right away."

"Mija, that doesn't matter. I am so happy. We'll miss you, of course, and it won't be the same without you, but what a wonderful opportunity. Sele is a strong girl, like you. She will do just fine."

I nod, but don't say anything. I fear that the minute I start to speak, tears will spill out.

Mami wipes at her eyes with a folded-up napkin. "Do you know how hard it was to leave you in charge after Papi died? To leave so much in your young hands? I cried every day when I left the house."

"You cried?" I ask her. Mami never cries. Except for now.

She nods. "You were such a young girl in charge of so much, and I felt so guilty about putting all that responsibility on your shoulders, but I had no choice. It was the only way. And hardship builds resilience and character. Look at you, Milagros. You are a strong young woman. You're ready to conquer this world. Sele is so much like you, and we can help her build resilience and character too, so that when she leaves too, she'll be ready, just like you are."

I nod, amidst tears, wondering how Mami can hold hers at bay, how she cries only when no one sees her. I bite my lip to stifle a sob.

"Papi is looking down on you, so proud. So proud. He's the one who wanted to name you Milagros. He would say that you're his little miracle. It was for you that he wanted to come here. He would never have left his home, his family, his mother if he hadn't wanted to give *you* the best." Mami reaches over to put a hand on my arm. "You are the reason we're all here. When he found out we were having you, he wanted you to be an American, to have all there is to have here, because you deserve it. You deserve Stanford. And you deserve Charlie Wheeler. You deserve to have what makes you happy."

Tears are falling down my face to the table. I reach for a napkin to wipe them away.

Mami gets up and comes around the table to give me

another hug. I stay in her arms, thinking that in just a short time, I won't have her this close to me anymore.

"I have some news too, Millie."

"What is it, Mami?"

"Mrs. Rosario and I are starting a cleaning business. She has a lot of contacts with a few offices and some families. I told Belinda that we are working to getting it going in a few months. She said the timing is good because she's thinking of cutting back her hours at work, and if Mr. Wheeler wins his election, they might all move to Washington, D.C."

I lean back to look at her. "Really? You're going to stop working for the Wheelers? And they might move?" The idea of Mami cutting work ties with the Wheelers surprises and pleases me. For her to start a business and make her own career choices would be fantastic.

"That's terrific, Mami. I'm so happy for you."

The coffee is done, my tears have subsided, and the kitchen begins to fill with yawning bodies. The phone rings, and Mami answers it. As soon as I hear her greet Detective Blake, I hang on her every word. It's mostly Detective Blake speaking with an occasional "I see" from Mami. It's a short phone call, and I stare at Mami as she hangs up the phone.

"Detective Blake said they arrested someone."

I gasp. "Who?"

Javi grabs Mami's arm. "From the fire?"

"Yes," Mami says. "They were able to investigate some of the latest online comments. They found someone local who was making comments. She said they questioned him and then found traces of those chemicals in his car. They arrested him this morning."

"Thank God!" Sele says, hugging Mami.

"So, he's in jail?" Ceci asks.

"Yes, mija," Mami says, crouching down to kiss Ceci on the forehead. "He's in jail."

"How long will he stay there?" Javi asks.

"I don't know," Mami says. Quickly, she changes the subject.

He's been arrested. The man who lit our house on fire, who hates us because of where we're from, is now sitting in a jail cell. I guess next there might be a trial, sentencing. There might also be news stories that will put us front and center in the media again.

Before I can think too much about it, though, I get a text from Susana. She'd like to drop off her donations this afternoon. I'd almost forgotten that I agreed to take two hundred pairs of shoes to a resource center in Potrillo.

≈

In the midafternoon, Susana and her mom arrive. Mami, Sele, and I help them carry in eight large cardboard boxes. They take up most of the living room. Mami gives Susana and her mother, Juana, a hug. She tells them to sit down and brings them iced tea. Mami and Juana immediately start talking like they're old friends, comparing stories of their kids.

"I can't believe you collected all these shoes," I tell Susana, gesturing at the boxes we've brought inside.

"I've been collecting all month," she tells me. "I got donations from church, my neighborhood, families my mom knows from work. Each box has a label telling if it's for men, women, boys, girls, and what sizes."

"That's great."

"I wish I could have brought more. Most of the families coming in have been wearing the same pair of shoes for weeks by the time they get out of detention. The shoes are dirty and wet. Their shoelaces have been taken away. They are all looking for a clean pair of shoes."

"I wish we had some to give," I say, thinking of all the old pairs of shoes under Javi's bed at the old house.

"Could you help me with these?" Susana asks. She's holding a large paper shopping bag. "I just picked them up on my way out of town and didn't have a chance to clean them before we left."

"Sure, no problem," I say, guiding her into the kitchen.

She wets two white sponges that she brought, and we sit down on the linoleum floor. "These sponges are like magic. They make things very clean." She hands me a sponge and begins taking tennis shoes out of the bag.

I watch her scrub the white trim around a pair of blue Vans, managing to clean off all the graying parts, so that the shoes look new.

"Oh, wow," I say. "That *is* like magic." I start scrubbing the bottom trim of a black tennis shoe.

"These are going to make a big difference for the asylum seekers," Susana says. "They have court dates, some of them have ankle bracelets for when they have to go back to have their case heard. Some of them haven't showered for weeks. They haven't had a proper meal for weeks. So, at the resource center, they can shower, get a set of clean clothes, clean shoes. Volunteers cook and serve them a meal. Then they have other people help them make travel arrangements. They go to stay with family or friends, whoever is sponsoring them. So they might take a bus or a plane to their new location, and the staff at the resource center helps them get in touch with their family or whoever is paying for the bus or air fare."

"So, what will we be doing when we get there?" I ask.

"Handing out clothes and shoes, serving the meal. I have been wanting to go so badly, but I just can't risk it. The Border Patrol checkpoint has really been scrutinizing people coming through lately."

"It must be so hard, feeling unsafe like that all the time."

Susana makes a neutral noise in her throat. "I was four when I came here with my parents from Mexico. We crossed at the border. My parents paid a coyote to get us across. I don't remember anything about that, but I can't imagine making it across the border, after that long journey, and then being taken away from my mom and dad, not knowing when I would ever see them again."

I think again about Ceci, now or even younger, being taken away from Mami, all by herself in a detention center. For all that we've been through, at least we haven't had to endure that. "I'm glad the child separation policy got reversed," I say. In truth, though, that doesn't comfort me much, because the sinister mind that thought up separating children from their parents is bound to come up with the next awful way of making immigrants suffer.

We clean about six more pairs of shoes, and then Susana helps me put them in the right box according to size and gender. "Thank you so much for taking all of this down. I hope one day to be able to go and help. It's so huge, for people to see a friendly face when they're just coming out of detention."

"Thank *you* for getting all of the shoes together and for bringing them all to me. I know it was a long drive for you and your mom. How's your situation right now?"

"We're doing okay. I got my diploma. I wasn't able to attend graduation or walk the stage, but at least I graduated. I'm starting college in the fall, and we're staying with family. I'm very lucky."

Mami and Juana come into the kitchen. Mami starts packing a bag of snacks, fruit, and drinks for them to take with them on their ride back home. Mami and Juana embrace and exchange phone numbers, vowing to keep in touch. Susana gives us all the information for the resource center—location, hours, contact numbers. I thank Susana and give her a hug before she and her mother head out.

≈

It's Monday morning. Mami takes the kids with her to the Wheelers' again. She leaves me with a can of white paint, two paintbrushes, and six very scraped, very graying kitchen cabinets.

I go over the dulling, dirty cabinets with a coat of fresh, snow-white paint. Words swirl around in my head. Mami's words, Susana's words, Sele's words . . . Charlie's words.

None of our differences change how I feel about you.

Finally, I pause to send Charlie a text: *I think I'd like to talk more after all, if you're still willing. When is a good time for you?*

≈

I hear a soft knock at the door, and I set my paintbrush down on the paint can lid to go answer it.

As I open the door to Charlie Wheeler, all rehearsed speech flies from my mind.

My arms go around his neck. I press myself to him, pushing him back a foot before he regains his balance and wraps his arms around my waist. He kisses me, and his hands work their way from my waist up to my back.

I pull my lips from his to look at his face. "I love you, Charlie. I want to give this another try."

He presses his forehead against mine. "I love you so much." He kisses me again. "I'm sorry for not listening before, for not trying harder to understand. I don't ever want you to feel like you can't be honest with me, especially when you're upset about something."

"I know," I say. "And I don't want to take all my frustrations and fears out on you. I want us to be a team." I pull away once more, taking his face in my hands. "Speaking of which, I told Mami about Stanford. I can't wait to go there with you."

Charlie beams at me and kisses my cheek. "Excellent. Meanwhile . . ." He lifts my arm and starts rubbing at a white paint stain. "Want some help painting?"

I smile and look toward the kitchen. "Sure. It's just a few cabinets. It shouldn't take long."

Charlie walks into the kitchen. "When we're done, we can go to lunch to celebrate, and talk things over some more."

"That sounds perfect," I say, picking up an unused paintbrush and handing it to him.

≈

The next morning, Dr. Wheeler and Charlie pick Mami and me up. Sele has offered to babysit Caroline, Javi, and Ceci while we go to the resource center in Potrillo. We fill the back of Dr. Wheeler's Land Cruiser with the boxes of shoes that Susana collected.

I notice that no campaign staff are tagging along to document this experience, to post about it on social media or share it with local news outlets. It's just us, doing this as people, not as symbolic public figures.

As we drive the two and a half hours to Potrillo, the thought lingers that Susana should be going with us. She's the one who collected all of the shoes. She painstakingly cleaned them to make sure they were in good condition. She should be the one to take the shoes to the families, instead of having to stay away from the border checkpoint.

Dr. Wheeler drives while Mami sits in the front passenger seat. They talk about when all of us were little, remembering stories from years ago. They both laugh at the time when Caroline was four, and she would only wear pajamas out of the house for about two weeks. Mami tells Dr. Wheeler that when Javi was little, he would only wear socks and sneakers to the beach. He threw a fit when Mami tried to force his feet into flip-flops. Mami finally compromised by buying him some water shoes.

Charlie and I sit in the middle, as close together as our seat belts allow. We're using his phone to look into our housing options at Stanford.

We also look at job opportunities on campus. I know I'll have to get a job to pay for any extras that my scholarship won't cover. Charlie says he wants to get a job too. He doesn't always want to be asking his parents for money. We search for job openings at the bookstore, the library, and a deli on campus.

Once we get into town, Dr. Wheeler has no trouble finding the resource center. We park in front and begin unloading the boxes. Two people come out to help us; one is Sister Magdalena, who I met last time we were in Potrillo, and the other is a man in his thirties.

Sister Magdalena takes my hand and thanks me for coming. She introduces us to Mario Jimenez, the manager of the center. We all sign in and get visitor badges, and then we follow Mario through a seating area into another large room. Behind a counter are almost-bare shelves of shoes. Mario helps us unpack our donated shoes and sort them onto the various shelves.

"So, there is a bus coming in about fifteen minutes," Mario says, looking at his watch. "When people get here, it gets a little chaotic. First, they get processed in, and then some of them will take showers, while others come to get clothes." Mario points to a door with a large sign that says *Showers/Las Duchas.* There's also a schedule posted for men, women, and children for various times throughout the day.

Mario leads Mami and Dr. Wheeler to the other end of the counter where the clothes are handed out. Meanwhile, two girls who seem to be in high school come up to Charlie and me. One with long black hair in a ponytail introduces herself as Sophia. The other one has short blond hair, and Sophia calls her Emily. They explain that most people will be coming in with dirty, wet, or tearing shoes. Those get replaced. Some of them will be in better condition, and all they will need are new shoelaces. Emily shows us a bin that holds new shoelaces.

"So, where are you two from?" I ask the girls, expecting them to tell me they're from one of the nearby towns—Donna, Edinburg, Harlingen.

"New Jersey," Emily says.

"New Jersey? Both of you?"

"Yes," Sophia says. "We're just here for the week."

"You're here on vacation?" Charlie asks.

Emily shakes her head. "No, we came to volunteer for the week."

"You came here for *this*?" I ask them, looking from Emily to Sophia.

"Yeah," Sophia says. "We came with a school group. Two of our teachers are here, and there are four other girls. They're making lunch right now."

"Wow," I say. I've been thinking all morning that *we* came from far away. These girls paid for airplane tickets to come almost two thousand miles to help families they've never met before.

"The bus is here," Emily says, peeking behind a curtain, covering a narrow window. "The staff will start processing people, and then they'll head over here."

Within moments, people start to trickle in. Some head to the showers first, others go to the clothing, and soon a long line forms in front of us.

"Que tamaño?" Emily asks a little girl whose eyes are turned downward. Her mother comes up behind the little girl and tells Emily, "Doce." Emily walks over to the girls' shelf to grab a pair of size twelve shoes.

A man steps forward behind her, and I make eye contact. "Hola, señor," I say.

He gives me a weary smile. "Hola. Cuarenta y uno, por favor."

I look at Sophia because he just said forty-one. She comes over and explains that some people will ask for shoe sizes in European sizes. She shows me that on some of the shoes, there is an EU and a number that correlates to the shoe sizes we use in America. I quickly see that a forty-one men's shoe size is an American size eight. I find him a pair of Nikes that I remember Susana cleaning two nights ago. He takes the shoes, and I sign a large manila envelope where I write the size of shoes he received.

I look over at Charlie and see him speaking to a young mom holding a toddler. Charlie picks out a pair of small shoes and puts the child's foot into it to see if it fits while mom still holds him.

Another man approaches, and I notice that he's wearing a very old pair of tennis shoes. The original laces have been taken out, and the shoes are laced with long strands of shiny material that look like aluminum blankets I've seen in images of the detention centers. He takes off his old pair of shoes and throws them away in a garbage can near the counter. He tells me his size, and I give him a pair of Adidas that also came from Susana's stash. I think about all the good that Susana's hard work is doing for these people, some of whom have been wearing the same pair of socks and shoes for weeks. I wish that she were here to see what a difference she's making in people's lives.

Glancing beyond our line, I see equally long lines at the clothing counter and the showers. I notice a man near the end of the shoe line clutching his son's arm. The boy looks to be about nine, and his dad does not let go of his arm. The boy looks around with lost eyes and stays very near to his father. I think about all of the families that have been separated, families like these, little kids with lost eyes being taken away from their parents in this strange place they don't know at all.

It takes more than an hour for families to cycle through all the lines. Afterward they gather in the large waiting room, sitting on chairs there or lying down on mats on the floor. Many of them get help with their transportation arrangements. I heard one woman say earlier that she needs to get to South Carolina. Someone is making flight arrangements for her, connecting her to the family members who are paying for it.

Sister Magdalena comes to tell us it's time to serve lunch. In the kitchen, we meet the other four girls from New Jersey and their two teachers who came with them. Sister Magdalena gives each of us plastic gloves and an assignment. When the families begin lining up at the counter for food, Charlie dishes out chicken and rice. I give each person two corn tortillas. Mami provides apple slices, and Dr. Wheeler adds a napkin and plastic fork at the end. Emily and Sophia are pouring drinks and taking juice boxes out of a cooler. The line is long, but we try to work quickly.

We dish up two plates for a woman carrying a baby and holding the hand of a toddler. She doesn't have a free hand to take the food, so Mami quickly comes around the counter and carries the plates to a table. While Dr. Wheeler covers Mami's apple-slice station, Mami removes her gloves and reaches out to take the baby.

"Síentense," Mami tells her. "Yo me quedo aqui con el bebe."

The woman looks at her for a long moment before she hands her the baby.

Mami stands next to the table while the woman and toddler are eating. She holds the baby, bobbing him up and down as she talks to the woman. The little girl, sitting beside her mom, eats quickly without pausing.

The rest of us continue handing out plates to the people coming through. They sit and eat while they wait to see when they can leave for the next stages of their journeys. Eventually an overhead speaker announces when vans are leaving to take people to the airport. The dining area thins out.

Two of the volunteers take full garbage bags out to the dumpster in the back alley. Charlie gets a broom and starts sweeping the dining area, and I wipe the tables down as people leave. We take a quick break in the kitchen and fix plates for ourselves before the next bus from the detention center comes at three o'clock.

We start all over with the next busload. Charlie and I pass out shoes with Emily and Sophia. Mami and Dr. Wheeler go back to the clothing line. We do the dinner line, and it's nearing seven-thirty when we finish cleaning up the kitchen and dining area with the rest of the volunteers. Sister Magdalena comes over to us again to collect our volunteer badges and say goodbye.

"Thank you so much for coming, Millie, Charlie, Belinda, Sandra." She squeezes our hands as she says each name. "Your presence has been a blessing. We always need volunteers. This is every day here. Every day, we have at least two busloads of families coming through. We couldn't do it without volunteers like you."

Dr. Wheeler gives her a hug. "I would definitely like to come again. I'm going to start collecting donations from my friends and neighbors."

"Me too," Mami says. "I am going to talk to people at church."

Sister Magdalena gives them each a list of the specific items the resource center is collecting and sends us on our way.

The image of the dad clutching his son's arm is the most vivid memory I walk away with. I imagine the fear and anxiety the dad felt about coming here in the first place. He probably knew he wouldn't be welcomed here, that his son could be taken from him, but he chose to come anyway. The conditions he left behind must be so much worse, so much more dangerous and miserable, that it was worth the risk. I can't imagine what he left behind, but I am glad that they're here, that they're together.

Once we get past the Border Patrol checkpoint, I lay my head on Charlie's shoulder, and he leans his head against mine. We sit in silence. I imagine he's doing what I'm doing, thinking over all the emotions that this day brought. There is sadness at the traumatic journey so many of the families have endured. Anger at the shameful policies that made their journey harder. Relief that these families are together now. Hope that they're bound for better situations, among loved ones—and that others, even strangers like Emily and Sophia, will step up to support them.

And fear that this is only a temporary relief for so many of these people, because there's still no guarantee that they'll be allowed to stay here.

≈

JULY 2018

Charlie and I are walking next to each other down the sidewalk in my new neighborhood. We're both wearing *Wheeler for Senate* T-shirts and holding clipboards. Anxiety is spreading throughout my body. This is something I never imagined myself doing—knocking on strangers' doors, asking them to vote for a political candidate.

Charlie takes my hand. "Thanks for coming with me. Are you feeling okay about it?"

I smile and squeeze his hand, thinking about how difficult it was to make the decisions that have brought me to this point. Charlie has been canvassing door-to-door for a couple of weeks, but this is my first time. I never thought I would be knocking on doors for any political candidate, much less for Charles Wheeler. He isn't a perfect candidate, of course. But I know he sees the humanity of people fleeing desperate situations. And that is not nothing. It's the people in power who control so much of what happens to immigrants, and if I can do a little to help shift that power by knocking on doors—then I have to do it.

I went through a training earlier today at Mr. Wheeler's campaign headquarters. The volunteer coordinator said that people respond to personal stories, and each of us should feel free to share why *we* plan to vote for Charles Wheeler.

I'm going to say that I will be casting my first vote in this election—an absentee ballot that I'll be mailing from Stanford. I'm going to say that if my father were alive, he would be so proud of me. My father was a dreamer when he named me Milagros; his dream for his family was that we would be Americans. I don't think there is anything more American than voting. And I'm going to vote for candidates who know that people like me, people like my father, deserve to be called Americans.

While I still don't think that I am miraculous in any way, I'm ready to add my small voice, to say that we do belong here.

AUTHOR'S NOTE

Guatemala is known as "País de la Eterna Primavera," or "Land of the Eternal Spring." One of its most important exports is bananas. United Fruit Company, an American company, had a monopoly on the banana trade in Guatemala for much of the twentieth century. UFC was known as el pulpo, the octopus, because it had its tentacles everywhere, including in building railroads and communication infrastructure to dominate the area. Guatemalan authorities gave UFC numerous privileges, allowed UFC to avoid paying taxes, and repressed labor unrest. This changed when Jacobo Arbenz was democratically elected as Guatemala's president in 1951. Arbenz advocated for fairer wages and agrarian land reform. He also wanted UFC to pay adequate taxes.

UFC lobbied the U.S. government to intervene to protect its financial interests. The company had many allies in the U.S. government. John Foster Dulles, who had previously represented UFC as a lawyer, was the secretary of state. His brother Allen Dulles, who did legal work for UFC and was on its board of directors, was the head of the CIA. John Moors Cabot, a major shareholder in the company and the brother of a former

UFC director, was the assistant secretary of state for Inter-American Affairs. Ed Whitman, a UFC lobbyist, was married to Ann C. Whitman, President Dwight D. Eisenhower's personal secretary.

In 1954, U.S.-backed forces armed, trained, and organized by the CIA invaded Guatemala to overthrow Arbenz. This coup was commissioned by the Eisenhower administration, and a military dictatorship was established under Carlos Castillo Armas. Armas was the first of several U.S.-backed leaders to govern a deeply destabilized Guatemala.

In 1960, a rebellion against Armas sparked a civil war. Over the next thirty-six years, more than 200,000 people—many of them civilians—were killed by the Guatemalan government. The U.S. continued to support the Guatemalan government despite its human rights violations. In 1999, after the conflict finally ended, the U.S. apologized for propping up dictators and for overlooking numerous atrocities, including acts of genocide, throughout the Guatemalan Civil War.

The war's legacy lingers in ongoing government corruption and violence, as well as in economic hardships for many Guatemalans.

It is in this context that so many people have left and continue to leave Guatemala. The circumstances they encounter upon their arrival have varied over time, but the struggles that drive them from their home country remain largely consistent, rooted in decades of U.S. involvement in Guatemala.

ACKNOWLEDGMENTS

Getting this book published has been a long journey, and it would not have been possible without the help of so many people. First, I would like to thank my husband, Nolan Mickelson. We are nearing three decades of knowing and loving each other. Your love and support have made everything I do possible. Thank you to my three boys—Omar, Diego, and Ruben— for being what matters most in my life. Being your mom will always be my favorite thing.

To my sister and childhood best friend, Claudia: I could not have picked a better friend to go through the journey of childhood and adolescence with. Throughout all of it, our weird imaginations were so in sync with each other. Feeding off each other's imaginings turned us into writers. I am so happy that we have each other to trade stories with.

Thank you to my friend Elodia Strain. I have been your fan since our old Ink Ladies blog days. You were one of the first people to read this manuscript. Your email's subject line—"At last . . . your beautiful book"—gave me hope and compelled me to keep working on it. Amanda Gignac, I am so glad we met so many years ago. Your friendship and your honest and amazing editing over the years have meant so much.

Thank you to Kay Pluta, Nicole Martin, Emilia Smith, Mikayla Oelschlegel, and Rebecca Latimer Jamison for reading this manuscript in its infancy and for all your essential feedback.

Thank you to my agent, Kathy Green, for your support. Our initial phone call gave me so much hope that I would be able to tell Millie's story. Thank you so much for believing in me and in her. Thank you to Amy Fitzgerald and everyone at Lerner Publishing for all the work that was done on this book. It has been an amazing experience.

Thank you to all my Blanche Moore friends. My years with you have been some of my favorites. Your love and laughs have meant the world.

Mami, gracias por todo tu amor, sacrificio, y apoyo. Gracias, Papi por traernos a este país donde pudimos realizar nuestros sueños.

ABOUT THE AUTHOR

Marcia Argueta Mickelson was born in Guatemala and immigrated to the United States as an infant. She is the author of several novels for adults and the young adult novel *The Huaca*. She lives in Texas with her husband and three sons.